# CROSS
# THE LINE

## JAMES PATTERSON

**LITTLE, BROWN AND COMPANY**

## LARGE PRINT EDITION

Copyright © 2016 by James Patterson

Little, Brown and Company
Hachette Book Group
1290 Avenue of the Americas, New York, NY 10104

Little, Brown and Company is a division of Hachette Book Group, Inc. The Little, Brown name and logo are trademarks of Hachette Book Group, Inc.

The publisher is not responsible for websites (or their content) that are not owned by the publisher.

ALEX CROSS is a trademark of JBP Business, LLC.

ISBN 978-1-62953-858-7

Printed in the United States of America

# Prologue

# A DEATH ON ROCK CREEK

# ONE

**HE CHANGED IDENTITY LIKE MANY** warriors do before battle. He called himself Mercury on nights like these.

Dressed in black from his visor helmet to his steel-toe boots, Mercury had his motorcycle backed up into a huge rhododendron bush by the Rock Creek Parkway south of Calvert Street. He sat astride the idling bike and cradled a U.S. Army surplus light detection and ranging device. He trained the lidar on every vehicle that went past him, checking its speed.

Forty-five miles an hour, on the money. Forty-four. Fifty-two. Routine stuff. Safe numbers. Boring numbers.

Mercury was hoping to see a more exotic and inflated figure on the screen. He had good reason

3

to believe a bloated number like that would appear before this night was over. He was certainly in the right place for it.

Built in the 1920s, Rock Creek Parkway had been designed to preserve the natural scenic beauty of the area. The winding four-lane road ran from the Lincoln Memorial north through parks, gardens, and woods. It was 2.9 miles long and split in Northwest DC. Beach Drive, the right fork, headed northeast, deeper into the park. The parkway itself continued on to the left and curled back northwest to the intersection with Calvert Street.

Forty-three miles an hour, according to the lidar display. Forty-seven. Forty-five.

These numbers were not surprising. The parkway was on the National Register of Historic Places and was maintained by the National Park Service; it had a set speed limit of forty-five miles an hour.

But the parkway's meandering route was about as close to a Grand Prix circuit as you could find in or around the District of Columbia. Elongated S curves, chicanes, a few altitude changes, straightaways that ran down the creek bottom—they were all there, and the road was almost twice the length of the fabled Grand Prix course at Watkins Glen, New York.

*That alone makes it a target,* Mercury thought. *That alone says someone will try. If not tonight, then tomorrow, or the night after.*

He'd read an article in the *Washington Post* that said that on any given night, the odds were better than one in three that some rich kid or an older prick sucking big-time off the federal teat would bring out the new Porsche or the overhorsed BMW and take a crack at Rock Creek. So might the suburban kid who'd snuck out the old man's Audi, or even a middle-aged mom or two.

All sorts of people seemed obsessed by it. One try every three nights, Mercury thought. But tonight, the odds were even better than average.

A few days ago, a budget crisis had closed the U.S. government. All funding for park law enforcement had been frozen. No salaries were being paid. Park rangers had been sent home for liability reasons. There was no one looking but him.

Hours went by. Traffic slowed to a trickle, and still Mercury aimed the lidar gun and shot, read the verdict, and waited. He was nodding off at a quarter to three that morning and thinking that he should pack it in when he heard the growl of a big-bore engine turning onto the parkway from Beach Drive.

On that sound alone, Mercury's right hand shot

out and fired up the bike. His left hand aimed the lidar at the growl, which became a whining, buzzing wail of fury coming right at him.

The instant he had headlights, he hit the trigger.

Seventy-two miles an hour.

He tossed the lidar into the rhododendrons. He'd return for it later.

The Maserati blew by him.

Mercury twisted the accelerator and popped the clutch. He blasted out of the rhododendrons, flew off the embankment, and landed with a smoking squeal in the parkway not a hundred yards behind the Italian sports car.

# TWO

**THE MASERATI WAS BRAND-NEW,** sleek, black; a Quattroporte, Mercury thought, judging by the glimpse he had gotten of the car as it roared past him, and probably an S Q5.

Mercury studied such exotic vehicles. A Maserati Quattroporte S Q5 had a turbo-injected six-cylinder engine with a top speed of 176 miles per hour, and it boasted brilliant transmission, suspension, and steering systems.

Overall, the Maserati was a worthy opponent, suited to the parkway's challenges. The average man or woman might think a car like that would be impossible to best on such a demanding course, especially by a motorcycle.

The average person would be wrong.

Mercury's bike was a flat-out runner of a beast

that could hit 190 miles an hour and remain nimble through curves, corkscrews, and every other twist, turn, and terrain change a road might throw at you. Especially if you knew how to drive a high-speed motorcycle, and Mercury did. He had been driving fast bikes his entire life and felt uniquely suited to bring this one up to speed.

Eighty miles per hour; ninety. The Maserati's brake lights flashed in front of him as the parkway came out of the big easterly curve. But the driver of the Italian sports car was not set up for the second turn of a lazy and backward S.

Mercury pounced on the rookie mistake; he crouched low, gunned the bike, and came into the second curve on a high line, smoking-fast and smooth. When he exited the second curve, he was right on the Maserati's back bumper and going seventy-plus.

The parkway ran a fairly true course south for nearly a mile there, and the Italian sports car tried to out-accelerate Mercury on the straight. But the Maserati was no match for Mercury's custom ride.

He drafted right in behind the sports car, let go of the left handlebar, and grabbed the Remington 1911 pistol Velcroed to the gas tank.

Eighty-nine. Ninety.

Ahead, the parkway took a hard, long left turn. The Maserati would have to brake. Mercury decelerated, dropped back, and waited for it.

The second the brake lights of the Italian sports car flashed, the motorcyclist hit the gas and made a lightning-quick jagging move that brought him right up next to the Maserati's passenger-side window. No passenger.

Mercury got no more than a silhouette image of the driver before he fired at him twice. The window shattered. The bullets hit hard.

The Maserati swerved left, smacked the guardrail, and spun back toward the inside lane just as Mercury's bike shot ahead and out of harm's way. He downshifted and braked, getting ready for the coming left turn.

In his side-view mirror, he watched the Maserati vault the rail, hit trees, and explode into fire.

Mercury felt no mercy or pity for the driver.

The sonofabitch should have known that speed kills.

# Part One

# A COP KILLING

# CHAPTER

# 1

**LEAVING THE GLUTEN-FREE AISLE** at Whole Foods, Tom McGrath was thinking that the long, lithe woman in the teal-colored leggings and matching warm-up jacket in front of him had the posture of a ballerina.

In her early thirties, with high cheekbones, almond-shaped eyes, and jet-black hair pulled back in a ponytail, she was lovely to look at, exotic even. She seemed to sense his interest and glanced back at him.

In a light Eastern European accent, she said, "You walk like old fart, Tom."

"I feel like one, Edita," said McGrath, who was in his midforties and built like a wide receiver gone slightly to seed. "I'm stiff and sore where I've never even thought of being stiff and sore."

"Too many years with the weights and no stretching," Edita said, putting two bottles of kombucha tea in the cart McGrath was pushing.

"I always stretch. Just not like that. Ever. And not at five in the morning. I felt like my head was swelling up like a tick's in some of those poses."

Edita stopped in front of the organic produce, started grabbing the makings of a salad, said, "What is this? Tick?"

"You know, the little bug that gives you Lyme disease?"

She snorted. "There was nothing about first yoga class you liked?"

"I gotta admit, I loved being at the back of the room doing the cobra when all you fine yoga ladies were up front doing downward dog," McGrath said.

Edita slapped him good-naturedly on the arm and said, "You did not."

"I got out of rhythm and found I kind of liked being out of sync."

She shook her head. "What is it with the men? After everything, still a mystery to me."

McGrath sobered. "On that note, any luck finding what I asked you about the other day?"

Edita stiffened. "I told you this is not so easy, Tom."

"Just do it, and be done with them."

She didn't look at him. "School? My car? My apartment?"

"I said I'd help you."

Torn, Edita said, "They don't give a shit, Tom. They—"

"Don't worry. You've got the warrior McGrath on your side."

"You are hopeless," she said, softening and touching his cheek.

"Just when it comes to you," he said.

Edita hesitated and then blew him a kiss before leading them to the checkout line. McGrath helped her unload the cart.

"Why do you look like the lonely puppy?" Edita asked him as the checker began ringing them through.

"I'm just used to a grocery cart with a little vice in it. Beer, at a minimum."

She gestured to a bottle on the conveyor belt. "This is better for you."

McGrath leaned forward and took it before the checker could.

"Cliffton Dry?"

"Think champagne made with organic apples, no grapes."

"If you say so," McGrath said skeptically.

As he loaded the food in cloth bags, Edita paid with cash from a little fanny pack around her waist. McGrath wondered what his childhood buddies would say about his hanging out with a woman who bought Cliffton Dry instead of a six-pack of Bud. They'd bust him mercilessly. But if apple bubbly was Edita's thing, he'd give it a try.

He knew their relationship was a strange one, but he'd decided recently that Edita was, for the most part, good for him. She made him happy. And she made him feel young and think young, which was also a good thing.

They grabbed the shopping bags. He followed her out into a warm drizzle that made the side-walk glisten. Traffic was already building in the southbound lane of Wisconsin Avenue even at that early-morning hour, but it was still light going north.

They turned to head south, Edita a step or two ahead of him.

A second later, McGrath caught red fire flashing in his peripheral vision, heard the *boom-boom-boom* of rapid pistol fire, and felt bullets hit him, one of them in his chest. It drove him to the ground.

Edita started to scream but caught the next two bullets and fell beside McGrath, the organic groceries tumbling across the bloody sidewalk.

For McGrath, everything became far away and slow motion. He fought for breath. It felt like he'd been bashed in the ribs with sledgehammers. He went on autopilot, fumbled for his cell phone in his gym-shorts pocket.

He punched in 911, watched dumbly as the un-broken bottle of Cliffton Dry rolled away from him down the sidewalk.

A dispatcher said, "District 911, how may I help you?"

"Officer down," McGrath croaked. "Thirty-two hundred block of Wisconsin Avenue. I repeat, officer…"

He felt himself swoon and start to fade. He let go of the phone and struggled to look at Edita. She wasn't moving, and her face looked blank and empty.

McGrath whispered to her before dying.

"Sorry, Ed," he said. "For all of it."

# CHAPTER

# 2

LIGHT RAIN HAD BEGUN TO fall when John Sampson and I climbed out of our unmarked car on Rock Creek Parkway south of Mass. Avenue. It was only six thirty a.m. and the humidity was already approaching steam-room levels.

The left lane was closed off for a medical examiner's van and two DC Metro patrol cars and officers. Morning traffic was going to be horrendous.

The younger of the two officers looked surprised to see us. "Homicide? This guy kissed a tree going ninety."

"Reports of gunfire before the crash," I said.

Sampson asked, "We have an ID on the victim?"

"Car's registered to Aaron Peters. Bethesda."

"Thanks, Officer," I said, and we headed to the car.

The Maserati was upside down with the passenger side wrapped around the base of a large Japanese maple tree. The sports car was heavily charred and all the windows were blown out.

The ME, a plump, brassy, extremely competent redhead named Nancy Ann Barton, knelt by the driver's side of the Maserati and peered in with a Maglite.

"What do you think, Nancy?" I asked.

Barton looked up and saw me, then stood and said, "Hi to you too, Alex."

"Hi, Nancy," I said. "Anything?"

"No 'Good morning'? No 'Top of the day to you'?"

I cracked a smile, said, "Top of the morning, Doc."

"That's better," Barton said and laughed. "Sorry, Alex, I'm on an old-school kick. Trying to bring congeniality back to humankind, or at least the humankind around me."

"How's that working for you, Nancy?" Sampson asked.

"Pretty well, actually," she said.

"This an accident?" I asked.

"Maybe," she said, and she squatted down again.

I knelt next to Barton, and she shone the light into the Maserati, showing me the driver. He was upside down, hanging from a harness, wearing a charred Bell helmet with a partially melted visor, a neck brace, and a Nomex fire suit, the kind Grand Prix drivers used, right down to the gloves and booties.

"The suit worked," Barton said. "No burn-through that I can see. And the air bag gave him a lot of protection. So did the internal roll bar."

"Aaron Peters," Sampson said, looking at his smartphone. "Former Senate staffer, big-time oil lobbyist. No wonder he could afford a Maserati."

Standing up to dig out my own flashlight, I said, "Enemies?"

"I would think by definition a big-time oil lobbyist would have enemies."

"Probably so," I said, squatting back down. I flipped my light on and probed around the interior. My beam came to rest on a black metal box mounted on the dashboard.

"What is it?" the ME asked.

"If I'm right, that's a camera inside that box, probably a GoPro. I think he may have been filming his run."

"Would something like that survive a fire?" Sampson asked.

"Maybe we'll get lucky," I said, then I trained the beam on the driver's blackened helmet. I noticed depressions in the upper part of it that didn't look right.

"You've photographed it?" I asked.

Barton nodded. I reached up and released the buckle of the chinstrap. Gently but firmly, I tugged on the helmet, revealing Aaron Peters. His Nomex balaclava looked untouched by the fire, but it was blood-soaked from two through-and-through bullet wounds to Peters's head.

"Not an accident," I said.

"Impossible," Barton agreed.

My phone rang. I was going to ignore it but then saw it was chief of police Bryan Michaels.

"Chief," I said.

"Where are you?"

"Rock Creek," I said. "Murder of an oil lobbyist in his car."

"Drop it and get to Georgetown. One of our own is down, part of a double drive-by, and I want our best on the scene."

I stood, motioned Sampson back toward the car, and broke into a trot, saying, "Who is it, Chief?"

He told me. My stomach turned over hard.

# CHAPTER

# 3

**SAMPSON PUT THE BUBBLE UP** on the roof and hit the siren, and we sped toward Georgetown. I noticed the light rain had finally stopped as I was punching in the number for Detective Bree Stone, my wife. Bree was testifying in court that day and I hoped she'd—

Bree answered, said, "Rock Creek an accident?"

"Murder," I said. "But FYI, Michaels just moved us to Georgetown. Two shooting victims. I'm afraid one is Tommy McGrath."

There was a long stunned silence before Bree choked out, "Oh Jesus, Alex. I think I'm going to be sick."

"Exactly my response. Anything I should know?"

"About Tommy? I'm not sure. He and his wife separated a while back."

"Reasons?"

"We didn't talk about personal stuff, but I could tell he was quietly upset about it. And about the fact that the new job kept him from working cases. He said he missed the streets."

"I'll keep it all in mind, and I'll text you when we get on the scene."

"Thanks," she said. "I'm going to have a cry."

She hung up, and my stomach felt sour all over again because I knew how much Tom McGrath meant to her. McGrath had been DC Metro's controversial chief of detectives and our boss. But back when Bree was a junior-grade detective, and McGrath was still working cases, he had taken her under his wing and guided her, even served as her partner for a brief time. He'd mentored her as she rose in the ranks and was the one who'd recommended that she move to the major cases.

As the COD, McGrath was a competent and fair administrator, I thought. He could be tough, and he played politics at times, the kind of cop who made enemies. One of his former partners even thought McGrath had turned on him, planting evidence and driving him from the force.

As a detective, though, Tommy had keen instincts. He was also genuinely curious about people and a good listener, and as I drove across the city toward his death scene, I realized I would miss him a great deal.

There were patrol cars with flashing blue lights, uniformed cops, and barriers closing off the 3200 block of Wisconsin Avenue. We parked down the street, and I took a moment to steel myself for what I was about to see and do.

I've spent years as an investigator with the FBI and with DC Metro, so I have been to hundreds of murder scenes, and I usually go to work inside a suit of psychological armor that keeps me at an emotional distance from all victims. But this was Tommy McGrath. One of the brethren was down, one of the good guys, and that put chinks in my armor. It made this all personal, and when I'm dealing with murder, I don't like it to be personal. Rational, observant, and analytical—that's my style.

I got out of the unmarked car trying to be that detached observer. When I reached the bloody scene, however, and saw McGrath in his workout shorts and T-shirt lying next to a beautiful woman in yoga gear, both of them dead of multiple gunshot wounds, the cold, rational Alex Cross took a hike. This *was* personal.

"I liked McGrath," Sampson said, his face as hard and dark as ebony. "A lot."

A patrolman approached and laid out for us

what seemed to have happened based on the initial statements he'd taken from witnesses. They said the car had come rolling toward McGrath and the woman. There were shots, three and then two. On that, all the witnesses agreed.

McGrath was hit first, then Jane Doe. Chaos ensued, as it always does when there's gunfire involved, witnesses diving out of the way, trying to find cover or safety, which is entirely understandable. Folks have the right to survive, but fear and panic make my job harder, because I have to be sure those emotions don't cloud their judgments or taint their memories.

The witnesses were waiting for us inside the Whole Foods, but before I went in, I walked the perimeter of the scene, seeing the organic goods strewn about the bodies: fresh produce, beeswax candles, and two broken bottles of kombucha tea.

Lying in the gutter about ten feet from the corpses was a bottle of Cliffton Dry, some kind of bubbly apple wine, which I thought was odd.

"What are you seeing, Alex?" Sampson asked.

I shrugged, said, "I thought Tommy McGrath always drank Bud."

"So it's her bottle. They together?"

"Bree said McGrath and his wife were separated."

"Divorce is always a possible motive in a murder," Sampson said. "But this looks gangland to me."

"Does it?" I asked. "This wasn't the normal spray-a-hail-of-bullets-and-hope-you-hit-something killing. This was precision shooting. Five shots fired. Five hits."

We looked over at the woman, who lay on her side at an awkward angle.

I noticed the fanny pack, put on gloves, and knelt down to open it.

# CHAPTER

# 4

**IN ADDITION TO THREE HUNDRED** dollars in fifties, the fanny pack contained a student ID card from American University's law school and a District of Columbia driver's license, both in the name of Edita Kravic. She was three days shy of her thirty-second birthday and didn't live far from the Whole Foods store.

I also found two business cards emblazoned with THE PHOENIX CLUB—THE NEW NORMAL, whatever that meant; according to the cards, Edita Kravic worked there as a Level 2 Certified Coach, whatever *that* meant. Below the club's name was a Virginia phone number and an address in Vienna, near Wolf Trap.

I stood up, thinking, *Who were you, Edita Kravic? And what were you to Chief of Detectives McGrath?*

Sampson and I went inside the Whole Foods and found the shaken witnesses. Three of them said they'd seen the entire event.

Melanie Winters, a checkout clerk, said the victims had just been in the store, laughing and joking with each other. Winters said they'd seemed good together, Tom and Edita Kravic, like they had chemistry, although McGrath had complained in the checkout line about her not letting him buy beer.

I glanced at Sampson. "What did I say?"

As McGrath and Kravic left, the checker said, she started moving empty produce boxes by the front window. She was looking outside when a dark blue sedan rolled up with the windows down and bullets started flying. Winters dived to the floor and stayed there until the gunfire stopped and the car squealed away.

"How many people in the car?" Sampson said.

"I don't know," she said. "I just saw these flashes and heard the shots."

"Where were the flashes?" I said. "Front seat or back or both?"

She winced. "I'm not sure."

Lucas Phelps, a senior at Georgetown, had been outside, about half a block south of the store. Phelps had been listening to a podcast over his Beats headphones when the shooting started. The student thought it was part of the program he was listening to until he saw McGrath and Kravic fall.

"What kind of car?" Sampson said.

"I'm not good at that," Phelps said. "A four-door car? Like, dark-colored?"

"How many people in the car?" I asked.

"Two, I think," Phelps said. "From my angle, it was kind of hard to say."

"You see flashes from the shots?"

"Sure, now that you mention it."

"Where were the flashes coming from? Front seat, back, or both?"

"Front," he said. "I think. It all happened so fast."

The third witness, Craig Brooks, proved once again that triangulation is often the best way to the truth. The seventy-two-year-old retired U.S. Treasury agent had been coming down the sidewalk from the north, heading to Whole Foods to get some "gluten-free crap" his wife wanted, when the shooting started.

"There were three people in that car, and one shooting out the window from the front seat, a Remington 1911 S, forty-five caliber."

"How do you know that?" Sampson asked.

"I saw the gun, and there's a fresh forty-five casing out there by the curb."

I followed his gesture and nodded. "You touch it?"

"Not stupid."

"Appreciate it. Make of the car? Model? License plate?"

"It was a GM of some sort, four-door, dark-colored but flat, no finish, like primer. They'd stripped it of any identifiers and covered the license plate too."

"Male? Female?"

"They were all wearing ball caps and black masks," Brooks said. "I got a clear look at the shooter's cap, though, as they went by me. Red with the Redskins logo on it."

We took phone numbers for possible follow-up, and I walked back outside. By then a team of criminalists had arrived and were documenting the scene.

I stopped to look at it all again now that we'd been given three versions of how the shooting had gone down. I could see it unfold in my mind.

"The shooter was more than good—he was trained," I said.

"Gimme that again," Sampson said.

"He'd have to be a pro to be able to shoot from a vehicle going fifteen to twenty miles an hour and still hit moving targets five out of five times."

"The difficulty depends on the angle, doesn't it?" Sampson said. "Where he started shooting and when, but I agree—he practiced for this scenario."

"And McGrath was the primary target. The shooter put three rounds in him before turning the gun on Edita Kravic."

One of the crime scene guys was taking photos, a dull aluminum lamp throwing light on the victims. I'd looked at McGrath in death at least six times now. Every time it got a little easier. Every time we grew apart.

# CHAPTER

# 5

**WORD GETS OUT FAST WHEN** a cop is killed. Wisconsin Avenue was a media circus by the time Sampson and I slipped out through an alleyway behind Whole Foods. We didn't want to talk to reporters until we had something to report.

The second we were back in the squad car and Sampson had us moving, I called Chief Michaels and filled him in.

"How many men do you need?" he asked when I'd finished.

I thought about that, said, "Four, sir, including Detective Stone. She and McGrath were friends. She'll want in."

"Done. I'll have them assembled ASAP."

"Give us an hour," I said. "We're swinging by McGrath's before we head in to the office."

"No stone unturned, Alex," Michaels said.

"No, sir."

"You'll have to look at Terry Howard."

"I heard Terry's in rough shape."

"Just the same. It will come up, and we have to say we've looked at him."

"I'll do it myself."

Michaels hung up. I knew the pressure on him to find the killer was already building. When a fellow cop is murdered, you want swift justice. You want to show solidarity, solve the case quick, and put someone in cuffs and on trial.

Then again, you don't want to leap to conclusions before you've collected all the evidence. With six detectives now assigned to the case, we'd be gathering facts fast and furious for the next few days. We'd be working around the clock.

I closed my eyes and took several deep, long breaths, preparing for the hard road that lay ahead and for the separation from my family.

The prospect of hard work didn't bother me; being apart from my family did. I'm better when I have a home life. I'm a more grounded person. I'm also a saner cop.

The car slowed. Sampson said, "We're here, Alex."

McGrath's place was a first-floor apartment in a converted row house near Dupont Circle. We got out the key our dead boss had been carrying and opened his front door.

It swung open on oiled hinges, revealing a sparsely furnished space with two recliners, a curved-screen TV on the wall, and a stack of cardboard packing boxes in the corner. It looked like McGrath had not yet fully moved in.

Before I could say that to Sampson, something crashed deep inside the apartment, and we heard someone running.

I drew my weapon, hissed, "Sampson, around the back."

My partner pivoted and ran, looking for a way into the alley. I went through McGrath's place, gun up, moving quickly, taking note of how few possessions the chief of detectives had had.

I cleared the floor fast, went to the kitchen, and found a window open. I stuck my head out. Sampson flashed by me. I twisted my head, saw he was chasing a male Caucasian in jeans, a black AC/DC T-shirt, and a black golf hat, brim pulled down over a wild shock of spiky blond hair.

He was a powerful runner; an athlete, certainly. He was carrying a black knapsack, but he still bounded more than ran, chewing up ground, putting a growing distance between himself and my partner. I spun around, raced back through McGrath's house and out the front door, jumped into the car, threw on the bubble and siren, and pulled out, trying to cut the runner off.

I came flying around the corner of Twenty-Fifth and I Streets and caught a glimpse of his back as he dodged a pedestrian and vanished at the end of the block. It was astonishing how fast he'd covered that distance. Sampson was only just coming out of the alley, at least a hundred yards behind the guy.

I felt like flooring it and roaring after him, but I knew we were already beaten; I Street jogs at the end of the block, becomes Twenty-Sixth Street, and dead-ends at Rock Creek Park, which had enough vegetation and terrain changes to swallow up any man who had that kind of wheels. Oddly, we weren't far as the crow flies from where the Maserati had crashed and exploded earlier in the day.

I turned off the siren, stopped next to Sampson, and got out.

"You okay, John?"

My partner was bent over, hands on his knees, drenched in sweat and gasping for air.

"Did you see that guy go?" he croaked. "Like the Flash or something."

"Impressive," I said. "Question is, what was the Flash doing in Tommy McGrath's place?"

# CHAPTER

# 6

**TWO HOURS LATER, DETECTIVE BREE** Stone drove into the tony West Langley neighborhood of McLean, Virginia.

"What do *you* think Tommy had on his laptop?" asked Detective Kurt Muller, the older man sitting beside her in the passenger seat. He was working the ends of his silver mustache so they held in tight curls.

"Something that got the laptop stolen and maybe also got him killed," Bree said, thinking back to the meeting they'd just left and the briefing they'd gotten from Alex and Sampson.

There was a lot to absorb, but they were sure that the fast-running burglar had taken McGrath's computer and probably his backup drive from his home office. They had DC Metro's IT experts going over McGrath's work files, and there was a detective looking at every security-camera feed within six blocks of the Whole Foods. Another top investigator was searching through all of McGrath's old cases to see if he had done anything that might warrant assassination.

Alex had asked Bree and Muller to pay a visit to McGrath's estranged wife at her home in McLean, Virginia. Alex and Sampson would focus on Edita Kravic and Terry Howard.

"Heard Howard's sick," Muller said.

"Hate to think that he was involved," Bree said as they drove.

"Me too," Muller said. "He used to be a friend of mine."

She slowed, spotted the mailbox with the address she was looking for, and turned into the long driveway of a sprawling Cape house with gray cedar-shake siding and a lushly landscaped yard.

"This must have cost a small fortune," Bree said.

"One point seven five million," Muller said. "I checked before we left."

"How does a chief of detectives afford a place like this?"

"Wife's money," Muller said. "She came with a trust fund."

That had Bree chewing the inside of her cheek. Parking, she said, "How come I didn't know that?"

"I take it you were never invited out here for dinner or a barbecue."

"I've never been here before in my life."

"I have," Muller said, and he climbed out.

Bree followed him as he crossed the driveway. When they were twenty feet shy of the door, it opened, and a tall, distinguished-looking man in a well-cut suit exited carrying a briefcase. The man stopped when he saw them.

A woman in her forties appeared in the doorway behind him. She had sandy-blond hair, a tennis-honed body, puffy red eyes, and a tortured expression on her face.

"Kurt," she called to Muller in a wavering voice. "I'm crushed to see you like this."

Muller nodded, said, "I am too, Vivian."

The well-dressed man half turned toward her.

Vivian McGrath gestured to the man absently. "Kurt, this is Lance Gordon, my attorney. Detective Muller used to work for Tommy, Lance."

"We both did," Bree said.

"I'm sorry for your loss, all of you," Gordon said. "Vivian, call anytime if you have questions."

"I appreciate it, Lance," she said. "Really."

The lawyer pursed his lips and nodded before

walking past Muller and Bree. When he went by, Bree noticed an oddly familiar odor trailing him. Weirdly sweet. But she couldn't place it.

Bree and Muller went to McGrath's widow. Muller said, "Got to be hard, Viv. Even after everything."

Bree forgot about Gordon and focused on Vivian as tears leaked from her eyes and she swallowed against emotion.

"It's true," she choked out. "I'd already lost him. But this. It's just…"

Muller patted her shoulder awkwardly, said, "Viv, this is Detective Bree Stone. We're part of a task force working on Tom's case. Alex Cross is leading."

Vivian smiled weakly. "Nothing but the best for Tommy."

Then she put a well-manicured hand on Bree's arm and said, "He talked of you often, Detective Stone. Please come inside. Can I offer you coffee?"

"Please," Bree said, and Muller nodded.

She led them through rooms that could have been featured in *Architectural Digest* and ushered them into a kitchen with exposed-beam ceilings, cream-colored cabinets, and a maroon stove.

Gleaming copper pots hung over a prep station. Every surface was spotless. Every knife and utensil looked in its place, so much so that it felt sterile to Bree. There were no pictures taped to the fridge, no stacks of mail on the counters, and no dishes in the sink.

"Sit, sit," Vivian said, gesturing to stools at a breakfast counter. "What do you want to know? How can I help?"

"We understand you and Tom were getting divorced," Bree said.

"We'd separated, yes." She sniffled. "What would you like? Espresso? A latte?"

Bree said, "Espresso would be fine."

"Latte," Muller said, and he touched his mustache.

In one corner of the kitchen was an espresso maker that Bree figured would have set her back a month's pay. Vivian pushed a button, and the machine steamed and hissed and spilled black coffee that smelled like heaven.

When Vivian set the cup and saucer down in front of her, Bree said, "The separation."

McGrath's widow hardened, crossed her arms, and said, "What about it?"

"Tom's idea?" Muller asked. "Or yours?"

"Tom never told you?"

"Assume we know nothing," Bree said.

"I suggested the separation, but it was because of Tom," she said forlornly. "I'd always believed we could make it work. He was so unlike anyone who ran in my social circles, but we worked for seventeen years, and then, for reasons I'm still trying to figure out, we just didn't anymore."

She broke down sobbing.

# CHAPTER

# 7

**BREE TOOK A BREATH, FEELING** more frustrated than sympathetic.

When Vivian got control again, Bree said, "Can you be more specific about *how* it wasn't working?"

She wiped at her eyes with a tissue, glanced at Muller, and then said, "He stopped touching me, if you must know. And it felt like he had secrets. He kept a second phone. Spent money he didn't have. I figured he had a mistress."

Bree didn't comment on that.

"*Did* Tommy have a mistress?" Muller asked.

"I don't know," Vivian said. "I think so. You tell me. I never hired anyone to look, I mean. But I could see Tom was unhappy with me, so three months ago I asked him if he still loved me. He wouldn't answer the question. I asked him if he wanted a separation, a divorce, and he said that was up to me."

"If you wanted to stay with him, why did you suggest the separation?" Bree asked.

Vivian wiped at her eyes, pulled herself up straight, and gazed at Bree evenly. "I thought it might knock some sense into him, make him come back to me."

"I gather he didn't," Muller said.

She looked humiliated. "No."

"Had you filed for divorce?" Bree asked.

"No."

"Why not?"

"Because I still loved him," she said. "I hoped..."

"Must have hurt," Bree said.

"It hurt, it demeaned, and it saddened me more than you can imagine, Detective Stone," she said with a stricken expression.

"And angered you?"

Vivian looked right at Bree. "Of course."

"Enough to kill him?" Muller asked.

"Never. We used to watch those television shows like *Forty-Eight Hours* and *Dateline* where there's always one spouse killing another. We always said we couldn't understand that; if the marriage wasn't working, you left. Found a way to be friends or not and just moved on."

"How did your marriage work financially?" Bree asked.

"There was a prenup, if that's what you're asking," Vivian said. "The day we married, seventeen years ago, Tom knew he'd get nothing if we divorced."

"He angry about that?" Muller asked.

Vivian snorted. "Quite the opposite. Tommy was fine with the agreement—proud of it, in fact. He said it proved he'd married me for…"

Tears welled in her eyes again. She took a deep breath. "He liked the personal independence it represented, and the self-reliance."

"How did your lives mix?" Bree asked. "I mean, you're out here, leading a country-club life, while Tom was in the city doing a dangerous job."

Vivian's face went through a slow flurry of emotions—resistance, then consideration, and finally acceptance. Her shoulders slumped.

"The more I think about it, Detective Stone, the more I see that Tom and I did live in separate worlds, right from the beginning. Here we had a safe, fairy-tale life, but out there in DC, on the streets—well, Tom liked to fight dragons. Being a cop made him feel alive, and all I could feel when I went into the city with him was fear."

Muller said, "He was killed with a younger woman."

"I heard that," she said. "Who was she?"

"Edita Kravic, early thirties, studying law at American University, damned attractive."

Vivian took the news that the woman her estranged husband had died with was in her early thirties and damned attractive like a one-two punch.

"Was she his mistress?" she asked in a strained voice.

"We don't know," Bree said. "He ever mention that name to you?"

"Never."

"Just for the record, Mrs. McGrath," Bree said, "where were you at seven twenty this morning?"

Vivian looked at her incredulously. "You honestly think I could kill Tom?"

"We have to ask, Viv," Muller said. "It's part of the job. You know the drill."

"I was probably taking a shower."

"Anyone see you?"

"I should hope not. I've been living alone."

"Who was the first person you saw this morning?"

"Catalina Monroe. My massage therapist. I had an eight o'clock."

"You have a way we can contact her?"

McGrath's widow rattled off a phone number, then said, "You know who you should be looking at?"

"Tell us," Bree said.

"Terry Howard," Vivian said with spite in her voice. "He threatened Tom on multiple occasions."

"Cross is working that angle," Muller said.

"Good. Good. I was afraid it might be…well, you know."

"Are you planning a memorial?" Bree asked.

Vivian seemed more confused than ever; she looked down and whispered, "Is that something *I'm* supposed to do? I don't know if Tommy would even want me to be involved."

Muller said, "I suppose you make that decision by first taking a moment to honor the good times you had with Tommy, figure out what they meant to you. If Tommy's love during those years was enough, you do it, you see him buried. And if those years of love weren't enough, you don't."

"If you decide not to do anything, I'll take care of the arrangements," Bree said.

McGrath's widow looked around as if in a daze, her chin trembling, and then said, "No, Kurt's right. Honoring our love and burying the husband Tommy *was* is the least I can do."

The dam burst, and she wept. "It's the only thing I can do for him now."

# CHAPTER

# 8

**EDITA KRAVIC'S APARTMENT IN** Columbia Heights looked like it had been decorated right out of the Sundance Catalog—high-end furniture, nicely framed prints on the wall—and given the place's location, the rent had to be two, maybe three thousand a month.

That was strange, I thought, because law students were usually starving. Edita evidently did quite well with the whole Level 2 Certified Coach thing.

The kitchen was stocked with culinary gadgetry, and there were fine wines chilling in the fridge along with gourmet cheeses and spreads. Nice crystal in the cabinets, but no photographs anywhere in the living area, nothing that suggested Edita Kravic's private life, nothing that could tell us more about her.

The apartment had three bedrooms. The smallest one had been turned into an office. There was a business phone with several lines and an open laptop on the desk.

"I'll look here," I said.

"I'll take the bedrooms," Sampson said.

Just as in the living area, there was nothing personal on the shelves or the walls. Just a basic desk, a backless chair, and two wooden filing cabinets. I tugged on the drawers of one and found them locked. The top drawer of the other slid open, revealing standard office supplies.

The next drawer down was full of files. I looked through them, found out that she owned a late-model Audi A5 and that she vacationed in the Caymans—a lot, as in three times in the prior year. But there was nothing that gave me a clear idea of how she'd paid for it all.

I was thinking she'd have to have an income of over a hundred grand to live like this. Did Level 2 Certified Coaches make that kind of money? If so, maybe I was in the wrong business.

I thought about breaking the lock on the first cabinet but decided to take a look at the computer first. To my surprise, when I ran my finger across the touchpad, the screen lit right up and showed me the desktop. Several different applications were running.

One was Edita's law school e-mail account. I sat down and scanned through the e-mails, seeing nothing from Tom McGrath. Most of the messages were to and from professors and classmates. One classmate, JohnnyBoy5, had sent six e-mails to her in the eighteen hours preceding her murder.

*Really?* read one sent around ten thirty the previous night. *Standing me up again? This was your meet, remember?*

I did a search of her entire in-box, looking for all e-mails from JohnnyBoy5. There were more than a hundred, going back eighteen months. I rearranged them so they were in chronological order and read a tale of growing obsession.

JohnnyBoy5 had evidently been smitten by Edita Kravic from the get-go, and he was not shy about saying so. Though she seemed to flirt with him at times, for the most part, she did nothing to encourage him.

For the first year, she'd managed to keep JohnnyBoy5 at bay. But after that, his tone became irate, and then depressed.

*I don't know what's come over me,* JohnnyBoy5 had written back in March. *I'm terrified that I won't see you again, Edita. I know it's irrational, but there it is. I can't shake this dark, dark feeling that I'm going to lose you somehow, that something bad is going to happen to you, that you're never going to see the real me, and that you'll never understand how much I truly care about you.*

Edita wrote back, *This is no good, Johnny. Go away or I get a restraining order. A third-year told me how to do it.*

For three weeks after that, there was no contact between Ms. Kravic and JohnnyBoy5. Then he e-mailed her again.

*I know what you are, Edita, what you do out of class.*

No return e-mail. No follow-up for months. Three weeks before Edita was murdered, however, JohnnyBoy5 wrote her again.

*Who is he? The big meathead who threatened to break my face? Really? This is how things are between us? What if I just posted on Facebook about you and the life you don't want anyone to know about? Will that do it?*

Two weeks passed.

*Sorry for the rants,* JohnnyBoy5 wrote. *God, I read back through some of it and that wasn't me, Edita. The doctor put me on this asthma medicine called montelukast and I had a rare but bad side effect, which put me in a dark way. But I've returned to the living! Study group's starting up again. Love to have you back, of course. No worries about anything else. Everyone's got skeletons in the closet, am I right?*

Edita did not respond. Every day after that, leading up to the day before her death, JohnnyBoy5 wrote—chidingly, in worry, in despair, and in anger.

*In so many ways, meeting you was the ruin of my life,* he'd written just two days before she died. *Everything I built was reduced to rubble the moment I met you. Ruin deserves ruin, Edita. Ruin deserves ruin.*

Obsession has been a staple in the recipe book of murder since time immemorial. Sometimes obsession is a major ingredient. Other times, obsession is the oven that makes things too hot to handle.

Some obsessives were taught to be that way through neglect or cruelty. Others developed hatred as the basis of their obsession. This was especially true of organized serial killers. They ritualized their killings, taking their rage out on surrogates for the people who'd spawned their hatred.

But love can be the basis of obsession too, especially if one party or the other is spurned. You see that kind of gradual *tick-tick-tick* change in a person as he goes from being smitten to being crazy in love to—when he's rejected—feeling sad, then worthless, then angry, then enraged, and then he grabs a gun because *If I can't have the object of my desire, no one will.*

Was that what had happened with JohnnyBoy5? Had he taken the romantic spiral toward homicide and killed Edita and Tommy McGrath, the big guy who'd threatened to break his face? Or was that someone else?

Sampson walked in. "I got something you need to see."

"Me too," I said, getting up. "She's got a stalker."

"That fits," he said. He turned and led me into her bedroom.

Big four-poster bed. Matched linens. New dresser. Nice mirror. A walk-in closet with racks bulging with clothes and shelves holding dozens of beautiful shoes.

There were built-in drawers at the far end of the closet.

Sampson had pulled two of them open. The first was filled with fine lingerie. The second featured a wide selection of sex toys and lubricants.

"So she had a kinky side," I said. "So what?"

He pushed shut the two drawers and opened the ones directly below. I took both in at a glance and said, "Oh, well, that changes things."

"Damn sure does," Sampson said, looking into the right drawer, which was filled with hard-core S&M equipment.

I was more interested in the drawer on the left, the deeper one, the one filled with stacks and stacks of banded fifty-dollar bills.

# CHAPTER

# 9

**SAMPSON AND I LEFT** Edita Kravic's apartment shortly after seven that evening. We'd found the sex equipment and the cash, which we estimated at forty thousand dollars, but little to explain how a second-year law student had come to have that kind of money stuck away in a clothes drawer.

When you see that much dough and the sex gear, your investigative instincts tend to drift toward hooking or drugs or smuggling or organized crime. But we'd found no direct evidence of anything illegal, not even in the locked file cabinet, which we'd opened after we'd located the key.

The cabinet had more of Edita Kravic's personal files, one of which revealed that she was from Slovakia and had a green card. Another file showed an account with Bank of America with a balance of fifteen hundred dollars. She owed less than that on her Visa and American Express cards. I found her lease. I'd predicted the rent would be two or three grand a month; it was actually four thousand. But she wasn't writing checks for the rent, or not any that I could see.

"She paid cash for everything," I said when we got back to the car.

"Bought high-end stuff with it," Sampson said. "Classic way to evade taxes."

"Still doesn't explain where the money came from," I said. "There were no files from the Phoenix Club, no record of payments."

"Maybe the club's evading taxes too," Sampson said, starting the squad car. "Where to?"

"Swing by Terry Howard's place before heading back to the office."

"Make the chief rest easier?"

"Exactly."

We drove to a shabby, four-story apartment building off New York Avenue in Northeast.

"This the right one?" I asked.

"Google Maps don't lie," Sampson said.

The seedy neighborhood sobered me, made me realize just how far and how hard Tommy McGrath's onetime partner had fallen since his days with the Major Case Unit. Terry Howard had had a formidable reputation for playing the tough guy. He had never been above intimidating a source to get what he wanted. In fact, he'd been accused of it multiple times, and because of that, and because Tommy had ultimately turned on Howard, we were here.

But the former detective who opened the door of his one-bedroom apartment didn't look like a tough guy; he looked like a tired man pushing seventy rather than fifty-five. He wore a faded Washington Redskins ball cap, a plain black T-shirt, and jeans that sagged off him. The big frame I remembered was still there, but he'd gone soft and lost weight. His eyes were rheumy. He smelled of vodka.

"Figured I'd see you two before too long," Howard said.

"Can we come in, Terry? Ask a few questions?"

"Not tonight, I got lots of jack shit to take care of. Sorry."

I said, "You know we have to talk to you, and you know why. Now, we can continue standing here in your doorway where everyone on the floor will know your business, or we can come in, or we can take you down to the station. Any way you want to do this is fine by us."

Howard's bleary eyes got hard and beady. "In here."

He stood aside. We walked into his sad little

world. The apartment reeked of cigarette smoke. The muted television was tuned to a cable station rerunning classic baseball games. Beer cans and three empty bottles of Smirnoff vodka crowded the coffee table. The parakeet in the cage between the easy chair and the couch looked like a miniature plucked chicken. It had no feathers except for a crown of baby blue and orange.

"That's Sylvia Plath," Howard said. "She's got issues."

He laughed uproariously at that and then started coughing hard. He picked up a tissue, spit into it, and then said, "Aren't you going to ask me where I was when Tommy got it?"

"We figured we'd dance with you awhile before that," Sampson said.

Howard sobered, said, "No reason to. I was right here at the time the TV guys say he was killed."

"Anyone see you?"

"Six of the fine ladies from my neighborhood Hooters were supposed to come over for breakfast and watch last night's game with me on the DVR," Howard said. "But, alas, they stood me up. Too bad. Good game. Senators demolished the Red Sox in interleague play. Harper went three for four."

"So you have no alibi," I said.

"Nope," Howard said, going to the kitchen and

pouring orange juice and vodka into a dirty high-ball glass. "But I know you can't put me on upper Wisconsin because I wasn't there. Hell, I can barely walk two blocks."

"You must have wanted to kill Tommy at one time," Sampson said.

"Man destroys your life, it crosses your mind," Howard said, shuffling back and settling into a recliner. "But I did not pull the trigger on COD McGrath."

"You own a Remington 1911?" I asked.

"I have always been a devotee of Smith and Wesson, so no."

"Mind if we look around?"

"Hell yeah, I mind," the disgraced detective said. "You got a warrant, Cross, have at her. Otherwise, and with all due respect, we're done here. Me and Sylvia P. got another game to watch."

# CHAPTER

# 10

**SAMPSON AND I DIDN'T ARGUE** with Howard. The former detective didn't strike me as being physically or mentally capable of shooting McGrath. He seemed to have given up and was at some bitter peace with that.

So we left and returned to the office, where I found Bree and Muller waiting with Rico Lincoln and Martin O'Donnell, the other detectives Chief Michaels had assigned to the murder of Tom McGrath. Bree and Muller described their meeting with Vivian McGrath and we brought them up to speed on what we'd found at McGrath's, Edita Kravic's, and Terry Howard's.

When we finished, I looked at Detective Lincoln, a tall, skinny marathoner who'd been smiling and acting impatient during our reports.

"You got something you'd like to share, Rico?"

"I do," Lincoln said. "I mean, we both do."

"You first," O'Donnell said.

Lincoln got on his computer and linked it to a large screen on the wall. The screen jumped to a traffic-camera perspective of upper Wisconsin Avenue. Cars in both northbound lanes came at the camera head-on so we could see each vehicle and its passengers best at a distance. With the rain, it was hard to get a good look through the windshields, especially the ones in the right lane.

Lincoln sped the video up, watching the data in the lower corner, and then paused at the time stamp reading 7:20 a.m.

"Tommy McGrath and Edita Kravic are gunned down at seven twenty," he said, and he hit Play. "Coming at you in the northbound right lane, dark-primer four-door sedan, stripped, almost looks like it's about to be repainted."

"That Treasury agent called it," Sampson said.

"Watch now," Lincoln said.

The car was passing, rain spattering its windshield, and you couldn't see a thing. Lincoln froze the screen when the front of the car was almost out of view. He pointed to the left side of the windshield. Up on the dashboard, there was a red Washington Redskins ball cap.

"We saw Howard wearing a red Redskins cap just like that not an hour ago," Sampson said.

It was true. Same hat.

Lincoln said, "Something else."

The detective advanced the frames so the windshield of the car and then the tinted driver-side window disappeared. When he stopped the film again, we had a side-angle view through the open rear window.

We could see the silhouette of a person with a wild mop of hair sitting in the middle of the backseat.

"Okay?" I said.

Lincoln advanced the film two frames. Here, the shadows were different. Three-quarters of the face was revealed.

I stared for a second and then said, "Raggedy Ann?"

"That was our reaction," Detective O'Donnell said. "At first we thought we had the wrong car and the cap on the windshield was just chance."

Lincoln said, "But the more we thought about it, the more we became convinced that there wasn't a third person in the backseat. A scarecrow was sitting there. See the shadows here and here? That's the shoulders of a dark coat. See the lapels?"

"I get it," I said. "Why's Raggedy Ann wearing a coat?"

"Exactly," Lincoln said.

Rubbing my chin, I said, "I agree that's our shooter's car. Have pictures of it at the best angles sent to every officer on the force."

"On it," Lincoln said, and he started typing.

Bree fought off a yawn. I fought off a yawn too and then nodded at O'Donnell, who said, "I started going through Chief McGrath's work files. Right away, I found a threatening e-mail."

He typed on his computer, and the screen changed from the close-up of the Raggedy Ann doll to a July 3 e-mail to McGrath from TL.

*You push too hard, we gonna push right back. Only it's gonna be lethal this time, Chief McG.*

"TL?" Sampson said. "That Thao Le?"

"Has to be," Bree said, sitting forward.

Muller said, "I thought Le got convicted in Prince George's last year."

"Got off on appeal four months ago," O'Donnell said, showing us an investigative file he'd found in McGrath's desk. "Tommy had evidently been running a solo investigation into Le's activities since his release."

"What did he find?" Bree asked.

"That Le was back in the game. Associating with

known criminals and members of his old gang. Drugs. Women. Loan-sharking. Extortion."

"Why wouldn't Tommy have told someone?" Sampson asked.

"Nailing Le was personal with Tommy," O'Donnell said. "He even wrote about it. He thought Le was the one who'd planted the evidence in Terry Howard's case, and even though Terry hated him, Tommy was out to prove it."

"So maybe Tommy got close enough to spook Le into making good on his threat," Bree said.

"Where's Le now?" I asked.

"No clue yet," O'Donnell said. "But the last two times Le was picked up on weapons charges, he was carrying a forty-five-caliber Remington 1911."

# CHAPTER

# 11

**I WAS UP BEFORE DAWN,** startled awake by a dream where a pistol-packing Raggedy Ann drove a motorcycle down Rock Creek Parkway, which was littered with fifty-dollar bills. The cash almost covered the corpses of Edita Kravic and Tommy McGrath.

I eased from bed, letting Bree sleep. We'd gotten home after midnight, wolfed down leftovers from the fridge, and gone straight to sleep.

After a shower, I went downstairs to find my ninety-one-year-old grandmother making breakfast.

"You're up kind of early, Nana Mama," I said, kissing her on the cheek.

"Big day ahead for you," she said. "I wanted to make sure it starts right."

"We appreciate it," I said. I poured myself some coffee and got the papers from the front porch.

The murder of Tommy McGrath and Edita Kravic led the front page of both the *Washington Post* and the *Washington Times*. Chief Michaels was quoted as saying DC Metro had lost one of its best men and that the department would be relentless in its pursuit of the killers. He announced the formation of an elite task force to investigate the murders, and he named me as team leader.

"Pop?"

I glanced up from the papers to see my oldest child, Damon, standing there, looking excited.

I smiled, asked, "You ready?"

"As I'll ever be."

"Sit down there and Nana will give you one last proper breakfast."

Damon's six foot five and towers over my grandmother. He scooped her up and gave her a kiss, which caused her to shriek with laughter.

"What was that for, young man?" she demanded, looking ruffled when he set her down.

"Just because," Damon said. "Can I get three eggs this morning?"

She sniffed. "I suppose I can manage it."

"Two for me," said my fifteen-year-old daughter, Jannie, who was still in her pajamas and rubbing her eyes when she came in. "I'll make my own shake."

Ali, almost eight and my youngest, ran in after her and said, "I want French toast."

"No sugar-bombing in my kitchen," Nana Mama said. "Eggs. Protein. Good for your brain."

"So's French toast."

I looked at him, said, "You'll never win that one."

Ali acted like the weight of the world was on him. "Can I get two sunny-side up with regular toast?"

"That you can have," my grandmother said.

Bree joined soon after. It was a nice treat, all of us sharing breakfast together on a weekday. All too soon, though, we were out in front of the house helping Damon load the last of his things into our car.

"That's it?" I said, shaking my head. "Really not that much."

"That surprises you?" Damon asked.

"I guess it does," I said. "Back when I left for school, I had twice the amount of stuff, or maybe my stuff was just bigger. That's it—there's no huge stereo system anymore. Everything's gotten smaller."

"That's a news flash, Alex," my grandmother said impatiently, and she rapped her cane on the sidewalk. "Now, Damon, you come over here and give your Nana Mama some love before you go, but do not pick me up again. You'll break my back."

Damon smirked before bending over and kissing Nana Mama good-bye.

"I'm so proud of you," she said, her eyes getting glassy. "You are a gentleman and a scholar."

Coming from my grandmother, a retired English teacher and former high school vice principal, that was high praise.

Damon beamed, said, "That's because you taught me how to study."

"You learned it and ran with it," she said. "Give yourself some credit."

He kissed her on the cheek again and then turned to Jannie. "You keep killing it, you hear?"

"That's the plan," she said, and hugged him. "You'll come to the invitational, right?"

Damon said, "Wouldn't miss out on watching the fastest woman on earth."

"Not yet," Jannie said, grinning.

"Dream it, own it, give it time," Damon said, and then he picked up Ali, who was looking morose. "Why the face, little man?"

Ali shrugged, said, "You're going away. Again."

"I'll be an hour away," Damon said. "Not six hours, like when I was up at Kraft, so I'll be home to see you a whole lot more."

Ali perked up. "Promise?"

"You know I need my Ali Cross fix," Damon said, and he tickled Ali until he howled with laughter.

Then he hugged Bree, told her to take care of me.

"Ready?" I asked.

"Whole new life waiting," Damon said, and even though he was trying to remain cool, I could see he was vibrating with emotion as we drove away.

# CHAPTER

# 12

**WE TOOK 295 HEADING NORTH** toward Baltimore and drove in a pleasant quiet. Part of me wanted to be a helicopter parent, remind him to do this or do that, tell him how to handle one academic crisis or another.

But Damon had left home at sixteen to chase his dreams. He knew how to take care of himself already, and that made me both proud and sad. My job as a parent had shrunk to the role of adviser, but once upon a time, I had been all he had.

Passing Hyattsville, Maryland, I flashed on the moment Damon was born, how my first wife, Maria, had sobbed with joy when the nurse laid him on her belly, a squirming, squealing miracle that I'd loved in an instant.

I managed to keep my mind from going to the

night Maria was killed in a drive-by. Instead, my memories were of those first few years after Maria died, how ripped apart I'd felt unless I was holding Damon or Jannie, who'd been an infant at the time. Without Nana Mama I would never have been able to go on. My grandmother had stepped in as she had when I was a boy. She was Damon's mother as much as she'd been mine.

Damon and I talked baseball near Laurel, Maryland, and both of us agreed that if Bryce Harper could stay healthy, he would put up Hall of Fame statistics. We'd gone to New York a few years ago for the All-Star Game and watched him hit in the Home Run Derby. Harper had freakish quickness and strength.

"He's like Jannie, you know?" Damon said. "An outlier. There's something special about them. You just see it when they move."

"You're not so bad yourself," I said.

"I'm good enough to be a seventh or eighth man in Division One."

"Never sell yourself short," I said.

"Just being honest, and I'm good with coming off the bench, Dad," he said. "Jannie, though? She's in a world where very few people get to live."

That was true. Seeing my daughter run on a track was like watching a gazelle chased by a lion and—

"Dad! Watch out!"

Six or seven car lengths in front of us, a twenty-seven-foot Jayco camping trailer attached to the back of a Ford F-150 pickup had started to swerve wildly. I got my foot on the brake a split second before the camper and pickup went into a wide, arcing skid and then jackknifed, flipped, and careened left, inches off our front bumper.

I hit the gas, shot forward, and went by it. The trailer smashed an oncoming car, the pickup slammed into something else, and then the whole mass of twisted metal went across the fast lane and down the embankment behind us.

"Holy shit!" Damon yelled. "Holy shit, we just almost died!"

My heart was slamming in my chest, and my hands were trembling on the wheel as I got over on the shoulder. We *had* almost died. The Grim Reaper had been right there but passed us by.

"C'mon," I said, yanking out my cell and dialing 911. "We've got to help."

Damon jumped out and ran back down the road to the embankment while I told the dispatcher what had happened.

When I reached the pickup, Damon shook his head. The driver was dead and hanging out the back window. We heard a baby crying in the car that had been hit by the travel trailer and flipped onto its roof.

"Help!" a woman yelled. "Someone please help us."

Damon got down on his knees by the car and I did too. The young mom's head was bleeding hard. The baby was upside down but appeared uninjured, mostly just upset about being upside down.

"We've got an ambulance coming," I said. "What's your name?"

"Sally Jo," she said. "Sally Jo Hepner. I'm bleeding like a stuck pig. Am I gonna die?"

"I think you'll need a lot of stitches, but you're not going to die. What's your baby's name?"

I could already hear sirens.

"Bobby," she said. "After my dad."

Damon had wriggled in through the window and gotten the car seat free. He squirmed back and pulled him out. Bobby Hepner was fussing, but just showing him his mother seemed to quiet him down.

Firemen and EMTs were on the scene within five minutes of the crash. We stayed until we saw the mom safely extracted from the car and put on a backboard with a neck collar, just in case. One of the EMTs carried her baby into the ambulance.

"Looks like our work here is done," I said. "Let's get you to school."

Damon smiled, but when we got back in the car, he was brooding. "Strange how life is. Here one minute and gone the next."

"Don't worry about it too much."

"I guess. But seeing that, it's like, what's the point? You never know when your time is up."

"Exactly," I said. "So live every minute like it's your last, and be grateful. The way I see it, that near miss was a message. We came close, but we weren't meant to be in a car accident today. We were reminded of how fragile and precious life is, but we weren't supposed to die. We were supposed to get you to college, and that's what we're going to do."

Damon dipped his head, but then he grinned, said, "Okay."

Johns Hopkins had changed in some ways since I was a student, but the Homewood campus was still an oasis of green quads and red-brick halls in the city of Baltimore, and I still felt the electricity of the place when we arrived. We were met by student volunteers, who steered us through the various lines and gave us a thick orientation packet for incoming freshmen.

We found Damon's room and met his roommate—William Clancy, a lacrosse player from

Massachusetts—and his parents. The boys seemed to click from the start. We helped them get squared away, and then there was an awkward moment when it was obvious they wanted the parents to leave.

"Walk me to the car," I said. "There's something down there that I want you to have."

"Uh, sure," Damon said, and he nodded to his roommate. "Be back, and then we'll go to the welcome picnic?"

"Sounds good," William said.

We got to the car, and I looked at him with fierce pride and love.

"What did you want me to have?" Damon asked.

I grabbed him and bear-hugged him, unable to stop the tears.

"Your mom," I choked out. "She would have been very, very happy to see who you've become."

Damon looked uncomfortable when I released him and stepped back. A few tears slipped from his eyes before he said, "Thank you, Dad. For everything."

I couldn't take it, and I bear-hugged him again and then told him to get going before I became a total, blubbering mess. He laughed. We bumped fists. And he was gone, into the place that had cut and sharpened me into a man.

Driving away was bittersweet; I was happy

beyond words for his achievements but already mourning a part of my life that had begun in the loving care of Damon, my helpless infant boy, and ended just a few moments before, when my young man had walked confidently away.

# Part Two

# A VIGILANTE KILLING

# CHAPTER

# 13

**I LEFT THE JOHNS HOPKINS** campus, drove around the corner, stopped, and put my head on the wheel. I'd known my son was leaving for months, but it had still flattened me.

My cell rang. John Sampson. I answered on the Bluetooth.

"You like pho?" he asked.

"If it's made right," I said, putting the car in gear. "Why?"

"Because one of O'Donnell's sources puts Thao Le at Pho Phred's in Falls Church at one o'clock this afternoon. Can you make it back in time?"

I looked at the clock, said, "With the bubble and siren, yes."

"I'd cut the siren when you get close," Sampson said, and he hung up.

I got back onto 295, put up the bubble, and took the car up to eighty-five, tapping on the siren to get folks out of the way and thinking about Thao Le.

He'd been a gangbanger from the get-go. Son of a California mobster, he'd come east at eighteen and formed his own criminal enterprise that focused on the trade in heroin, cocaine, and marijuana, but he'd later branched out into human trafficking.

He'd been arrested twice on racketeering charges, and twice he'd walked because of insufficient evidence or, depending on your source, because of the money Le paid in bribes. Soon enough, though, Le came on the radar of Detective Tommy McGrath and his partner at the time, Terry Howard.

A year into the investigation of Le, Internal Affairs caught Howard with cocaine and money taken during a drug bust. Howard had always maintained his innocence, even tried to blame it on McGrath, but in the end, he'd been fired, and it had been ugly for him ever since.

McGrath believed Le had framed his partner. But six years after the fact, Tommy had not turned up enough evidence to exonerate Terry Howard because, as he'd noted in the file O'Donnell found, the Vietnamese gangster was *slippery and careful.* The most time Le had ever served was three and a half years for assaulting two police officers attempting to take him into custody. Both cops had ended up in the hospital.

Which is why I decided that if we were going to talk with Le, we would bring a small army with us. I started making calls.

At ten minutes to one, I pulled into a lumber-yard just down the street from Eden Center, a Vietnamese and Korean entertainment and shopping hub in Falls Church. I found Bree, Sampson, and Muller waiting for me as well as four SWAT operators, two patrol units, and a sergeant detective named Earl Rand whom I'd worked with successfully before. All were with the Fairfax County Sheriff's Department.

"How'd it go?" Bree said. She'd already armored up in the sweltering heat.

"Heartbreaking in some ways, the proudest moment of my life in others."

"Good for you. You should be proud of him. He's an amazing kid."

"He is that," I said, and I put on my own armor as Detective Rand placed a map on the hood of one of the cruisers. It showed the Eden Center, a mall laid out in a lazy U shape with a large parking lot in the middle.

Pho Phred's was near the Viet-Royale restaurant

in the northeast corner of the U, part of a section called the Sidewalk Stores that was set up to resemble an outdoor market in old Saigon. Rand showed us the access to the area from the south off the main parking lot and from the north off a smaller parking lot that abutted Oakwood Cemetery.

Rand said we'd want to cover both entrances as well as send in Fairfax officers familiar with the center through both ends of the bottom of the U.

"You'll have him cut off in four directions," Rand said. "There's nowhere else to go."

"Let's do it," I said, and I got in a car with Sampson.

"It'd be nice if Le's good for McGrath, Kravic, and Peters," he said.

"It would be," I said. "I could take some time off, go watch Jannie run."

"No reason that can't happen," Sampson said, starting the car and heading for Eden Center.

From there, everything went downhill fast.

# CHAPTER

# 14

**WE WERE ALL IN CONTACT** over the same radio frequency. Two Fairfax County officers entered Eden Center through Planet Fitness, on the far west side of the Sidewalk Stores. Two more came in from the east.

Bree and Muller came in the north entrance. Sampson, Detective Rand, and I went in through the south door. This section of Eden Center was painted light blue, which Rand said was believed to promote prosperity.

The area was certainly doing a thriving business. At one o'clock on a Friday afternoon, there were hundreds of Vietnamese Americans roaming around, shopping for fresh fish in one store, embroidered silk dresses in another, taffy candy in a third. And the air smelled savory and sweet.

Sampson and I stood out like sore thumbs, but being tall among short people had its advantages. We later figured that one or all of us must have been seen entering the center, because we were inside for no more than ninety seconds before, not fifty yards away, Thao Le blew out of Pho Phred's, looked around, and saw us.

Le was wiry, fast, and agile. He turned and ran north.

"He's coming right at you, Bree," I said, breaking into a run.

"I see him."

Detective Rand said, "Take him clean if you—"

Le must have spotted Bree and Muller, because he suddenly darted into a packed restaurant. Bree left Muller in the dust and dashed in after Le, her badge up. We heard screaming.

"There's got to be a back way out of there!" I yelled, dodging into a fish store forty yards shy of the restaurant.

With my badge up, I yelled at the startled merchant and his customers, "Back door!"

His eyes got big and round, but he gestured to rubber curtains behind the counter.

I heard Rand calling for patrol cars as I went through the rubber curtains into a cold storage area off a small loading dock. The overhead door was raised. A wholesale-seafood truck was backing up.

I jumped off the dock before the truck could block it, landed in a putrid-smelling puddle, and stumbled. Sampson was right behind me; he grabbed me under the arm and got me upright just as we heard a crotch-rocket motorcycle start up and then saw it squeal out from behind a dumpster fifty yards away.

Helmetless, Le handled the bike like an expert, rear wheel drifting and smoking before he shot north and away from Bree, who had her gun up but wisely held her fire. Le accelerated toward the corner of the mall, then downshifted, braked, and disappeared to our right.

"I've got cars coming right at him!" Rand gasped as he caught up to us.

We were all running now. Bree got around the corner and held her ground. We reached her just in time to see the Fairfax patrol car turn Le.

The gangster came right back at us with the patrol car in pursuit. Another patrol car was entering the hunt from behind us. I was thinking Le was as good as in cuffs.

Le stopped about halfway down the parking lot, near another dumpster and a haphazard pile of wooden pallets stacked by the rear chain-link fence. The first cruiser was almost to Le when he looked our way and smiled.

He flicked the accelerator on the motorcycle,

covered fifteen yards in a second, shot up that pile of wooden pallets, and was in the air for maybe ten feet before he landed almost sideways on the dumpster.

Le buried the throttle the instant he touched down, then he shot across the dumpster lids diagonally, jumped up on the pegs as the bike went airborne again, and sailed over the chain-link fence that separated the parking lot from Oakwood Cemetery.

The motorcycle landed on a service road and almost tipped, but Le got his foot down, righted it, and sped off, leaving us angry at losing him and slack-jawed at his mad skills.

Then a Fairfax patrolman still inside Eden Center came over the radio and said, "I've got Le's girlfriend here at Pho Phred's. You want to talk to her?"

# CHAPTER

# 15

**WE FOUND THE OFFICER AND** a zip-cuffed Michele Bui outside Pho Phred's. Ms. Bui was, to put it mildly, unhappy.

"I got my rights," she said. "I'm U.S. born and raised, never put a toe in Hanoi or Ho Chi Minh City. So I don't have to say a thing because I have not done a thing other than order lunch. This is harassment, pure and simple."

Bui was tall for a Vietnamese female, almost five six, and slender. Her hair was shaved on one side and long on the other. She sported tattoos of yellow butterflies on her left arm, and red ones swarmed on the right. Two hoops in each nostril completed the look.

Bui began to shout in Vietnamese, and many

people in the halls and other stores came to the doorways and looked at us.

"We just want to have a chat," Bree said calmly.

"You usually bring guns and zip cuffs to a chat?" Bui asked.

"When Thao Le is who we want to chat with, yes," I said.

"When are you guys going to leave Thao alone?" she said. "You arrest him, he gets off. You arrest him, he gets off. When you going to figure out that he can't be had?"

She watched our faces and smiled knowingly. "You don't have him, do you? You didn't catch him!"

Bui started laughing and then called out something in Vietnamese that got the other people there laughing.

She looked at me. "You in charge?"

I jerked my head toward Detective Rand.

Bui rolled her eyes, said, "Can you take the cuffs off? They're starting to hurt, and I smell a lawsuit coming on."

Bree said, "If we take them off, you'll talk to us?"

"Why would I do that?" Bui asked. "I am under zero obligation to talk to you because I have done nothing wrong."

"How about aiding and abetting a cop killer?" Sampson said.

That seemed to come out of nowhere to Bui, and her chin retreated fast.

"Thao's no cop killer," she said.

"We think he is," Bree said. "The cop was Tommy McGrath, a guy who had a jones to put Thao away for the rest of his life."

Bui said nothing, her eyes darting back and forth.

"You've heard the name before? McGrath?" I asked.

The way she shook her head said she *had* heard of the late COD.

Bree picked up on it too. She said, "When someone kills a cop, the net gets big and wide. That net is forming around your boyfriend. Question is, which of his fish will get caught in the net with him?"

"What's that mean?"

"It means your boyfriend is disloyal," I said. "He keeps three different women in three different apartments, rotates among them."

Bui's face hardened, but she said nothing.

"How's that make you feel, sharing him with two others, good for only one night in three?"

Le's girlfriend blinked, stared at the floor, and said, "If that."

"Right. And suppose his other two girlfriends decide it's better to tell us what they know than get caught in Thao's net. Where's that going to leave you?"

Tears began to well in her eyes. "Up a creek," she said. "Take off the cuffs, and I'll tell you what I can."

# CHAPTER

# 16

**BREE BUILT UP A QUICK** rapport with the twenty-four-year-old, so we decided to let her and Muller run the questioning when we returned to DC.

I went back to the office I share with Sampson and found a GoPro camera in a sealed evidence bag along with a note from the medical examiner Nancy Barton.

*From the Maserati,* she'd written. *You'll find it interesting.*

Barton had included a cable to hook up the camera to my computer. I attached it and turned the camera on. I had to fiddle until I got it in play-back mode, and then Sampson and I watched the most recent MPEG file.

We watched it again. We talked about what we'd seen, and then we watched it a third time.

"I think we need to tell Michaels sooner rather than later," Sampson said.

"Agreed," I replied.

Ten minutes later, we were in the office of DC police chief Bryan Michaels. A welterweight fighting a paunchy belly, Michaels took a sip from his coffee cup and made a sour face.

"Damn it, I'll never get used to this," he said, shuddering and setting the cup down on his desk. "Hot lemon water. Supposed to be good for me, change my alkalinity."

"Add honey," I said.

"But first call up that video we sent you," Sampson said.

"I could use a latte." Michaels sighed, put on reading glasses, and turned to his computer.

A few keystrokes later, the MPEG video appeared.

"What is this?" he asked.

"Film of the last minutes of Aaron Peters's life," I said. "He had a GoPro Hero mounted in a fireproof housing on his dashboard. He must have hooked it up to his speedometer somehow, because—well, you'll see."

The chief clicked on the video, blew it up to full screen.

The camera gave us a view from the center of the dash, looking over the sleek hood and down along the headlight beams of the Maserati. In the lower right corner of the video, there was a digital speedometer. Lower left, a timer set at 0.

"Here we go, epic run," said Aaron Peters off camera as he left Beach Drive for Rock Creek Parkway.

The timer started running as the engine roared, and the Maserati accelerated from thirty to seventy-five in under four seconds.

Peters laughed and then said, "Sonofa—"

The sounds of downshifting and brakes squealing filled the chief's office.

"Watch for it, Chief," Sampson said.

Coming out of a backward S curve, a single headlamp cut the pavement beside the Maserati.

"Motorcycle?" Michaels said.

"What the…hey, asshole!" Aaron Peters said.

The headlights slashed again to the right, and you could hear the powerful whine of the motorcycle over the Maserati's engine. But then Peters began cutting back and forth, trying to keep the motorcyclist from passing. He braked poorly in the next curve and tried to accelerate.

"Catch me if you can," Aaron Peters said, and his speed climbed to ninety.

It didn't seem to matter. The single headlight swung, and the motorcycle's engine sounded almost as loud as the Maserati's before two shots rang out. The sports car went out of control, smacked a guardrail, and did a whip-fast 360-degree skid that almost lit up the escaping motorcyclist for a split second before the car vaulted into the woods, hit the trees, and exploded into flames.

"Jesus," Michaels said. "The guy shot from a motorcycle as he was going ninety?"

"Exactly our reaction," I said. "Now call up the pictures I sent you."

A minute later, the screen split into two photographs. One showed the wounds on COD Tom McGrath as photographed during his autopsy earlier in the day. The other picture was a close-up of Peters's two head wounds.

"Okay?" Michaels said.

"In both cases, the shooting was extraordinary," I said. "And in both cases, every bullet fired was a forty-five, perhaps from a Remington model 1911."

Chief Michaels squinted one eye. "You think it's the same shooter?"

"We have two slugs from Peters's Kevlar helmet. We should have solid comparisons to the bullets that killed McGrath, but in the meantime we have to consider the possibility of one shooter, and I thought you should know."

The chief thought a moment, said, "I don't want any of this getting out until we've got a confirm or no-confirm on the ballistics. Are we clear?"

"We are," Sampson said, and I nodded.

"Any connection between Peters and McGrath?" the chief asked.

"Nothing yet," Sampson said.

"Keep me posted."

"Every few hours, sir," I said.

When we turned to leave, Michaels said, "Alex, could I have a word with you?"

I glanced at Sampson, said, "Sure."

When the door closed behind my partner, Michaels said, "I need a chief of detectives."

"Who are you considering?"

"You."

"Me?"

"Who better?"

I felt all sorts of conflicting emotions roil through me.

"Well?" Michaels said.

"I'm flattered, Chief," I said. "And humbled that you think highly enough of me to offer me the job. But I need some time to think, to talk to Bree and my family."

"You'd have more regular hours. Be able to

see them more consistently, if that matters to you."

"It does, but I still am going to need some time to—"

"Take all the time in the world. Just give me an answer by eight o'clock tomorrow morning."

# CHAPTER

# 17

**NANA MAMA WAS IN RARE** form that night. She'd seen Rachael Ray make chicken Provençal and decided to make it herself, doctoring the dish a bit by adding a little of this and a little of that until it was the kind of meal where you fought for seconds.

"Good, isn't it?" I said.

"I'll say," Ali said.

"More, please," Jannie said.

"Is that cumin?" Bree asked, smacking her lips.

"And a touch of curry powder," Nana Mama said. "That and the way the onions and the chicken skin get so crispy? I'd pay for a meal like this."

"Nana?" Ali said. "Did you check the lottery?"

Nana Mama had been playing numbers since I

was a little kid. It was one of her few vices. Every week since I'd moved into her home all those years ago, she'd played a number.

"Already looked," I said. "No one won Powerball. It'll be up over fifty million the next draw."

"No, Dad," Ali said. "The charter-school lottery."

My grandmother said, "Ali wants to go to Washington Latin, and I want him to go. He'll be challenged academically in a charter, just as Jannie has been."

"I should get in, right, Dad?" Ali said. "I scored ninety-six percent in math."

"In the ninety-sixth percentile in math," Nana Mama corrected him.

"And ninety-one percent, uh, tile, in reading," Ali said.

"That will get you at least one more number in the lottery."

"Two more," Nana said. "He'll have a good chance."

Ali grinned down the table at me. He was such an affable brainiac, interested in so many subjects it was sometimes hard to believe he was only seven. "I'm getting in if I have to go down the chimney," he said.

"Always better to go in the front door," Bree said.

She was up clearing dishes. I joined her, and we cleaned the kitchen to a high gloss that pleased Nana Mama enough for her to go out to watch *NCIS,* her latest favorite television show. Bree looked ready to join her, but I said, "Take a walk in the rain with me?"

Bree smiled. "Sure."

The air was hot and saturated with the light rain that had begun falling. It felt good to walk in it, loosened up my legs a little after I'd eaten so much.

"What did Michele Bui have to say?"

"Nothing that pins the murders on Le, but she gave us enough promising leads to make it worthwhile," Bree said. "She says he does have a Remington 1911 in a forty-five caliber. Several, evidently. And he had mentioned Tommy McGrath numerous times in the past few months, and always in anger. Le told Michele that Tommy was persecuting him. It's amazing how they squeal when someone's getting close."

"I know," I said. "Listen, Michaels offered me chief of detectives."

Bree stopped and beamed at me. "Really? Oh my God, Alex. This is big."

"I know."

"You should do it. You deserve it, and I think you'd be great at it. Kind of like Tommy was, a mentor, an ally for every detective in Metro."

We started walking again. "I've thought of that. It's appealing on that level."

"You'd also have more regular hours for the first time in longer than you've known me," Bree said. "Jannie's gonna be a sophomore. She won't be home forever."

"I know," I said. "And I'd get to see all of her races and attend science fairs with Ali. It's really tempting."

Bree stopped again. There were raindrops on her cheeks that looked like tears. I brushed them away.

"I hear a *but* coming," she said.

"There's always a *but* coming."

"And yours is?"

"Right here," I said, patting my rump.

"You're avoiding the issue," she said.

"I am. Let's go back."

"Not before you kiss me," she said.

"Excuse me?"

"You're kind of sexy in the rain."

"That so?"

"Oh yeah," she said, and she got up on her tip-toes, put her arms around my neck, and kissed me long and deep.

"Wow," I said. "I'm going to have to walk in the rain more often."

She grinned and started strolling away coyly.

"Can you imagine me in a steamy-hot rain forest, Chief Cross?"

"Vividly," I said, and we both laughed our way back to the house.

I went upstairs to our bedroom and punched in the number for my recently found long-lost father. He answered on the second ring.

"Haven't heard from you in a bit, Alex," my dad said.

"You either, Dad. Retirement got you busy?"

"Picking up more work than I can handle with the Palm Beach County prosecutors," he said, sounding as if he couldn't believe it.

"Why does that surprise you?" I said. "They may have thrown you out of sheriff's homicide, but they're not going to waste talent."

"I'm still pinching myself I'm not in prison."

"You paid your dues. You became a good man, Jason Cross or Peter Drummond or whatever it is you're calling yourself these days."

"Pete's fine," he said. "End of that. What's up with you and the family?"

I told him about the job offer.

He listened and then said, "What turns you on, son?"

"Being a detective," I said. "It's what I'm good at. Being an administrator—not so much."

"You can always delegate," he said. "Stick to the

stuff you'd enjoy about being COD and get rid of the rest of it. Negotiate it with your chief up front."

"Maybe," I said. "I'll sleep on it."

"Sounds to me like you've already made your decision."

# CHAPTER

# 18

**ON THE EVE OF BATTLE,** he always changed his identity to suit his role. That night he thought of himself as John Brown.

Brown rode in the front passenger seat of a tan panel van that bore no markings. Perfect for a predator. Or a pack of them.

"Seven minutes," Brown said, rubbing at a sore knee.

He heard grunts from behind him in the van and then the unmistakable *ker-thunk* of banana magazines seating and the *chick-chink* of automatic weapons feeding rounds into breeches.

They left Interstate 695 and crossed the bridge over the Anacostia River, heading toward the part of DC few tourists ever ventured. Drugs. Apathy. Poverty. They were all here. They all festered here, and because they were an infection, they had to be cut out, the area doused with antibiotics.

They left the bridge, headed south on I-295 and then east again on Suitland Parkway. They exited two miles later and went south of Buena Vista.

"Be smart and disciplined," Brown said, pulling a sheer black mask down over his face. "Nothing gets taken, and nothing gets left behind. Agreed?"

Grunts of approval came from the blackness of the van behind him. Brown leaned over and took the wheel while the driver put on his mask.

A female voice in the back said, "Work the plan."

"Smart choices, smart fire," a male said.

"Surgical precision," another male said.

Brown pressed the microphone taped to his neck. "Status, Cass?"

His headphones crackled with a woman's voice

"Good to go," Cass said. She was in the van trailing them.

Brown said, "Fifty seconds out."

More rounds were seated in chambers. A few soldiers coughed or blew their noses. The tension in the van was remarkably low, given the task ahead. Then again, the men and women following Brown were highly trained. This was neither a new drill nor an unfamiliar assignment.

They pulled onto a spur road that hooked around back to the west, where it met the Lincoln

Memorial Cemetery. The van stopped where three streetlights had gone dark thanks to Crosman pellet guns two of his men used the night before. Brown's driver killed the headlights. The rear of the van opened, and four men dressed head to toe in black spilled out.

Brown got out after them. Before clicking shut the passenger-side door, he said, "Oh three thirty."

The driver nodded and drove away. The second van disgorged its passengers as well, and soon eight men and two women were climbing up and over the wall and into the cemetery. They turned on night-vision goggles. They wove through the green shadows and tombstones on a route that had been scouted repeatedly in the past three weeks. The intelligence was solid. So was this entry and exit route.

Now it was just a matter of executing the plan.

With his sore knee, Brown struggled to keep up, but he soon joined the others strung out along the tree line as they looked across a junky parking lot toward a dark and abandoned machine-tool factory. He listened, heard the purr of gas-fired electric generators, several of them, which was all the evidence you really needed to know that there was more to that relic of a factory than met the eye.

"See them, right there?" Cass whispered. "Two by the door, one on either end? Just like I told you."

Cass was a big woman in her early thirties with short blond hair, and she was extraordinarily strong from years spent training in CrossFit. She was also one of the most competent and loyal people Brown had ever met. He'd had her scout the machine shop, knowing she'd do the job right.

He turned up the magnification on his night-vision, peered across the lot, and spotted the first two guards. They were lying on mattresses on either side of a double door. A third smoked a cigarette at the far corner. The fourth sat on his haunches at the opposite end of the building.

"Formation is the same," Brown murmured into his microphone. "Cass and Hobbes, take the center. Price and Fender, the flanks."

They padded softly toward their prey. The two guards sleeping at the doors didn't have a chance to stir or make a peep before Cass and Hobbes snapped their necks. And the two watching the corners of the factory had no warning as Price and Fender came up behind them, flipped loops of piano wire over their heads, and crushed their throats.

# CHAPTER

# 19

**IN THE MISTY AUGUST DAWN,** six patrol cars with lights flashing formed a broad perimeter around an abandoned machine-tool factory in Anacostia. Despite the early hour, small groups of people were standing outside on stoops and sidewalks, peering at the old brick building as if it were some cursed place.

Bree, Sampson, and I had responded because we were closest, and we found the two patrolmen who'd made the discovery shaken.

They laid out the situation, which began with an anonymous call to 911 and ended with what they'd found in the old factory.

"We saw enough to fall back and call in the cavalry," one said.

"You did right," I said. "Show us."

The officers led us around the rear of the building. We could hear generators rumbling inside when we turned the corner and saw the first strangled man sprawled ten feet away on gravel and weeds.

The piano wire that had killed him was embedded in his flesh. Early twenties, Hispanic, better than six feet tall and well over two hundred hard pounds, he wore a black wifebeater, baggy denim, expensive Nike basketball shoes, and lots of gold bling.

"Took somebody awful strong to do this," Bree said.

"You know it," Sampson said.

I dug through the victim's front pockets and came up with cash and a vial of pinkish powder.

"Tastes like meth," I said after dipping a gloved finger into it.

There was something odd about the angle of the dead man's hips, so I pushed the body forward. Nothing on the ground. But when I lifted the tail of his shirt, there was a 9mm Ruger in a concealed-carry holster at the small of his back.

"He never got the chance to go for his gun," I said.

"So somebody awful strong and awful sneaky quiet," Bree said.

There were three other dead men outside the

factory. The two by the doors were African American and had suffered broken necks. The one at the far corner was Caucasian and had also been strangled with piano wire. All of them were buff. All of them were armed. Not one of them carried an ID.

"So how did it work?" Sampson asked. "One killer?"

"He'd have to be a ninja or something," I said. "I'm thinking four."

"At the same time?" Bree said.

I looked around, saw no lightbulbs in any of the exterior light fixtures.

"At the same time and in the dark," I said. Then, gesturing toward the steel doors, I asked, "If they were guards, what were they guarding?"

Sampson went to the near door, turned the knob, and pushed. The door creaked open. We got out Maglites and, pistols drawn, entered the abandoned factory. I led, my beam flickering down the cement-floored hall to swinging double doors, which I pushed through.

Big machine tools had once occupied the large open space. You could see the outlines of them on the floors beneath a film of grit and dust; you could smell the oil of them in the air. There was also a faint smell of engine exhaust.

Pigeons flew through broken windows two

stories above us. The sun was starting to light up the area, but I kept the flashlight on, peering around, seeing that about halfway across the factory, the vault met the walls of a second story. In the space below that upper floor, there were two large gas-fired electrical generators idling, the source of that exhaust smell.

"No one move," Bree said.

I turned and found her studying the factory floor. She scuffed at the grime with the toe of her shoe and then turned her light back the way we'd come.

"We're leaving footprints here," she said. "But not back in the hallway. It's been swept. Maybe mopped."

I got what she was saying and trained my flashlight on the floor by the double doors. The floor there was clean as well. On either side of the doors, there was a cleaned path about twenty inches wide that ran the length of the room tight to the wall; each ended at a steel industrial staircase.

We didn't need the flashlights to see that the stairs climbed to two catwalks and that the catwalks led to doors, one at either end of the second story. We walked along the left path, our flashlight beams finding mounds of junk, old pipes, conduits, and metal fittings, all coated in filth.

But the steel staircases looked freshly swept. The catwalk too.

One door was ajar, and I could see light shining beyond.

"Alex?" Sampson said. He'd stopped on the catwalk behind me and was shining his light down at the factory floor and onto a fifth dead man sprawled on his belly there.

"He's been shot in the head," Bree said, focusing her beam on the nasty exit wound at the back of his skull. "I'm calling in a second forensics team."

"Smart," I said, shifting my attention to the open doorway. I moved closer and pushed the door inward, revealing a short passage that was blocked from floor to ceiling and wall to wall with black, heavy-gauge plastic sheeting.

There was an industrial-strength vertical zipper in the sheeting and two small square windows through which light was blazing. I stepped up, looked through one of the windows, and felt my stomach fall twenty stories.

"Alex?" Bree said from behind me. "What is that?"

"An air lock," I said, twisting away from the window.

She must have caught the shock on my face, said, "What?"

"Call in two more forensics teams," I replied, hearing the tremor in my voice. "Better yet, call the FBI, Ned Mahoney. Tell him we need a team of the best from Quantico. And have them bring chemists and hazmat suits."

# CHAPTER

# 20

**BY THE TIME MY OLD** friend and partner Ned Mahoney and two FBI chemists arrived, there were news satellite trucks setting up and news helicopters circling overhead.

I was on the phone with Chief Michaels, having just given him an overview of what we'd seen inside.

"Jesus," he said. "The FBI will take this over, won't they?"

"Not yet," I said. "Which brings me to your question from last night."

"Okay?"

"I'm honored, but my place is in the field, and right now it's inside this factory."

"Goddamn it, Cross, I need someone managing my detectives."

"Chief, they're bringing me my hazmat suit. I'll call when we're out and know the full extent of things."

I hung up before he could challenge me. I went to the FBI van, where Mahoney, his chemists, and Sampson were climbing into protective suits.

"How many did you see?" Mahoney asked.

"At least five more bodies," I said.

"Wait until the cable shows get hold of this," Sampson said.

"They already have," said Bree, coming up behind us and eyeing the hazmat suits. "Someone needs to talk to them."

"Once we know what to tell them," I said. "You coming?"

She made a sour face and shook her head. "I'd get claustrophobic in one of those things. And we don't even know what's in there yet."

"Which is why we have to go look," I said, and I kissed her.

I donned the hooded visor. The temperature outside was pushing ninety, and inside the suit, it had to be well over one hundred degrees as we started back into the factory. Sampson let the chemists go through the air lock first. I heard one of them inhale sharply.

"Be careful in here," he said. "No sudden moves."

"Believe me, there won't be," I said, and I ducked through the flaps of the air lock into a room set up as a sophisticated laboratory.

The FBI chemists were already studying the mind-boggling array of equipment and the various chemical processes that had been under way at the time of the massacre. Sampson and I went to the five dead people in the room, two women and three men, sprawled by various workbenches.

They wore hospital scrubs, lab goggles, booties, and surgical hats and masks. Every one of them was shot either through the head or square in the chest.

I scanned the floor all around, said, "I haven't seen a cartridge casing yet."

"No," Sampson said. "They policed their brass, swept their way out."

"Professional gunmen," I said.

Mahoney and the chemists came over.

"What do you think?" I asked.

Pitts, one of the chemists, said, "It's no Walter White setup, but this has the makings of a serious drug lab. Meth and ecstasy."

"Any danger of this place exploding?" I asked.

"Lots of potential danger," Pitts said. "But now that we know what we've got, we'll start shutting down the reactions. Then we'll do an inventory and take the samples we need. We'll call for a full team to dismantle the entire lab and store it for trial."

Trial. I couldn't begin to think how long it was going to take to investigate this case, much less bring the killers to court. Sampson and I headed toward a second air lock at the other end of the laboratory.

We went through it, and in the next twenty minutes we found the rest of the illegal drug factory as well as twelve more bodies. Five females, seven males of various races and ages. Twenty-two dead in all.

Three of the females were found in a packaging room with long stainless-steel tables, large mortars and pestles, digital scales, hundreds of boxes of zip-lock bags, and four vacuum-sealing machines. Six kilos of raw meth were piled on the table. Sampson figured there was at least twice that amount already wrapped, sealed, and boxed for delivery.

"If this were a case of assassins hired by rival drug lords, you'd figure they would have taken the drugs with them," Sampson said.

"Maybe they were after money," I said. "An operation this size has to be generating millions in cash."

In the last room we found the cash. On a pallet, there were banded fifty-dollar bills, similar to the ones we'd seen at Edita Kravic's place, stacked three feet high and wrapped in cellophane. Next to that were two guys in their mid- to late thirties wearing suits and ties. Both had been shot between the eyes.

"Has to be at least a million dollars right there, and they leave it," Sampson said. "I don't get it."

"I don't either," I said.

"Revenge?"

"Maybe. Not one of the victims seems to have put up any kind of resistance. It's as if every single one of them was surprised and killed with a single shot."

"Which means suppressors on all the weapons."

"Definitely."

Sampson said, "Everything about this is scary smart and precise. The shooting. Picking up the brass. Sweeping as they left. The lack of a reason."

"Oh, there's a reason, John," I said. "You don't kill twenty-two people if you don't have a damned good reason."

# CHAPTER
# 21

AN HOUR LATER, IN THE full heat of the day, Bree stepped up in front of a bank of microphones outside the factory fences.

"I know this has been frustrating, but we wanted to give you accurate facts and it took time to gather them," she said in a clear, commanding voice. "We are dealing with multiple homicides in the unstable environment of an extremely large methamphetamine lab. Twenty-two are known dead."

Gasps went up. Reporters started bellowing questions. Screams of horror and grief gathered force in the crowd beyond the media throng.

"Please," Bree said, holding up her hands. "The bodies have been stripped of identification. Someone out there knows someone who worked in this factory—a wife, a mother, a friend, a husband, a father, a son or daughter.

"If you're that someone, we ask that you come forward to identify the body and help us understand who might be responsible for committing these cold-blooded killings and why."

The media went nuts and bombarded Bree with questions. She kept calm and told them essentially the same thing over and over again.

"Well done," I said when she walked away from the microphones after promising to update them on the hour.

"Just have to know how to feed them," Bree said. "Bit by bit."

No one came forward initially, not even those people openly grieving. Then the bodies started leaving the factory in black bags, and the massacre was real, and their loss was heartbreaking.

Vicky Sue Granger was the first to talk. In her late twenties, she looked devastated, and she said she was sure her husband, Dale, was in there.

"He work in the lab?" Bree asked.

"Shamrock City," she said weakly. "That's what they called it. If you were lucky enough to get inside, and you worked hard, the money just came pouring—"

She stopped talking. I guess she figured the less she said about illegal cash, the better.

I said, "Who was in charge?"

Mrs. Granger shrugged, said, "Dale got in through T-Shawn, his cousin."

Other relatives started coming forward once we'd moved the bodies to an air-conditioned space at the medical examiner's office. Family after family was forced to walk down the line of corpses lying in open bags on the cement floor. One man was looking for his eighteen-year-old son. Two girls were there for their older sister. A grandmother broke down in Bree's arms.

Dale Granger *was* there. He worked in packaging and had taken a bullet to the chest. His cousin Tim Shawn Warren, a part-time bouncer at a strip club, was one of the muscular guys who'd been strangled outside.

Few of the relatives wanted to talk. The ones that did come up to us claimed to know little of what their loved ones had been doing, only that they'd gotten jobs and suddenly had a lot of cash on hand.

Then Claire Newfield walked in. She saw her younger brother, Clyde, a guard with a broken neck, and became hysterical. When she finally got herself under control, she said Clyde had told her that he worked for scientists.

"He said they were like geniuses," Newfield said. "They'd figured out a new way to make meth and they were going to rule the entire East Coast."

"You have names?"

"No, I didn't want to know."

Around eight that night, we were left with seven bodies on the chill cement floor, and no one waiting outside. Two Jane Does. Five John Does. Two were the older Caucasian males in suits who'd been found with the cash; the remaining five were all in their late twenties and had been discovered in the meth lab.

I knelt next to the bodies and looked at them. What had brought them to this? Who the hell were they?

"Let's get these bodies on ice," I said.

"Dr. Cross?" called one of the patrolmen by the door. "There's a young lady out here who wants to look for her friends."

"Okay, one more."

Alexandra Campbell shuffled in as if against her will, shoulders rolled forward, looking everywhere but at the bodies. She was a reedy woman in her twenties with a colorful sleeve tattoo and blond hair dyed peach in places.

"You think you know someone here?" I asked after introducing myself.

Campbell shrugged miserably, said, "Gotta look. Make sure."

I led her over. Campbell stopped eight or nine feet from the remaining seven bodies. Her hand trembled up to cover her mouth.

"Carlo," she choked out. "Now look where you've left me."

She kind of folded down into herself then, wrapped her arms around her knees at the feet of the body bags, and sobbed her poor heart out. I gave her some time and then crouched at her side and offered her a tissue box.

Bree brought her a bottle of water, and Campbell told us everything she knew.

# CHAPTER

# 22

**WE DIDN'T REACH HOME UNTIL** well after midnight. We ate cold leftover chicken in the kitchen and tried to forget the things we'd seen and heard.

"You believe her?" Bree asked, getting up from the table to wash her plate. "Alexandra Campbell?"

"The bones of it," I said.

"God help us, then," she said. "Tomorrow's going to be a zoo."

"Just be the calm tortoise," I said.

"You're asking me to act like a turtle at work?"

"No, like a tortoise, with a big armored shell and the ability to stand back from it all and keep plodding toward the finish line."

Bree looked at me sleepily, came into my arms, and said, "I have a feeling this is going to be all-consuming for a while, and you telling me to act like a land turtle wasn't exactly the advice I expected from you. But I love you and let's not lose track of each other."

"Deal," I said, and followed her upstairs to bed.

I don't remember my head hitting the pillow. I don't remember dreaming.

There was nothing but darkness until the alarm went off at six fifteen. Bree was already up, showered, and dressed, and eating in the kitchen with Nana Mama. Jannie was drinking a protein shake and wearing her warm-ups.

I yawned, said to Jannie, "You're up early."

"Trainer's waiting. He wants my workouts done before the heat comes up."

"You on the track?"

"Gym," Jannie said. "I'm being introduced to Olympic weight lifting."

"You're going to be one of those bodybuilders?" my grandmother asked. "They're not fast."

"No, Nana," Jannie said. "This is exactly the opposite of bodybuilding. The Olympic lifts require every muscle in your body to engage and fire. So doing them in addition to running will get me much stronger and more explosive, and it'll do it without making my body look freakish."

"Oh, well, that's good," Nana Mama said. "No freakish in this family."

I smiled through another yawn, poured myself

coffee. Bree rinsed the dishes and got ready to leave. I followed her into the front hallway.

"Why are you in such a rush?" I asked.

"Chief Michaels texted me, asked me to be in his office by nine."

"For what?"

"To brief the mayor and the commissioner. How do I look?"

"Like a badass crime fighter."

Bree smiled at that, pecked me on the lips, and said, "Thanks for making my life easier."

"Anytime. Day or night."

# CHAPTER

# 23

**THE MURDERS OF AARON PETERS,** Tom McGrath, and Edita Kravic were put on the back burner after the massacre. Chief Michaels ordered virtually the entire Major Case Unit to work on the factory slayings.

The FBI put another ten agents on the case. The help of the DEA was enlisted as well. A task-force meeting was called for early that afternoon in a room normally used for patrol roll call.

The room was packed when Chief Michaels came in; he was followed by Ned Mahoney, a guy with a shaved head I didn't recognize, and Bree. We hadn't seen each other all morning, since I'd been back at the factory, watching the FBI neutralize and dismantle the meth lab.

She smiled and opened her eyes wide at me, mouthed the word *Text*.

I frowned, reached in my pocket, pulled out my smartphone, and realized that I'd shut the alerts off. There were several texts from Bree. The first three said *Call*.

The last one said *Oh, well, hold on to your hat*.

"This kind of slaughter will not go unanswered," Chief Michaels began. "You cannot kill twenty-two people and not face punishment."

Everyone in the room sobered. Many nodded their heads.

"The FBI, DEA, and DCPD have pledged total cooperation in that effort," Chief Michaels said. "Our new chief of detectives, Bree Stone, will be supervising liaison with Special Agent Mahoney of the FBI and the acting DEA special agent in charge for the District, George Potter."

Sampson whispered in my ear, "Your mouth's hanging open."

I shut it and grinned, prouder than proud. How could I not have seen that one coming?

Bree stepped up to the mike and nodded to me, all business.

Multiple photographs appeared on a screen in the corner.

"As of now, we have twenty out of twenty-two confirmed identities for the victims," Bree said.

"Any one of these people could be linked to the killers, so we are going to need workups on all of them."

She nodded to someone, and the photos were reduced to five.

"This has not come out yet, but we know quite a bit about these five from a witness who came forward late last night," she said. "All five are classmates in the graduate chemistry program at Georgetown University."

That sent a rumble through the crowd. Georgetown? Chemists from a prestigious university running a meth lab?

Bree gestured to a photo of a dark-complected curly-haired man and said, "This is Laxman Dalal. Twenty-two years old. PhD candidate. Born in Mumbai, he went to the University of Southern California on a full academic ride and finished in two years. We believe he was the brains and driving force behind the drug lab."

From there she gave them a story of four very smart, very driven people who'd been seduced into crime and easy money by Laxman Dalal, a man whom Campbell had described as "brilliant, charismatic, and morally corrupt."

"Dalal evidently didn't think the laws applied to him," Bree said. "By sheer force of brains and personality, he convinced his fellow students, including Alexandra Campbell's ex-boyfriend Carlo Puente, that they could earn a whole lot of cash by making meth at night, on weekends, and during their summer breaks."

They got good fast, and their illegal business started to grow even faster. Campbell said it had started in a small garage in Southeast DC, but they'd soon moved to the factory in Anacostia.

"Campbell said her boyfriend showed her bags of money back in March," Bree said. "That's when she said she called it quits with Puente. She says she told him Dalal was going to get him killed. And he did. That's it for me. Special Agent Potter?"

Bree stepped away from the lectern, and the DEA SAC took her place.

Potter said, "Before last year, I would have told you that there was no drug gang brazen enough or capable enough to pull off this kind of massacre. But in the last six months, across northern Mexico and the desert Southwest, we've seen a rise in deadly turf wars. Traffickers shot and left for dead. Labs like this one blown up. When I was in the El Paso office, it looked like some group was bent on cornering the market in illicit drugs, forming kind of a supercartel that was willing to kill anyone in its way."

"We have a name for this supercartel?" I asked. "People involved?"

Potter looked at me, said, "I wish we did, Dr. Cross. In El Paso, it was like chasing ghosts, and then I was transferred here."

"Did you have any intelligence about that factory?" Sampson asked.

Potter looked at his men, who shook their heads.

"It was as big a surprise to us as it was to you," Potter said, and then he sighed. "But then again, we've been shorthanded. Budget cuts."

Ned Mahoney cleared his throat, said, "I don't know about a supercartel, but I think you're right about brazenness being a factor here. You'd have to be stone-cold to do this, so I think we have to agree from the start that this was professionally done and proceed from there."

"No doubt," Potter said. "These guys were highly trained."

"SWAT level?" Bree asked.

"I think we're dealing with a group that's quite a few steps above SWAT," Mahoney said. "This feels commando-trained, at a minimum."

"So, mercenaries?" Sampson asked.

"Could be," Mahoney replied. "There are a lot of private security contractors around, now that Iraq and Afghanistan are winding down. I don't think you'd have trouble putting together an elite team if the money was right."

"Hold that thought," Bree said, and nodded.

Photos of the remaining two John Does, the ones dressed for business, got bigger on the screen.

"We think these two are the moneymen," she said. "Either they funded the lab's construction and equipment or they were involved in the sale of—"

Mahoney's phone started beeping. So did Bree's. And Potter's.

They all went for their phones. Bree's was right in her hand. She scanned the screen, stiffened, and said, "Two more drug labs have been hit. One in Newark. Another in rural Connecticut. Multiple deaths confirmed in both places."

# CHAPTER

# 24

BOTH METH LABS HAD BEEN taken down within minutes of each other, and with the same attention to detail. All the people inside the drug factories were dead. There were no cartridge casings at either scene. In each case, hundreds of thousands of dollars and multiple kilos of methamphetamine were left untouched.

Ned Mahoney and the FBI seized control of the larger investigation at that point. Three different massacres across state lines demanded it, though Chief of Detectives Bree Stone remained in charge of the Anacostia slayings.

It was a little odd at first, having my wife be my boss, but then I realized she and Nana Mama ruled the roost at home anyway, and I got over it. Even better, Bree was good at being a chief. Right off the bat. She had a knack for pulling the levers, getting you what you needed.

But despite her efforts, for several days we made little progress. Then, ninety-six hours after we arrived at the massacre scene in Anacostia, we identified the two dead businessmen through missing-persons reports in Virginia and Maryland.

Chandler Keen of Falls Church ran a small investment firm currently under investigation by the SEC. Matthew Franks was a Bethesda-based real estate developer who'd been hit with several multimillion-dollar legal judgments in construction-default lawsuits.

The FBI raided their offices and homes, but it was going to take some time to cull through the seized evidence. It was clear, though, that both men had had adequate reasons to get involved in the lucrative business of illegal drug manufacturing. But how it had happened and why they and the twenty others had been targeted for death remained a mystery.

Cable news, not surprisingly, went bonkers over the case, especially the Georgetown University angle. Students were back on campus and some of them were more than happy to talk. As a result, we knew a lot more about the five genius victims, but nothing game-changing.

On the sixth morning after the massacre, I told

Bree I was going back to work the Tom McGrath case while we waited for forensics to give us some kind of tangible lead on the factory killings.

"Wish I could go with you," she said, sitting behind her desk with a stack of papers before her. "But between fielding calls from the brass and making decisions on overtime, I'm going to be here for a while."

"I feel for you. Take my dad's advice: delegate the worst of it."

"I can't delegate anything until I understand the job."

"True," I said. "You're doing great, by the way."

"You think?"

"Not just me. Keep trusting your instincts."

Bree laughed. "They're all I've had so far. Where are you going?"

I told her I was going to look for an American University law student named JohnnyBoy5.

# CHAPTER

# 25

SAMPSON AND I MADE A trip to the administrative offices of American University's law school. We explained we were working on Edita Kravic's murder case, and that got us fifteen minutes with the dean, who told us Kravic had been a star student, a role model for foreign students and women entering school at a relatively late age.

"We could use some help, then," I said, and I told him about JohnnyBoy5. "That's his online name, but he's a student here, and we want to talk with him. Can you figure out who he is?"

"May I ask why?" the dean said.

"He was obsessed with Ms. Kravic," Sampson said. "Maybe enough to kill her and Chief McGrath."

The dean cringed at the idea that one of his

students might have murdered another as well as the police chief. He hesitated, said, "There are privacy issues."

"More important than bringing a double murderer to justice?" I said flatly. "Do we have to go to the press and tell them that the dean of a law school is being obstructive in the hunt for a cop killer?"

Five minutes later, we had a bead on one John Boynton, aka JohnnyBoy5, a second-year law student from Indiana who was attending a summer class on torts in the school amphitheater. The dean texted us his photo.

We waited in the hallway on the second floor of the law school for the lecture to end. A crowd of students began exiting the amphitheater, and I soon had eyes on JohnnyBoy5, who was still inside the room, about ten feet back from the door.

"Check out the hairdo," I said.

"I see it," Sampson said. "Flashy."

I don't know what about us tipped Boynton. Maybe it was his Spider-Man instincts. Or maybe just the memory of a big guy threatening to break his face. Whatever triggered it, the guy with the spiked blond hair took one look at us and shoved several students forward hard, causing people in the crowd to stagger and fall like dominoes. Then he spun and took off deeper into the lecture hall.

"Sonofabitch, he's running!" Sampson roared. He drew his service weapon and sped after him, throwing students out of his way and yelling, "Police! Get down!"

I went another route, running down the hall toward an exit sign. I shouldered the door open and took the stairs four at a time. When I hit the bottom I threw open a second door, saw students fleeing the amphitheater through an exit at the end of the hall.

A girl looked over her shoulder and screamed. I stepped into a janitor's closet next to the stairwell, leaving the door open.

Boynton came out of the amphitheater, smashing people out of his way, then sprinted down the hall right at me. I waited until he was just past me and then hit him hard across his back with the head of a heavy, wet industrial mop.

JohnnyBoy5 smashed into the stairway door and fell in a heap, groaning.

# 26

**BOYNTON SAT ON THE FLOOR,** held his nose, which was gushing blood, and moaned. "I'm suing. Whoever you are, I'm suing."

"No, you're not," I said as Sampson came up behind me. "We're homicide detectives investigating Edita Kravic's murder. We saw the e-mails you sent her."

That rocked him. He wiped at his nose, groaned, muttered, "I had a bad reaction to a generic version of Singulair, an asthma drug. Talk to my allergist. He said in rare cases, it could make you manic. It definitely made me that way."

"Some of the things you wrote sounded threatening and psychotic," I said. "She was going to file a restraining order against you."

His shoulders slumped. "I swear to you, Detective, that wasn't the real John Boynton writing those things. It was a hopped-up, crazed version of me. Two days after getting off that goddamned drug, I was fine."

The way he said it, exposed and defeated, made me believe it was possible that some of the messages had been fueled by a bad reaction to a drug.

"Okay, let's put those particular e-mails aside," I said. "The fact is, you seem to have had an escalating obsession with Edita Kravic from the first day of law school. Did you love her?"

Boynton looked ready to deny it but then surrendered and nodded. "I thought she was perfect."

"But she didn't feel that way about you?"

"She liked me at first, then I got all weird with the medicine."

"You wrote to her once accusing her of hiring muscle to threaten you."

"Said he'd take a baseball bat to my face if I didn't end all contact with Edita."

"Who was it?"

Boynton shrugged. "The cop she was sleeping with, and died with." Something about the way he moved just then made me recognize him—this was the guy with the knapsack who'd run out of McGrath's apartment.

"Can I go to a hospital, please?" he whined.

"When we're done talking," I said. "You're not

going to die from a nosebleed. Why did you break into Chief McGrath's place?"

He hesitated. Then he said, "She asked me to."

"Bullshit," Sampson said.

"She did," he insisted.

Boynton claimed that Edita had called him and said that she'd done some research and now believed him about the medicine. She'd also said she was in trouble and needed his help. They met, and she asked him to steal McGrath's laptop.

"She said McGrath had stuff on the computer that could get her in big trouble, prevent her from becoming a lawyer," Boynton said.

"Like what kind of stuff?"

"She wouldn't tell me, but she was convincing," Boynton said. "You could hear it in her voice and see it in her body language. She was scared by whatever he had on the laptop."

Recalling the e-mails I'd seen in Edita's computer, I said, "You were supposed to meet at ten the night before she was killed?"

He nodded and said she'd come over later than that, around eleven, to give him McGrath's apartment key and to have sex.

"Edita was sleeping with you both?" Sampson asked, eyebrows raised.

"She was going to break up with McGrath after

I gave her the laptop," he said, looking crestfallen. "She was finally going to be mine."

Before she'd left Boynton's apartment that night, Edita had told him she was taking McGrath to an early-morning yoga class and then to breakfast at her place. Boynton would have plenty of time to use the key and get the laptop. I thought about it, remembered Boynton running with the backpack from McGrath's place. It all fit in a strange way.

Boynton said he had the laptop at his apartment. We got him to his feet, handcuffed him, and told him we'd swing by his place on the way to the hospital.

"Am I under arrest? They'll throw me out of school."

"You're in custody for now," I said.

In the car on the way to his apartment, I turned around in the front seat and looked at him.

"In one of your e-mails during your manic phase, you wrote something like 'I know what you do, Edita, and I'll tell everyone.' What was that all about?"

Fear flickered across Boynton's swollen face. "I was just bluffing, you know? Everyone has a secret, so I figured—"

"You're lying to me, Mr. Boynton," I said with a sigh. "Every time you lie, you get closer to an arrest and the end of law school. So what do you know?"

"I...I followed her a few times."

"You stalked her?" Sampson said.

"Just followed her. I wanted to see what she did when she wasn't at school. That's all."

"Get to it," Sampson said. "Where did she go?"

"This place in Vienna, Virginia, called the Phoenix Club."

Edita went there three or four days a week, he told us. She'd often stay until after midnight. Boynton tried to get inside once but was told it was a private club. He said he stopped following her once he realized someone else was following her.

"Who?" Sampson said.

"Another cop," Boynton said. "At least, he talked like a cop."

"He caught you following Edita?"

"Twice. The second time he told me he had her under surveillance and I had to stop or he'd have me arrested for obstructing justice."

"Name?"

"He never said."

"Never showed you a badge?"

Boynton shook his head. "But like I said, he acted like a cop."

"What did he look like?" I said.

"Tall, big, but he didn't look too good, like he was sick or something. He coughed a lot. And he wore a red Redskins cap."

# CHAPTER

# 27

**BREE MANAGED TO GET AWAY** from all her paper-work, and three hours later, Kurt Muller, Bree, and I pulled up in front of Terry Howard's depressing apartment building in Northeast DC.

We'd retrieved McGrath's laptop and taken it and Boynton downtown. The laptop went to Detectives Lincoln and O'Donnell, along with marching orders to look for anything related to Edita or the Phoenix Club. Sampson stayed behind to take Boynton's full statement.

We stood in the foyer and buzzed Howard's apartment three times but got no answer. We buzzed the other five apartments, but it was a weekday and everyone was out. No response.

"Call him," I said.

Bree looked up Howard's number and punched

it into her cell phone. No answer. Straight to voice mail.

We were turning to leave when Muller noticed a beater Dodge four-door parked across the street. "That's Howard's. He's here, just not answering."

"He could have walked somewhere," Bree said. "Taken the Metro."

"Not the way he was coughing and wheezing the last time I saw him," I said.

"Where's his apartment?"

"The third floor, back."

We walked around into the alley and located Howard's apartment and the fire escape. I picked Bree up; she grabbed the ladder and pulled it down. We climbed up the three flights and stopped outside the kitchen window.

The sink overflowed with dishes. Liquor and beer bottles crowded the small table and just about every other surface. A second window was raised slightly and looked into a small dining area and part of the living room where Sampson and I had spoken with Howard. We could see the television was on, tuned to ESPN.

"Call his number again," I said.

Bree did, and almost immediately I heard the jangle of an old-fashioned rotary phone coming from the apartment. The ringing stopped.

"Voice mail," Bree said.

"That's probable cause to do a well-being check, don't you think, Chief?"

She hesitated, and then said, "No fruit of the poisonous tree."

Nodding, I pushed up the sash and climbed in, calling, "Terry Howard? It's Alex Cross. We're just checking on your well-being."

No voice replied, but almost immediately I heard a bird squawking.

"That's Sylvia Plath," I said, helping Bree and Muller inside. "His neurotic parakeet."

"Howard always had a twisted sense of humor," Muller said.

We moved deeper into the apartment, past a dining table buried in stacks of old newspapers to the parakeet that was pacing back and forth on its perch, screeching, bobbing its head, and pecking viciously at its featherless skin, clearly agitated.

We stepped into the living area and saw why.

Terry Howard sat in his easy chair facing the television; a film of blood and gore spattered the ceiling and walls around him. He had apparently put a gun in his mouth and shot himself. A sizable chunk of his skull was gone. A bloody, red Redskins cap was on the floor beside him.

An empty bottle of Smirnoff and a Remington 1911 .45-caliber pistol, the same kind of gun that had killed Tom McGrath, lay in his old partner's lap.

On the floor beside him, there was a note scrawled in ink.

*Rot in hell, Tommy McG,* it read. *You and your lying bitch of a girlfriend.*

# CHAPTER

# 28

**"CASE CLOSED?" SAMPSON ASKED AS** we drove past the Wolf Trap National Park for the Performing Arts in Northern Virginia.

"Bree thinks so," I said. "So does Michaels. Tough one to swallow, but there it is."

"You're not sold?"

"Just trying to understand the entire situation before we declare it a revenge killing and a suicide. Take a right."

Sampson did, and then he made a left, and we were into big-money properties, sprawling estates, some with high walls and security gates. It was dusk and lights were blinking on.

"Coming up on your right," I said.

Sampson slowed, put on a blinker. We drove up a narrow road maybe a hundred feet long with gardens on both sides. At the end of it was a guardhouse, a turnaround, and a steel security gate set in a high wall.

The polished brass sign on the guardhouse read THE PHOENIX CLUB. PRIVATE. MEMBERS ONLY.

We'd no sooner reached the turnaround than a big, muscular dude stepped out in a blue polo shirt with the Phoenix Club logo on the chest and a Glock pistol holstered at his waist.

He held up his hand and came to the driver-side window.

"Are you members?" he said in a thick Eastern European accent.

"No," Sampson said, and he showed his police badge and ID. "We need to talk to someone about Edita Kravic."

"I don't know her," the man said, seeming unimpressed that we were cops.

"She worked here, and now she's dead," Sampson said. "So go inside and call whoever would know and tell them we're not leaving until we speak with someone about her."

The guard stared at Sampson. Sampson glared back. Then the security guy bit his lip and went into the guardhouse.

Twenty minutes later, the gates opened and out came a golf cart driven by a bald man in a finely tailored blue suit. He stopped the cart and got out. He was in his thirties, with slightly cauli-flower ears, pale blue eyes, and extraordinarily large hands with knuckles that had been broken a few times.

"I am Sergei Bogrov," he said, taking my hand and then laying his other mitt-like hand on top of mine, swallowing it. "I help manage the club. How may I help?"

"Edita Kravic," I said. "She worked here."

Bogrov's face fell and he let go of my hand. "Yes, we hear this. Very sad. She was well liked by the staff and members."

"What did she do?"

"She taught a hybrid of yoga and Feldenkrais therapy."

"Level Two Certified Coach?" I asked.

"That's right," Bogrov said. "She also worked in the spa as a masseuse. She was an excellent one."

"Good money in that?" Sampson asked.

"If the member is a generous tipper, it can be," he said.

"So, what is the Phoenix Club?" I asked. "Health spa and…"

"Pools, tennis courts, fitness center, an excellent private restaurant, an extensive wine cellar, the best bar in Virginia, and the company of others who have achieved much in life and deserve more," Bogrov said.

"You sound like you're doing a marketing pitch," Sampson said.

Bogrov smiled. "You caught me."

"Can we get a tour?" I asked.

"I'm afraid that's impossible," Bogrov said. "Our members belong to the club as much for its strict privacy as for its amenities."

"We could get a warrant," Sampson said.

Bogrov dropped the facade of friendliness and said, "On what basis, Detective?"

"The murder of a DC police chief and his confidential informant."

Bogrov's eyes narrowed. "I ask again, on what basis? Yes, I know who Edita was killed with, but where do you connect this to my club?"

"At the moment, I'm not at liberty to say."

"This means you have nothing," Bogrov said with a dismissive flap of a giant hand. "And since you are from the District of Columbia and not the Commonwealth of Virginia, you have no jurisdiction here. So I ask you politely but firmly to leave the property."

# CHAPTER

# 29

**I WOKE OUT OF A** dead sleep to find Jannie standing by the bed holding her running shoes.

Dazed, I glanced at the clock. Ten minutes to six. Then I remembered I'd told her to wake me and we'd run together. I'd been working so much I wasn't getting in my normal workouts and had put on five pounds I didn't need.

So I nodded and got up, leaving Bree blissfully snoozing. I dressed in the bathroom, went into the kitchen, and made a cup of instant coffee. As I sat there drinking it, I tried to muster up the will to tie my shoelaces. This wasn't going to be a fun run. More like torture.

"Dad?"

Stifling a yawn, I looked up and saw Ali standing there, rubbing his eyes.

"What are you doing up so early, kiddo?" I asked.

"I couldn't sleep," he said, coming over to snuggle with me, which didn't help my workout plans. I could have drifted off right then and there with my little boy in my arms.

But I said, "You couldn't fall asleep? Or you couldn't stay asleep?"

"Both," he said. "I had too much to think about."

"Really?" I said, closing my eyes. "Like what?"

"Time," Ali said. "And how it, like, curves at the speed of light. Neil deGrasse Tyson said that's what happens, so it has to be true."

I opened my eyes, thinking how strange it was to be having this conversation with a seven-year-old. "I think Einstein figured that out."

"I know that," Ali said. "Which makes it doubly true, and that's the problem, and that's why I can't sleep."

"I don't understand."

"I can't see it in my head—you know, time curving."

"And that's why you fell asleep late and woke up early?"

"Yes," he said, snuggling deeper into my lap. "Can you explain it to me?"

I had to fight not to laugh.

"Uh, no," I said. "Physics isn't one of my strengths even when I'm well rested."

"Oh," Ali said. "I was thinking that maybe it was like when you're dreaming and time seems like it goes on forever, but scientists studying your brain say you're only dreaming for three to eight minutes. Does that make sense?"

That woke me up for good, and I looked down at my son and wondered what he would become. I'd told all my kids that they could be anything their hearts desired as long as they were willing to work for it. But at that moment, Ali seemed limitless.

"Dad? *Does* that make sense?"

"I've never heard Einstein's theory of relativity explained that way, and I honestly can't tell you if it makes sense, but you certainly showed imagination coming up with that idea."

Ali smiled and then chewed on his lip. "You think Neil deGrasse Tyson would know if that's how dreams work? You know, at the speed of light and bending time?"

"I would imagine that if anyone knows, it would be Neil deGrasse Tyson."

"He's not here," Ali said. "At the Smithsonian, I mean."

"No, he's in New York. At the Natural History Museum, I believe."

"Think I could call him up and ask him?"

I laughed. "You want to call Dr. Tyson up and tell him about your theory?"

"That's right. Can I, Dad?"

"I don't have his number."

"Oh," Ali said. "Who would?"

Jannie appeared in the doorway. "Dad, do you even have your shoes on?"

"They're on, just not tied," I said, giving Ali a nudge.

He got off my lap grudgingly and said, "Dad?"

"I'll look into it and get back to you. Okay?"

Ali brightened, said, "I'm going to watch *Origins* until Nana Mama gets up to make breakfast."

"An excellent idea." I grunted and tied my shoes.

# CHAPTER

# 30

**"FINALLY," JANNIE SAID WHEN I** walked out onto the front porch and found her stretching.

"Your brother had lots of questions."

"As usual," Jannie said, sounding slightly miffed. "Where does he come up with that stuff? Dreams and time and, I don't know, the universe?"

"Those shows he watches," I said, trying to stretch my hips and failing miserably. "And the Internet."

"He's the only kid I know who thinks like that," she said.

"It's a good thing."

"I guess," she said. "But it's like guaranteed now he's going to be a nerd."

"Nerds rule the world these days, or hadn't you noticed?"

Jannie thought about that, said, "Well, I guess it would be okay if my little brother grew up to rule the world."

"In a manner of speaking."

"Right." She grinned. "Now, are we going to run or not?"

"To be honest, I would vote for not."

"Do I need to remind you about the ten pounds you need to lose?"

"Ouch," I said. "And it's five."

Jannie crossed her arms and raised her eyebrow skeptically.

"Okay, seven," I said. "And let's go before I decide to get doughnuts."

Jannie turned, started to move, and became someone else. It was a very strange thing, I thought as she started to lope down the sidewalk with me puffing already. There was my daughter, Jannie, who had to struggle to sit still and succeed in school. And there was Jannie Cross, who ran so effortlessly.

She picked up her pace all the way to the end of the block and then glided back to me.

"Show-off," I said.

"You're breaking a sweat," she said. "This is good."

"How far are we going?" I asked.

"Three miles," she said.

"Thank you for being merciful."

"The idea is to make you want to show up again tomorrow."

"Right," I said without enthusiasm.

We ran past the Marine barracks and heard them doing PT. We ran past Chung Sun Chung's convenience store, the best around. It was doing a brisk business, as usual. In the window, the Powerball sign said the pot was nearing fifty million dollars.

"Remind me to stop and get Nana Mama's tickets on the way back," I said.

"You ever won anything?"

"No."

"Nana Mama?"

"Twice. Once ten thousand dollars and once twenty-five thousand."

"When was that?"

"Before I went to college."

"So a long time ago."

"Paleolithic era," I said.

"Must be why you run like a mastodon."

She laughed and took off in a burst of speed, ran all the way to the end of the block, then jogged back to me again.

"Mastodon?" I said, trying to act offended.

"Saber-toothed tiger trying to get back in shape?"

"Much better."

We ran on for several minutes before Jannie said, "So why were you and Bree fighting last night?"

"We weren't fighting," I said. "We were arguing."

"Loud argument."

"Passionate subject," I said. "And Bree's under a lot of pressure from the top brass to make something happen, something that shows the public that DC Metro is still on top of things."

"Like what?" Jannie asked as we ran past the armory.

"Like clearing a major murder case. The Tommy McGrath murder case."

"Are you close to making an arrest?"

"No, because the prime suspect shot himself yesterday."

Jannie shook her head. "I don't know how you deal with that kind of stuff."

"Like anything, it takes practice."

"So why did he shoot himself? Because you suspected him and he knew you were after him?"

"That's what Bree thinks," I said. "It's also what Chief Michaels thinks."

"But you don't?"

I struggled with how much to tell her. "There are other explanations of why the suspect would want to commit suicide."

"Like what?"

"I can't tell you."

"Oh."

"And no more questions about that, okay?"

"Sure, Dad. I was just interested."

"And I appreciate your interest in that and in getting me out of bed this morning."

We ran to the National Arboretum, and on the way back, the running wasn't half the torture I'd expected. When we passed Chung Sun Chung's store, the line for lottery tickets was ten-deep, so I skipped it and we went home.

Nana Mama was up cooking scrambled eggs and bacon, and Ali was engrossed in *Origins.* I went upstairs; Bree was in the shower.

"Hey," she said when I climbed in.

"Sorry we argued last night."

Bree nodded, hugged me, and said, "I still think Howard did it, shot Tom, Edita, and then himself."

"Or Howard shot himself because he had stage four lung cancer. Or he was telling you the truth about not owning a Remington 1911."

"Or he was lying about it."

"Or he was lying about it. Or he didn't kill anyone, and someone associated with the Phoenix Club did. Truce until we know more?"

Bree hugged me tighter. "Being chief of detectives is hard."

"I think you're doing a great job."

"Chief Michaels doesn't think so."

"Sure he does. He's just getting heat from the mayor and the city council."

"I am going to get through this, right?"

"*We* are going to get through this."

# CHAPTER

# 31

**THE BALLISTICS REPORT ON THE** .45-caliber Remington 1911 that killed Terry Howard came back around ten fifteen that morning. It was the same pistol that had been used to kill Tom McGrath and Edita Kravic.

"Case closed?" Chief Michaels asked. "We can tell the media that?"

"Yes," Bree said.

I said nothing.

The chief noticed, said, "Alex?"

"You might want to say there's strong evidence that Howard did it, but there are still some loose ends to take care of before we put the file in boxes."

"What loose ends?"

"The car used in McGrath's murder. It wasn't

Howard's. And I'd like to see a bill of sale saying Howard actually owned a Remington 1911. All records I've checked say he *was* a Smith and Wesson guy."

Chief Michaels looked at Bree, said, "You're confident?"

"Terry Howard hated Tom," she said. "Howard had lost his job and had cancer. Tom was chief of detectives with a younger girlfriend. So Howard's bitterness built into rage, and he shot Tom and Edita. Then he shot himself, figuring we'd eventually put two and two together."

"Kind of convenient."

"Or true."

"Sorry, Alex," Chief Michaels said. "I agree with Chief Stone."

"Not my call, but I can live with it," I said.

"Good. And the drug-lab massacre?"

"We've had everyone pressuring informants, but there's no talk on the streets about the hired gunmen. Just the victims."

"Which means?"

"They're an outside force," I said. "Highly trained. Probably ex-military."

"Probably hired by a rival drug interest," Bree said.

"Or they're vigilantes," I said.

"Alex," Bree said with a sigh.

"Vigilantes?" the chief said, eyes narrowing. "Where do you see that?"

"No drugs were taken in the three attacks. No money was taken in the three attacks. If you think about it, a message was being sent loud and clear."

"What message?"

*"Stop making meth or we'll kill you too."*

Chief Michaels thought about that for several moments before he looked at Bree. "No talk about vigilantes until we have something more solid."

Bree glanced at me, then said, "Done, sir."

Sampson and I watched Bree's press conference in our office. Even though Bree and I disagreed on both cases, I thought she handled the situation skillfully, and I was grateful when she said that the evidence indicated Howard killed his former partner but that there were loose ends that had to be dealt with before the investigation could be considered closed.

When discussing the mass murder at the drug factory, however, she made no mention of vigilantes and supported the theory that we were dealing with a drug gang war and mercenaries.

"I hope she's right," Sampson said.

"I do too, actually," I said.

"No attack in days."

"It is possible that there won't be any more, that what needed to be done has been done."

"Uh-huh," Sampson said. "What's your Spider-Man sense telling you?"

"I don't have a Spider-Man sense. I can't even pick a good lottery number."

"Okay, what are your years of experience telling you?"

I thought about that, said, "This isn't over. Not by a long shot."

Detective Lincoln knocked, said, "McGrath had serious encryption on his computer. We're going to have to send it out."

"Send it to Quantico," I said. "I'll try to get it moved to the front of the line."

"Right away," Lincoln said, and he left.

Sampson said, "I feel like we're banging our heads against a wall on every aspect of every case we've got."

"You've got a hard head; you'll break us through."

"No match between Howard's gun and the Rock Creek shooter."

"I saw that. You talk with Aaron Peters's fellow lobbyists? Family?"

Sampson nodded, said the Maserati's driver had been divorced for five years. No kids. Played the field. He had a reputation for ruthlessness, but not in a way that provoked animosity or revenge.

"His partners said Peters could make you

smile while he was cutting your throat," Sampson said.

"Lovely image," I said. "What about other shootings like these?"

Sampson frowned, said, "I'll look. You?"

"I think I'll go hunting for mercenaries."

# CHAPTER

# 32

**THREE DAYS LATER, SAMPSON AND** I drove south on Maryland's Eastern Shore. Looking west across Chesapeake Bay, I saw something pale and white in the sky far away. I squinted. The sun caught it.

"There's a blimp out there," I said. "A couple of them."

"Don't see those too often. There a big sports event?"

"No idea," I said before losing sight of them.

Forty minutes later, we were on the Nanticoke Road in Salisbury, Maryland. Farmers were cutting hay and harvesting corn in a shimmering heat.

"Feels like we're going to kick a hornet's nest," Sampson said.

"Or a basket with spitting cobras inside," I said, and I wondered whether we might be biting off more than we could chew, coming here without an entire SWAT team to back us up.

"This guy's background is spooky."

I nodded, said, "In some ways, he's got the perfect résumé for a mass murderer."

"That's it up ahead on the right, I think," Sampson said, gesturing through the windshield at a gated pull-off in a large woodlot between two farms.

Hand-painted signs hung from the locked gate: DOGS ARE THE LEAST OF YOUR WORRIES; DON'T EVEN THINK ABOUT IT; BLAST ZONE; and, my favorite, THE LUNATIC IS IN THE GRASS.

"We might want to rethink this," Sampson said.

"Dolores said he's good until sundown usually," I said and pulled the squad car over on the shoulder beyond the gate.

I got out, felt the breeze, smelled the salt air, and heard the sawing of cicadas in the hardwoods. I looked at the signs on the gate again, thought about the path that had taken us here, and wondered if Sampson was right, if we should rethink this unannounced visit.

Three days before, I'd started looking into mercenaries living in the Washington, DC, area, and I was shocked at the high numbers. But once it was explained to me, it made sense.

In 2008, at the height of the Iraq War, there

were 155,826 private contractors operating in Iraq in support of 152,000 U.S. soldiers. Private contractors outnumbered the U.S. military in Afghanistan as well. Between the two wars, best estimates are that as many as forty thousand men and women were involved in security and other private military activities. In other words, guns for hire. In other words, mercenaries.

Most of them were highly trained former elite soldiers working through security companies like Blackwater, which had been based in Northern Virginia. These companies and ex-soldiers had made a lot of money for nearly a decade.

And then the spigot closed. President Obama ordered the troops withdrawn from Iraq, and with them went the need and the money to hire scads of private security personnel. Men who'd been making a hundred and fifty thousand to a half a million a year in the war zones were suddenly looking for work.

A friend of mine at the Pentagon told me there were probably five thousand of these guns for hire living in and around the nation's capital. But it wasn't like there was a directory of them.

I'd asked my friend if there was someone who knew a lot about that world, someone who might point us in the right direction. He'd called back yesterday and given me a phone number.

When I'd called it, a woman answered and said, "Don't bother doing a trace, Detective Cross. It's a burn phone. And call me Dolores."

"I'm just asking for advice, Dolores."

"Ask away."

I asked Dolores if she'd read about the massacre at the drug factory in Anacostia. She had. I told her how clean an operation it was and how we believed ex-military were involved.

"Makes sense," she'd said.

"Any candidates you can think of? Someone with military training, and maybe a beef with drug dealers? Someone willing to go outside the law and lead others into mass murder?"

There was a long, long pause, and finally Dolores had said, "I can think of only one offhand."

Startling me from my thoughts, Sampson cleared his throat and gestured at the gate. "After you, Alex."

With a sour feeling in the pit of my stomach, I walked to the gate of Nicholas Condon's place and climbed over it.

# CHAPTER

# 33

**SAMPSON AND I HAD LOOKED** at Condon's hundred-and-twelve-acre empire on Google Earth the night before. The dirt road beyond the gate wound through woods to a modest farm with several fields.

Now we could see that the road was not frequently used and even less frequently maintained, with wild raspberry and thorny vines trying to choke it off on both sides.

"Get your badge out," I said. "You see him, you raise both hands and identify yourself."

"Think he'll care that we're cops?"

"I have no idea," I said. "But someone with his background probably realizes that killing a cop would be a stupid move."

"Comforting when you're going to talk to a guy who considers himself a lunatic in the grass."

I couldn't argue with Sampson's concern. Condon had graduated from the Naval Academy and been a sniper, a damned good one, with a SEAL Team 6 unit. A week after he had mustered out of the military for medical reasons, a company called Dyson Security gave Condon a contract and sent him to Afghanistan.

Condon's reputation for having a cool head even in the most extreme conditions continued after he left the military, and he soon led a Dyson team that specialized in protecting political and corporate dignitaries and rescuing private contractors taken hostage by the Taliban.

One of those private contractors was an American woman named Paula Healey who worked trying to improve the lives of Afghani girls, which had made her a target for the fundamentalists. Healey was also the love of Condon's life.

She and three other women were taken outside of Kandahar. After several months, Condon learned where Healey was being held—in a remote village in a region known for poppy cultivation and opium production.

Condon and a team of his men went in under cover of night. After a firefight with the local Taliban, he found Healey strung out on opium and stabbed in the chest. She was the only one of the four women left alive. She'd been raped repeatedly and died in Condon's arms.

What happened then depends on whose testimony you believe. Either the Taliban counterattacked and Condon risked his life repeatedly to kill and drive them back, or Condon went berserk with grief and rage and gunned down every male over the age of fourteen left in the village.

There'd been an investigation, and every one of the Dyson Security operators backed up Condon's version of events. The widows and mothers claimed their dead were not Taliban and that they had been slaughtered.

Ultimately, Condon was exonerated. But losing his love changed him, made him violent and unpredictable. Dyson decided he could not be put in the field and paid off his five-year contract in a lump sum.

Condon had used the money to buy the land we were walking through.

Dolores said Condon was a hermit who liked to farm and go fishing on his boat out on the ocean alone. He distrusted anybody involved in the government. His only visitors, and they were rare, were the men and women who'd served with him in Afghanistan and Iraq.

I'd asked Dolores how she knew so much about him.

She'd hesitated and then said, "Once, a long time before he met Paula, *I* was the love of Nicholas's life."

There was a picket stake in the trail with a piece of orange tape fluttering off it. We went around it and entered the field forty yards from its eastern end, where there was a ten-foot-high dirt embankment with a large red tub of Tide detergent sitting on top.

The field to our right lay fallow. It was long and narrow, three hundred yards to the other end and maybe fifty yards to the far tree line.

"The house is in the next field?" Sampson said as we started across.

"That's the way I—"

We never heard the shot, just the bullet ripping the air before the Tide detergent tub on the embankment erupted like a land mine, throwing dirt, rock, and melted plastic everywhere and sending a plume of gray smoke toward the sky.

# CHAPTER

# 34

**AS SOON AS WE HEARD** the bullet ripping past us, instinct kicked in. We were both diving when the bomb went off.

Sampson and I hit the ground and put our arms over our heads as debris rained down on us. My left ear rang and for a moment I was disoriented.

Then, like a boxer recovering from a glancing blow, I became more alert. I dug at my back for my service pistol and then followed Sampson as he squirmed forward into high grass and weeds.

"Where'd the shot come from?" Sampson asked in a harsh whisper.

"From Condon's sniper rifle?"

"I meant from what direction?"

"No idea, but it had to have been far away if we

didn't hear the report before whatever was in that Tide thing exploded."

"We need to reach the trees and call for backup," Sampson said.

"Backup first," I said, and pulled out my cell. "Great—no service."

"I had it over by the road."

"Not here," I said, and then I heard something over the ringing in my left ear.

Sampson heard it too, rose up to look, and then ducked down.

"That's an ATV," Sampson said. "He's coming for us. Two hundred yards out. Near the tree line."

We stared at each other, thinking the same thing: Do we run for the trees and risk getting shot by a world-class sniper? Or—

I pushed myself to my feet, held out my badge, and aimed my pistol at Condon, who was less than a hundred yards away in a green Polaris Ranger. Sampson stood up beside me and did the same.

Condon pulled up at ninety yards, snaked a scoped rifle over the wheel, and shouted, "You trying to get yourselves killed? Didn't you see the goddamned orange flag in the road?"

"We didn't know what it meant," I shouted back. "We're detectives with Washington Metro Police. We just want to ask you a few questions."

Condon was hunkered over the rifle, aiming at us through his scope. At ninety yards, any shot we might take with the pistol would be a Hail Mary. But ninety yards with a precision sniper rifle was a chip shot.

I had a funny feeling in my chest, as if he'd put the crosshairs there. Then he lifted his head. "You *the* Alex Cross? FBI profiler and all that?"

"I was," I called back. "That's right."

That seemed to satisfy Condon because he slipped the rifle into a plastic scabbard mounted to the side of the ATV and started driving toward us.

"How'd he know your name?" Sampson asked.

"I'm thinking he read our credentials through his scope," I said, lowering my gun but not holstering it.

Condon pulled up about ten yards away. Late thirties and rawboned, he had silver-and-red hair and a matching beard. Both needed cutting.

"Azore," he said. "Denni."

Two German shepherds jumped down from the flatbed carrier behind the sniper. They stopped and stood there, panting, at Condon's side.

"You mind telling us what the hell that was all about?" Sampson asked. "Shooting at us?"

Condon said, "Practicing my trade. You walked into a hot rifle range, my place of business, unannounced and forewarned. That's what happened."

I said, "You didn't see us before you shot?"

He looked at me, blinked, said, "Hell no, I was in the zone. In the whole wide world, there was nothing but the *I* and the *D* and the trigger and me."

"What's the *I* and the *D*?"

He spelled it out. "T-i-d-e."

"What was in that container?" I asked.

"Tannerite," he said. "Exploding target material. Shot indicator."

Sampson said, "You almost killed us with that stuff, which is illegal in Maryland, by the way."

Ordinarily the mere presence of a pissed-off John Sampson was enough to shake the toughest of criminals. But Condon looked at ease.

"Not for me," he said. "I have a federal permit through Alcohol, Tobacco, and Firearms. And, like I said, I didn't know you were there. If I'd wanted to kill you, Detectives, you'd already be dead, and I'd have a shovel-and-shut-up mission on my hands. Know what I mean?"

I did know what the sniper meant and absolutely believed him.

# CHAPTER

# 35

**CONDON CROSSED HIS ARMS AND** said, "So go ahead, ask your questions."

"Somewhere we can sit down?" Sampson said. "Get out of this heat?"

Condon considered that, said, "Two weapons each? Primary and backup?"

I nodded.

"Azore," Condon said. "Denni."

The dogs circled us in easy lopes. Both hesitated, turned noses toward our ankles, then wagged their tails.

The sniper whistled and they went back to his side.

"Always like to know for sure," Condon said, and he started up the Ranger. "One of you can sit up front. One in the back."

"I'll take the back," I said, then I holstered my pistol and climbed up onto the little flatbed carrier beside several toolboxes that presumably held the tools of Condon's trade.

Sampson had to duck his head to squeeze into the passenger seat.

Condon put the Ranger in gear, glanced at Sampson, and said, "Guys big as you don't last long when the shit hits the fan."

"Which is why I like to be holding the fan at all times," Sampson growled.

Condon almost smiled.

The German shepherds ran along as we drove to the tree line, where another picket with orange flagging blocked the road. The sniper got out, drew it from the ground, and handed it to me.

A minute or two later, we pulled up by a black Ford F-150, a Harley-Davidson, and a John Deere farm tractor parked in front of a white ranch house in need of scraping and painting. A Grady-White fishing boat sat on a trailer near a red barn in need of shoring and paint.

The long field in front of Condon's house was shoulder-high in corn. His grass needed mowing, and the air smelled of stale dog dung and urine.

Condon turned off the ATV, tugged the rifle

from the black scabbard, and got out. He walked with a slight hitch in his stride to retrieve one of the toolboxes.

"Nice gun," I said.

"Designed it myself," he said, grabbing one of the toolboxes and showing me a .338 Lapua with a Timney trigger, a Lone Wolf custom stock, and a Swarovski 4 to 18 power scope.

No wonder he'd been able to read my credentials at ninety yards.

"How far can you shoot something like that?" Sampson asked.

"Wind's calm and I'm right, a mile," Condon said, and he went with a slight hitch in his gait up a cracked walkway to the front porch.

He came up with a heavy ring of keys and used them to open three dead bolts. Opening the door, he called, "Denni. Azore."

The dogs streaked into the house. Two minutes later, they returned.

"Kennel up," he said.

The dogs trotted over to cedar beds and lay down.

Condon gestured for us to follow him inside and flipped on the light in a small living area off a kitchen. The place reeked of marijuana. Beer cans and an empty bottle of Jack Daniel's crowded a coffee table between a couch with busted springs and a large TV on the wall. An image from *Game of Thrones* was frozen on the flat-screen.

The drapes were drawn. Condon crossed to an air-conditioning unit mounted on the wall and turned it on.

"Beer?" he asked.

"We're on duty," Sampson said.

"Suit yourself," Condon said, and he went into the kitchen.

I looked around, saw Sampson had gone to a small table in the corner and was looking at several framed photographs, all of the same beautiful young woman in a variety of rugged outdoor settings. In the largest picture, an eight-by-ten, she was in Condon's arms and he glowed like he owned the world.

"That what you're here about?" Condon asked. "Paula and all?"

Even with the limp, he'd come up behind us so quietly we both startled.

When I turned, the sniper popped his Bud can, looked at us coldly.

"We'd heard about her. I'm sorry for your loss."

Condon softened slightly, said, "Thank you."

"What's it been? Four years?"

"Four years, six months, three days, nine hours, three minutes. Was this what you came all the way from DC to talk about?"

In the car, Sampson and I had hashed out how best to approach him. Trying to bull or bluff a guy like Condon wasn't going to work, so I opted to come at him from the side.

"We need your help," I said. "Do you keep up with the news?"

"I try not to," Condon said.

"There was a mass murder in a methamphetamine factory in Washington, DC," I said. "Twenty-two people died. The assault seemed professional, as in highly trained. Probably ex-military."

As if he were seeing an enemy in the distance, the sniper's eyes hardened.

"I know where this is going," he said. "I'll save you some time. I had nothing to do with that. Now, unless you have a warrant, Detective Cross, I'm going to have to ask you to get out of my house and off my land."

"Mr. Condon—"

"Now. Before I get all loony and PTSD, start thinking you're the Taliban."

# Part Three

# MERCURY RISING

# CHAPTER

# 36

**MERCURY RARELY RODE HIS MOTORCYCLE** in broad daylight.

He generally took the bike out only at night and on patrol. But heading south on Interstate 97, he felt like nothing could shake him today, as if more balance were coming into the world, and into his life. He had been the avenger now in more ways than one, and he rather liked the role.

Hell, he loved everything about what he'd been doing these past few weeks—taking charge and acting when no one else would. Certainly not the police. Certainly not the FBI or NCIS. Do-nothings, one and—

Mercury noticed a beige Ford Taurus weaving in the slow lane just south of the Maryland Route

32 interchange. He hung one car back and one car over.

The Taurus drifted, and the Porsche SUV in front of Mercury honked at it. The Taurus wandered back into its lane.

The Porsche accelerated. Mercury sped up as if to pass the Taurus too and got just far enough to see what was really going on.

"Stupid bitch," he muttered, anger beginning to build, boiling away all that good feeling. "Don't you read? Don't you listen?"

He backed off, telling himself that this wasn't the time or the place.

But as he entered a long, slow, easterly curve in the four-lane highway, Mercury realized that, except for the Taurus, the southbound lanes were clear in front and behind him.

He made a split-second decision and zipped open his jacket. With his right hand he twisted the throttle, and with his left, he drew the pistol.

The motorcycle sped up until it was right beside the Taurus. The stupid bitch driving didn't look at him, and she wasn't looking at the road ahead.

She was texting on an iPhone while driving sixty-two miles an hour.

Years of practice had made Mercury an ambidextrous shot. He was about to pull the trigger when Ms. Textaholic actually took her eyes off the goddamned screen.

She looked over. She saw the gun.

She dropped the iPhone and twisted as he shot.

The tail end of the Taurus swung violently into his lane, almost knocking over the motorcycle, and then it veered back the other way, did a 360-degree spin, ran up an embankment, and flipped over onto its roof.

He put away the pistol and drove on at a steady sixty-three, two miles below the speed limit.

No need to draw any attention now that the traffic laws were being obeyed and a sense of balance, a sense of order, had been restored.

# CHAPTER

# 37

**THAT AFTERNOON AFTER WE TALKED** to Condon, we went to Bree's office and gave her our report.

"So Condon threatened two law enforcement officers?" she asked, looking as stressed and tired as I've ever seen her.

"Oh yeah," Sampson said.

"In a manner of speaking, anyway," I said. "He's highly intelligent. Knew what we were up to the second we mentioned the massacre."

"You ask him where he was on the night in question?"

"He wouldn't answer," Sampson said. "Said he'd learned the hard way never to talk with an investigator of any kind without an attorney present."

"But you put him on notice that he's a suspect," Bree said. "That can be a good thing."

"It can," I said. "But we can't exactly put him under surveillance from here, and we don't have evidence to support a search warrant."

"Find me one thing that links Condon to that factory, and I'll call in some favors with the state police in Maryland. Have them put him under surveillance."

"I find one thing that links Condon to that factory and I think Mahoney will take over and call in the FBI cavalry, and it will be out of our hands."

Sampson said, "I'm going to check if Condon has a Tannerite waiver. If not, he's stockpiling explosives and we can walk in his front door with an army behind us."

"Good," Bree said.

We started to leave, but Bree called after me, "Alex? Can we talk?"

"Fine," Sampson said. "I know when I'm not wanted."

He closed the door as he left. Bree sagged back in her chair.

"You okay?" I said.

"Not today," she said. "This morning, the mayor and the chief took turns using me as their verbal punching bag over the massacre."

"And a few days ago, you helped them get the pressure off their backs by naming Terry Howard as Tom's killer. You can't go up and down emotionally along with *their* roller-coaster whims. Accept the fact that getting pressure from above is part of the job but doesn't define it. Focus on doing the best you can. Nothing else. Three months from now you'll have a whole different outlook on things."

Bree sighed. "Think so?"

"I know so," I said, coming around to massage her shoulders and neck.

"Ohhhh, I need that," she said. "My lower back's hurting too."

"You're sitting down too much," I said. "You're used to being up and active, and your body's protesting."

"I'm a desk jockey now. Part of the territory."

"Get the chief to buy you one of those stand-up desks. Or better yet, a treadmill desk."

"That's not a bad idea," Bree said.

"I'm full of good ideas today." I bent over and kissed her on the cheek.

"I miss you," she said.

"I miss you too," I said and nuzzled her neck. "But we're good, right?"

"Always."

There was a knock at the door.

Sampson called out, "You still dressed?"

"No, we're buck-naked," Bree called back. "C'mon in."

He opened the door cautiously, saw me massaging her neck, and said, "Sorry to disturb you in the middle of things, but I had a ViCAP going on drivers who were shot like Mr. Maserati there in Rock Creek."

I stopped kneading Bree's neck. "You got a hit?"

"You tell me."

# CHAPTER

# 38

**A FEW WEEKS BEFORE AARON PETERS** was shot to death by a motorcyclist on the Rock Creek Parkway, thirty-nine-year-old Liza Crawford, a successful real estate agent in Gettysburg, Pennsylvania, was found dead in her brand-new Corvette on a winding rural road lined in places with stacked stone walls.

The investigator said Crawford was traveling at a high rate of speed when she hit a stone wall. The Corvette flipped over and landed on its roof, crushing her.

The extensive damage to Crawford's head had initially hidden the .45-caliber-bullet entry and exit wounds, but they were discovered during the autopsy. She'd been dead before the crash. The slug was retrieved from the passenger-side door and it was now being processed at Pennsylvania's state crime lab.

Samuel Tate, twenty-three, died two months before Peters and Crawford. An auto mechanic, Tate was found dead inside his souped-up Ford Mustang, the front end of which was wrapped around an oak tree on a rural road west of Fredericksburg, Virginia.

Tate was known to be an excellent driver who never drank or got high. There were no skid marks on the road, and yet he'd been going well over one hundred miles an hour when he lost control. A medical examiner found a hole made by a .45-caliber bullet in the left side of his head. The bullet had already been processed.

"Look at that," Sampson said now, tapping on his computer screen, which displayed the report on Tate's bullet and the report on the bullets taken from the Rock Creek victim. "They're a dead-on match."

"Crawford's will be too," I said, studying a map. "She died about the same distance from Washington as Tate did, but she was to the north of it and he was to the south. So a ninety- to ninety-five-minute radius."

"Which means what?"

"We've got a serial killer. A hunter on a

motorcycle. Draw a ninety-minute circle around us. That's his hunting ground."

"What's he hunting?"

"Maseratis. Corvettes. Mustangs."

"High-performance cars," Sampson said.

"Well, the people who drive high-performance cars."

"And drive them very fast."

Tapping my lip with one finger, I thought about that.

"What's the point?" Sampson asked. "Is it a game?"

"Could be," I said. "That video from Peters's car shows they were playing cat and mouse, and the motorcyclist was better at being the cat."

Sampson shook his head. "The media's going to have a field day with this one too. Remember the Beltway Sniper attacks?"

"How could I forget?"

I was still with the FBI on the morning of October 3, 2002, when four people were randomly shot to death in suburban Maryland. That night, inside the District, a seventy-two-year-old carpenter was shot and killed while taking a walk on Georgia Avenue.

The press called them the Beltway Sniper attacks. But it soon became clear to the FBI that the shooting spree had started eight months before in

Tacoma, Washington. In all, we found twelve people who'd been wounded or killed by the snipers prior to October 3, from Arizona to Texas to Atlanta to Baton Rouge, Louisiana.

We eventually caught the two troubled men with a Bushmaster AR-15 rifle, but before it was over, seventeen people died. Another ten were wounded but survived.

"Malvo and Muhammad did it for sport," Sampson said. "It could be what we're looking at here."

"Possibly," I said. "A challenge to the motorcyclist, chasing the fast car down and getting off a lethal shot at the driver."

"And escaping unharmed?"

I nodded, thinking how bad this could get. The country had been caught up in twenty-three days of fear when the Beltway Snipers were shooting and killing. Those twenty-three days had been some of the most stressful of my life.

"You going to tell Bree? She's got a lot on her shoulders already."

Before I could answer, my wife appeared at the door to my office, breathless.

"O'Donnell, Lincoln, and two patrolmen came under automatic-weapon fire in Northeast five minutes ago," she said. "Lincoln was hit. So was a patrolman. O'Donnell says Thao Le was one of the shooters."

# CHAPTER

# 39

**WE RACED THROUGH THE CITY,** blues flashing and sirens wailing. I drove. Sampson struggled into body armor in the seat beside me. Bree was in the back, fielding calls, fighting to get a full understanding of the situation, and coordinating with the other chiefs to send the right personnel to the scene.

Evidently, Detectives Lincoln and O'Donnell had been tracking Thao Le through his girlfriend Michele Bui. She had texted O'Donnell that Le was moving a load of drugs through a row house in Northeast that afternoon.

The detectives had gone to check it out and called for backup. One patrol car drove into the alley behind the house. Another patrol car came onto the block at one end, and Lincoln and

O'Donnell came from the other. They saw Le and three of his men chilling on the front porch.

O'Donnell had stopped his vehicle just shy of the house. The other patrol car did the same. All four officers jumped out, guns drawn, and ordered the men on the porch to lie down. Le came up with an AK-47 and opened fire.

Lincoln and a patrolman were hit; Lincoln took a bullet through his thigh and another through his hand. O'Donnell had been able to pull him behind a car across the street. The injured patrolman, Josh Parks, had been shot through the pelvis, but he'd dragged himself up against the base of the porch, where he could not be seen or shot at from inside.

"How are you, Parks?" Bree asked over the radio.

"Feel like I got a drill bit through my groin to my spine, but otherwise peachy," the officer said.

"O'Donnell?"

"We need to get Lincoln and Parks to the hospital without getting shot."

"I hear you," she said. "Cavalry's on its way. ETA four minutes."

"I heard a lot of screaming inside. I'm thinking he's got hostages."

We heard shouting and automatic gunfire, and then the connection died.

"Shit!" Bree shouted.

She tried to redial, but her phone rang before she could.

"O'Donnell?" Bree said, and listened. "Where are you?"

Bree punched the speaker button, and out came the terrified voice of Michele Bui.

"I'm hiding inside a closet upstairs," Thao Le's girlfriend said, clearly on the verge of tears. "Thao and his friends have been snorting coke and meth for days, and they're out of their minds and paranoid. He's got them convinced they're next."

"Next for what?"

"Next to be killed," she said. "They were so whacked, they thought the cops were those vigilantes killing meth cookers."

"Who else is in the house with you?" Bree asked.

"I don't know exactly," she said. "I was upstairs sleeping, but I heard a few of the cutters and packagers come in and work through the night. After the shots, I heard screams and—"

"What?"

"Thao's yelling for me," she said. "I gotta go."

The line went dead.

# CHAPTER

# 40

**METRO PATROL CARS WERE PARKED** in V formations blocking the street at both ends of the road. Other officers were moving through the alleys to evacuate residents closest to the row house Le was in.

A pair of ambulances had already arrived. We left our squad car down the street and got our first look at the situation through binoculars.

Halfway down the block on the east side, Officer Joshua Parks was on his side by the stoop to the row house, contorted in agony.

"We're here, Parks, with more on the way," Bree said over her radio.

"Good," he said. "I'm getting one hell of a leg cramp lying on the cement like this."

Bree couldn't help but smile. "We'll have that cramp looked into. Talk to me, O'Donnell."

Detective O'Donnell was across the street from Parks on the sidewalk behind a white Ford Explorer. He was holding Lincoln, who looked weak.

"O'Donnell, talk to me," Bree said again.

"Lincoln's conscious, but hurting bad. What's the plan?"

"Working on it," Bree said.

She looked at me, said quietly, "I've never handled anything remotely like this, Alex. You have, so I'm all ears."

I scanned the scene again and then said, "We need to be inside the house directly across the street from Le's and also in the house directly behind it. And we need Le's cell phone number."

"I'll try Michele Bui again," Bree said.

The SWAT van pulled up. Captain Matt Fuller, dressed head to toe in black body armor, climbed out and hurried toward us.

"Shit," I muttered.

"What?"

"I'd hoped Captain Reagan was on duty," I said. "Fuller's good at what he does, but he wants to do it as often as he can, if you know what I mean."

A burly man with soft, almost saggy facial features, Fuller said, "Dr. Cross. Chief Stone. Sampson. How's the officer down?"

"Two are down, Captain," Bree said. "Lincoln, who's one of my men, and Officer Parks. Both are in critical need of medical attention, especially Parks."

Fuller looked at the scene through binoculars. When he put them down, he said, "We're going to want to be in the house opposite and the one behind."

"You took the words right out of my mouth," I said, and then I looked to Bree again. "Call Michele. Get that number."

Captain Fuller, four of his men, Sampson, and I used an alley to reach the row house directly in front of Detectives O'Donnell and Lincoln and across the street from Parks. A frail older woman had been evacuated from the house. She'd given her key to one of the patrolmen who'd helped her, and we used it to go through the back door into her kitchen.

We passed a steep staircase on our way into the living area, barely taking in the dated furniture, the photos of a lifetime, and a baby grand piano.

"Maxwell and Keith, you're upstairs," Captain Fuller said behind me. "Stay back from the windows, keep it dark."

While the two SWAT officers climbed the stairs, Bree pushed aside the window curtains just enough for us to see O'Donnell and Lincoln right there on the sidewalk, backs to the Explorer, no more than fifty feet away. O'Donnell had his belt around Lincoln's thigh, but Lincoln looked wan, like he'd lost a lot of blood.

"Lincoln needs medical help now," Bree said.

"Both of them do," I said, watching Parks go through some kind of pain spasm that made him arch in agony.

The SWAT commander was quiet for several moments and then said, "We're going to handle this one at a time. Easiest first, which means Lincoln."

Fuller looked at his two other men. "How fast can you get out the door, go down those steps, grab Lincoln, and get your asses back inside?"

"Twenty seconds," Sergeant Daniel Kiniry said.

"Maybe less," Officer Brent Remer said. "Unless we come under fire."

"O'Donnell? How long since the last shots?" Fuller asked.

"Ten, maybe twelve minutes," the detective came back.

The captain thought a moment and then spoke into his radio. "Wilkerson?"

"Go ahead, Captain."

"Break me out a couple of grenades."

# CHAPTER

# 41

**BREE AND I LOOKED AT** Captain Fuller like he'd lost his mind.

"Grenades?" Bree said. "Isn't that a little extreme?"

"No," Fuller said, and then he explained what he wanted to do.

I considered it, decided once again that Captain Fuller was good at his job, and admitted, "That could work."

"It could," Bree said. "Your move, Captain."

Three minutes later, on Fuller's command, two flash-bang grenades went off behind the row house where Le and his fellow gangbangers were holed up.

I had my binoculars trained on the windows across the street and saw movement inside, figures running to investigate the explosions. Then Bree threw up the window sash, and we stuck our service weapons out the window.

"Go," Fuller said, and he yanked open the front door to the old lady's home.

Kiniry and Remer bolted across the porch, leaped off the stairs, and landed beside Lincoln. O'Donnell let go of his partner.

The SWAT guys got their hands under Lincoln and came up fast. O'Donnell jumped up, his gun, like ours, aimed at the row house as he backed up, covering Kiniry, Remer, and Lincoln.

They got Lincoln inside, and O'Donnell was almost there when Le or one of his men opened up with an automatic weapon. Bullets blew out the windows of the Explorer and pinged and cracked off the cement stairs while Sampson, Bree, and I emptied our weapons at the house.

O'Donnell sprinted and dove inside. Fuller slammed shut the heavy oak door as bullets strafed the side of the house and then stopped.

"Fuck!" O'Donnell screamed, crawling and clutching at his shoe. "He shot me through the foot!"

"Get this man medical attention!" Bree yelled back into the house.

Two EMTs came running from the kitchen.

While they started to work, I reloaded. Over our headsets, a voice said, "Cap, this is Maxwell."

"Go, Maxwell," Fuller said.

"I've got the shooter. Full chest exposed."

"Identity?"

"Unclear, but subject is armed with an AK."

"Take him," Fuller said without a moment's hesitation.

"What? Wait!" Bree said.

There was a rifle crack overhead, followed by a death scream across the street.

"Slow down, Captain!" I shouted.

"You're not giving them any options!" Bree said.

"Options?" Fuller looked at us like we were addled. "That shooter, Le or not, just tried to kill four—count them, four—of my fellow officers. In my mind, that makes that person a potential cop killer with active intent, so I ordered him shot. End of story."

Bree started to argue but her phone buzzed. Angry, she looked at the screen, rocked her head back, and said, "Oh Jesus."

"What?"

"It's Michele Bui. She says we just shot and killed one of the female hostages."

# CHAPTER

# 42

**FULLER DIDN'T HEAR. HE WAS** barking orders into his radio while EMTs rolled a morphine-happy Detective O'Donnell through the kitchen toward the back door. The siren of the ambulance bearing Lincoln was already wailing away.

"Captain!" I shouted at Fuller.

The SWAT commander put his radio on his shoulder, peered at me angrily. "Detective Cross, stand down."

"I won't stand down, Captain," I said.

"Nor will I," Bree said. "One of your men upstairs, Officer Maxwell, just shot an innocent hostage on your orders."

Fuller lost color. "No."

"Le's girlfriend, who is in there, says yes."

The captain pulled himself together and clicked his radio. "Maxwell?"

"Right here, Cap."

"How did you identify the shooter?"

"White T-shirt and weapon."

"No head?"

"Negative."

"How long did you have the shooter in your scope?"

"From right before he started shooting at O'Donnell," Maxwell replied. "When he stopped, he ducked out of sight for maybe three seconds and then returned, like he'd reloaded."

"That was not a reload," Bree said into her radio. "Officer Maxwell, you shot a hostage."

There was a long, terrible silence before Maxwell said, "Cap?"

"Maxwell?"

"Permission to stand down, sir."

Fuller glared at Bree, said, "Permission denied. I need you up there."

Bree said, "Captain, for the time being, *you* are going to stand down and let me try to save Officer Parks and avoid more bloodshed. Or do I call Chief Michaels to have you relieved of command?"

Fuller blinked slowly at Bree, said, "I guess it's your show, Chief."

"No, it's Dr. Cross's show," she said, looking at me. "I've got Le's phone number. Try to talk to him."

I took a moment to mentally adjust, to become less a police detective and more a criminal psychologist. Then I entered the phone number and hit Send.

The phone rang three times before Le answered in a jittery, cocaine-fueled voice. "Who the hell's this?"

"The only chance you have of not dying today, Mr. Le," I said. "My name is Alex Cross."

# CHAPTER

# 43

**LE'S BREATHING WAS RAPID AND** shallow in my ear.

"Do you understand, Mr. Le?" I asked. "There are SWAT officers preparing to storm in and kill you. I'm offering you a way out."

After a long, long pause, he said, "How's that?"

"Start by not making it worse for yourself," I said. "Two police officers have been wounded and a hostage killed."

"That's not on me," Le said. "Some cop shot her."

I wasn't going to quibble and point out that he'd shoved her into the line of fire with a weapon in her hand; I needed to keep him talking, establish rapport.

"You're a hell of a motorcycle rider," I said. "Saw you in action at Eden Center a while back."

Le chuckled. "You never saw anyone pull that kind of shit before."

"Never," I said. "You are a rare talent. Now, how are we going to keep you, and your talent, from dying today?"

During a long pause I heard him snorting meth or coke or both. Then he said, "I dunno, Alex. You tell me."

"How about you show me you can be trusted?" I said. "Let us retrieve our wounded officer."

"What's in that for me?" Le said.

I said, "We're in this together."

"Give me a fucking break," he said. "We're not together. We're traveling different roads."

"Different roads that are at an intersection. I'm trying to prevent a crash that you would not survive. Is that what you want too?"

He didn't say anything for almost a minute.

"Mr. Le?" I said.

When Le spoke, his voice was softer, more thoughtful. "I figured things would turn out different for me."

"What was your dream? Everyone's got one."

Le laughed. "X Games, man."

"On the motorcycle?"

"That's it," Le said. "All I thought about. All I did."

"When did you let the dream die?"

"I crashed too much and needed something strong enough to get through the pain," he said. "Going into the business of killing pain just made sense."

Le was smart, articulate, and self-aware. No wonder he'd been able to build a small empire.

"Can we come for Officer Parks? Things will go worse for you if he dies."

Le thought about that and then said, "Do it. We won't shoot."

# CHAPTER

# 44

**"THANK YOU, MR. LE,"** I said. "We appreciate it."

I muted my phone and said to Bree and Fuller, "Get me EMTs. I'm going across with them. I'll keep him talking until Parks is clear."

"I don't like it," Fuller said.

"Neither do I," Bree said.

"Le needs to see me. It will change things."

I didn't wait for a reply. I cut the mute and said, "Mr. Le? You there?"

I heard him snort something again. "I'm here. You coming?"

"I am," I said. "I'll be the tall unarmed man with the ambulance workers."

The EMTs came in pushing a gurney. I hit the mute button again.

"He says he won't shoot," I said. "But it's your call. I'll go alone if I have to."

The male EMT, Bill Hawkins, said, "He mentally stable?"

"Surprisingly so, at the moment," I said. "But an hour ago he evidently thought Officer Parks and the others were part of a vigilante gang and opened up on them. So there's got to be some delusion there."

"You trust him?" said Emma Jean Lord, the other EMT.

"Enough to lead the way," I said.

They looked at each other and nodded.

"Be quick about this," Bree told them. "Let Alex talk. You go straight to Parks, everything crisp and businesslike, no different than if he'd had a heart attack on his front lawn."

"Okay," Hawkins said. "Let's go."

Looking to Captain Fuller, Bree said, "You'll cover them?"

"What are the rules of engagement?" he said with the hint of a sneer.

"Protect them."

"Okay," Fuller said. "I can live with that."

"Good," I said, thumbing the mute button off. "We're coming out, Mr. Le. We will be moving fast to get to Officer Parks."

"Come on, then," Le said.

I holstered my gun, opened the door, and trotted off the front porch, saying, "You're seeing me?"

"We're not looking out windows and getting shot," Le said. "Do what you have to do."

Still, I couldn't help feeling as if crosshairs were on my forehead as the three of us went to Officer Parks, who was gray and sweating with pain.

Hawkins swung the gurney next to him.

Lord said, kneeling beside Parks, "Can you feel your legs?"

"Yeah, too much," Parks said through gritted teeth. "Like they're on fire, and it hurts insanely bad around and above my hips. I think my pelvis is broken on both sides. And I'm thirsty."

"Because you're gut shot," the EMT said, taking his vitals.

"Am I gonna live?"

"If we have anything to say about it," Hawkins said.

Lord and Hawkins worked fast, getting an IV into Parks's arm and then putting him on a backboard. They lifted him onto the gurney, strapped him down, and headed for the street.

I waited until they were out of range before saying, "You did a good thing, Mr. Le. Officer Parks will live. Why don't you do another good thing and come out onto the porch to talk to me face-to-face?"

There was a moment of silence before Le said, "You must think I'm an idiot. I take one step out that door and I go *boom-boom* away."

"Not if I have anything to do with it," I said. "At least let some of the hostages go."

"No."

"No, you won't come out and talk, or no, you won't let the hostages go?"

"The hostages stay," Le said, and I heard him set his cell down.

Then I heard him snorting yet again.

A female voice in the background said, "Go talk to him. Figure this the hell out, because I'm not dying for you and your meth paranoia!"

After several moments, the phone was picked up again. Le said in a slow, weird voice, "Uhhhh, sure, Cross. I'll come out, and we'll have us a chitchat."

"When?"

"Why don't we do it right the fuck now?"

Before I could reply, the line went dead, and inside the house a woman screamed.

# CHAPTER

# 45

**BREE'S VOICE BARKED IN MY** earbud, "What's going on in there?"

"I have no idea—" I started, and then the front door flew open.

A dazed Michele Bui shuffled out, her face a spiderweb of blood from a head wound. Thao Le stood behind her, one arm around her neck, the other hand pressing a .45-caliber 1911 pistol to her temple.

Le looked as wired as any snort-head I had ever seen. His eyes were sunk in their sockets, and the whites were the color of a freshly painted fire-alarm box. Blood seeped from his left nostril over skin and lips that had turned so waxy from the drugs they would have looked dead were it not for the odd twitches in his cheeks and cracked lips.

I turned my palms up to show I had no weapon, said, "Mr. Le?"

On the porch, two feet out from the open doorway, Le tracked me. "You…Cross?"

"That's right," I said. "What are you doing? We agreed to talk man-to-man."

"What, did you think I was coming out alone? Without a shield? Let you all shoot me down? You cops been wanting to take me out for years."

"Why don't you let Michele go? She's bleeding. She needs medical help."

Le blinked and cocked his head but said nothing.

"C'mon, Mr. Le. She's your girlfriend. Do you really want to—"

"You know her name, Cross?" he said. "And that she's my girlfriend?"

He laughed and pressed the muzzle of the gun tighter against her head. Michele Bui winced and tried to cringe away, but he held her close.

"I am not stupid, Cross," he said. "You know her name means you talked to her, and she's been talking to you. And my girlfriend? Hell no. This skank's a throwaway blow-up sex doll, means nothing to me."

Something started to change in Michele Bui's expression. She came up out of the daze and her eyes went hard.

"Michele seems interested only in keeping you

alive," I said. "In my book, that's caring, Mr. Le. That's love."

Le glanced at his girlfriend and laughed. "Nah. That's survival. Without me, she's on the street selling her ass."

"So what do you want?"

"A way out of here," Le said.

"That can be arranged."

"Not in cuffs. Not in a cruiser. I mean gone."

"Gone is not happening. But you can do yourself some good. Let her go."

"No," Le said. "I know stuff. There's got to be a trade here. I tell you the stuff I know, and you let me walk."

"You'd have to know something of great value for that to happen," I said.

"Like what?"

"Like who are the vigilantes? Are they mercenaries hired by rival drug gangs?"

"Hey, I don't know, man," Le said. "Seriously. I know a lot, but not that."

I thought a moment. "Did you kill Tom McGrath?"

"No way," Le said. "I wanted to, but that ain't on me, and I can prove it. Can't I, Michele?"

Bui looked at me and nodded. "We were in bed when that happened."

"See?" Le said, relaxing his hold around her

neck. "Sex dolls are important in other ways. What else do you want to know?"

I was just doing my best to keep him talking when something popped into my head.

"Did you frame Terry Howard?" I asked. "Did you plant the cocaine and the money? He's dead, you know. It would help clear things up."

"Nah," Le said with a smirk. "I never did nothing like—"

Michele Bui opened her mouth and chomped down on Le's forearm.

Le howled in pain and yanked his arm free. A ragged chunk of his flesh tore away, and his arm poured blood. In his drug-agitated state, Le looked at the wound in disbelief and trembled from adrenaline.

Bui smiled, spit, and said, "A throwaway sex doll that bites!"

She tried to kick Le in the balls, but he swatted the kick away, which threw her off balance, and she fell, half on the porch, half on the stairs to the front yard.

Le raised his gun, screaming, "I'm throwing you away now, bitch! You see it coming?"

"Le, don't!" I shouted.

But it was too late.

From the second story of the house across the street, a sniper rifle barked.

Le lurched at the impact and fired his pistol, but the bullet went a foot wide of Bui's legs and splintered one of the corner posts of the porch. The gangbanger staggered backward, hit the doorjamb, and slid down it.

I raced up, jumped over Bui, and got to Le. He gasped something in Vietnamese.

I knelt next to him, said, "There's an ambulance coming."

He laughed. "Won't make it."

"Did you frame Terry Howard?"

Le looked up at me, smiled, and seemed to try to wink before blood spilled from his lips and the light in his eyes turned a dull shade of gray.

# CHAPTER

# 46

**JOHN BROWN APPRECIATED OVERCAST NIGHTS** like these, when it was so dark he couldn't see his hand in front of his face. Blinded, Brown found his other senses heightened. He smelled manure and ripening tobacco, heard a barn owl hooting, and tasted the bitter espresso bean he was chewing to stay alert.

"Three miles out," Cass said in his earpiece.

"Copy," Brown said, shifting his weight on the corrugated steel. "Hobbes?"

"We're ready."

"Fender?"

"Affirmative."

Brown bent to dig into a knapsack at his feet. A stabbing pain drilled through his knee, and he grunted through the spasm.

He managed to get out his iPad and stand, feeling the bones in his knee crack and settle. In a cold sweat, Brown turned on the tablet and signed into a secure website.

"Coming at you," Cass said. "Lead car's a blue Mustang, Florida plates. Behind the trucks, there's a black Dodge Viper, Georgia plates."

"Copy," said a male voice.

Brown clicked on a link that opened a private video feed from a camera carried by one of Hobbes's men. The scene was an interchange on Interstate 95 near the town of Ladysmith, Virginia, roughly one hundred and fifteen miles south of Washington, DC.

I-95 below the interchange was under repair. Crews were down there laboring under bright lights, and a detour forced all northbound traffic off the Ladysmith exit ramp. Another of Hobbes's men stood at the top of the ramp.

He was dressed in a workman's jumpsuit, a yellow reflective vest, and a hard hat, and he held a flashlight with an orange cover that he was using to direct the sparse traffic west, toward Ladysmith and the Jefferson Davis Highway.

The blue Mustang came into view, followed by the first of three eighteen-wheel refrigerated semis bearing the logo of the Littlefield Produce Company of Freehold Township, New Jersey. The black

Dodge Viper brought up the rear as Hobbes's flagman waved them *east*, to State Route 639.

When the flagman had done the same to Cass, who was driving a white Ford Taurus, Brown changed the feed to a camera held by one of Fender's men, who was standing in the road directing traffic a mile west of the interstate. He waved the little convoy north on Virginia Route 633.

When Cass's taillights disappeared, Brown said, "Stick to the plan. Execute the plan. Surgical precision in every move."

Brown did not bother to watch the feed of the flagmen turning the convoy off Route 633 onto a little-used, unpaved county road that cut through woodlots and agricultural fields. He could already see the headlights of the Mustang turning off the county road, following the detour signs.

"Come to Papa," Fender said.

Hearing guns being loaded all around him, Brown watched the semis make the turn onto the farm road and saw the Viper coming behind them. He knew he was going to suffer, but he knelt and gritted his teeth at the agony in his knee. The headlights came closer, revealing Brown on the corrugated steel roof of an old tobacco-drying shed.

There were six such long, low sheds in all, three set back on either side of the road that passed between them. The Mustang slowed at the blinking red light next to the sign they'd put up beyond the southernmost shed; it read TIGHT SPOT, 15 MPH.

Brown watched through the sheer black mask he wore as the Mustang kept coming. He could see the driver and the passenger now, both wearing T-shirts and looking around as if to say *Where the hell is this detour taking us?*

"Patience," Brown said as the Mustang passed below him and beyond the northernmost shed.

He glanced at the semis but then focused on the Mustang as it followed a curve in the road and stopped at a high berm and dead end.

The trailer of the first semi was almost beyond the sheds when it stopped. The second one was completely between the sheds, and the third had its cab and half of the trailer between them.

Brown waited until he heard shouting from the men in the Mustang before he said, "Take them."

He saw it all unfold in headlight glare and shadows.

Before the driver of the Viper behind the semis could even get out of his car, Cass came up fast behind him and head-shot him with a .223 AR rifle mounted with a suppressor. From the roof of the southern shed, one of Hobbes's men armed with an identical weapon shot the passenger through the windshield.

Others positioned on the roofs of the sheds took out the drivers and passengers in all three semis. The six men died in their seats even as the Mustang's driver and passenger realized what was happening. They came out of the Mustang fast and low, carrying automatic weapons.

Fender rose up from behind the berm in front of the Mustang and shot both men before they got twenty yards from their vehicle.

"Clear," Fender said.

"Clear," said Hobbes.

Brown said, "Leave the trucks and cars running. Police your brass, sweep your way out; we'll meet on the road."

Cass said, "Are you sure we shouldn't check the produce?"

Brown grimaced as he fought his way up out of the crouch. They'd been over this before and she was still challenging him on it.

"Negative," Brown said emphatically. "Nobody gets anywhere near that cargo."

# CHAPTER

# 47

**MIDMORNING, AN FBI HELICOPTER PICKED** up Sampson and me on the roof of DC Metro headquarters. Special Agent Ned Mahoney, grim and quiet, sat up front.

Ninety minutes earlier, a Caroline County sheriff's deputy had been driving by a tobacco-drying facility northeast of Ladysmith, Virginia. A heavy chain usually blocked the entrance, but he noticed that today the chain lay in the mud next to the tracks of many large vehicles.

The deputy thought it odd because the harvest was still weeks off, and he drove in. He saw enough to call the state police and the FBI.

"Who's been through the scene other than the deputy?" I asked.

"No one," Mahoney said. "As soon as I heard, I

was on the horn to Virginia State Police to seal off the area. We should be looking at it fairly clean."

Forty-five minutes later we were dropping altitude over mixed farmland and woods, rolling terrain, mostly, with some creek beds and rivers. After the chopper soared over a last stand of towering oaks, the forest opened up and we flew in an oval pattern around the scene.

The grille of a blue Mustang was nosed up against an earthen barrier, the vehicle's doors open. Two bodies, both male, were sprawled nearby in the grass. Between the long drying sheds, three gray, refrigerated semitrailers were lined nose to tail like elephants on parade. The truck windows and windshields were shot through and spiderwebbed. Behind the last semi was a black Dodge Viper with two dead men in the front seat.

The pilot landed out by the highway, where a perimeter had been established. After checking in with the Virginia State Police lieutenant and the county sheriff, we went to the crime scene on foot.

It was hot. Insects buzzed and drummed in the forest around the tobacco facility. Truck engines idling swallowed the sound of blowflies gathering around the Viper.

"They've swept their way out again," Mahoney said when we were ten yards from the Dodge.

I looked at the glistening dirt road between the Viper and us. I saw faint grooves in the moist dirt and said, "Or raked."

The door to the muscle car was ajar. The window was down. The driver had taken a slug through the back of the skull, left occipital. Blood spattered the windshield and almost covered two bullet holes, one exiting, and one entering. The passenger in the Viper had been rocked back, his left eye a bloody socket and a spray of carnage behind him.

"Two shots, two kills," Sampson said. "Driver was shot from behind."

"And at a slight angle," I said. "The passenger was shot from one of those roofs, probably the left one."

We walked on, seeing the trucks parked grille to bumper and the signs that said they belonged to the Littlefield Produce Company of Freehold Township, New Jersey. Two dead men in every cab. Each of them shot once.

"They were suckered in here and then executed from above," I said, wondering if Nicholas Condon and his buddies could have dreamed up this ambush. Yes, I decided, probably relatively easily.

"Shot from one shed roof or another," Mahoney agreed. "The roofs are slanted toward us and yet we haven't seen a single spent casing on the ground."

"If each sniper shoots once, there's no reloading, so no brass," I said.

We walked past the forward semi and looked to the Mustang and the two dead men lying in the field with tape up around them and a crew of FBI criminalists documenting the scene. Figuring we'd better not disturb them, we walked back to the rear semi, the only one without a truck grille up against its rear bumper.

Deputy Max Wolford, who'd discovered the massacre, was waiting with the bolt cutters.

Sampson said, "How much do you want to bet we don't find radishes and baby greens in here?"

"I vote for drugs and money," Mahoney said, and he nodded to Wolford, who centered the lock shackle between the cutter's blades and snipped it off. Sampson worked the lever and threw up the door.

A cloud of cold humid air billowed from the refrigerated unit, and sunlight poured inside. It wasn't what we'd expected. Not at all.

"Jesus Christ," Sampson said. "I didn't see that coming."

I swallowed my reaction, drew my gun, held up my badge, and climbed in.

# CHAPTER

# 48

**FOUR BLUE CORPSES IN UNDERWEAR** were laid out on tarps on top of stacks of wooden produce crates marked CUCUMBERS, TOMATOES, and LETTUCE. Three of the dead were young women, late teens and early twenties. The fourth was a young boy, maybe a year older than Ali, no more.

Beyond the bodies and the crates, far back in the container, I could see the shoulders, heads, and fearful eyes of at least thirty people of various races and colors, mostly young women and a few young boys dressed in ragged winter clothes, all pressed tight together, teeth chattering, trying not to freeze to death.

"Move the trucks so we can get the other containers open," I told Mahoney. "We've got to get emergency medical crews in here."

"And a lot more support," Mahoney said, pulling out his cell phone.

I pulled off one of the tarps, gave it to Sampson, said, "Cover the Viper. They don't need to see that."

He took it, and I started clearing a path through the produce boxes.

"I'm with the police," I said. "We're getting you all help."

They stared at me either shyly or blankly.

"Any of you speak English?" I asked.

A few of them shifted their eyes, but not one replied.

When I reached them, some were crying, and some shrank from me, would not look at me, as if they were both afraid and ashamed somehow. I tried to smile reassuringly and gestured toward Sampson. At first, no one moved.

Then a pretty young woman with black hair wearing a gray snorkel parka broke from the group and hurried past me. A stream of them followed. Only a few glanced at the corpses on the way out.

Sampson helped them off the truck, and they lay down in the grass in the baking sun beyond the shrouded Viper, weeping, hugging, and consoling one another in at least five languages.

State troopers brought jugs of water and boxes of PowerBars, which they tore into ravenously.

After the cabs of the other trucks had been photographed, we had the miserable task of removing the dead and placing them on the plank floors of the drying sheds.

In the other two containers we found a total of five corpses and sixty-seven survivors.

"We have no idea how long they've been in there," Sampson said, frustrated as the scope of the situation sank in. "We have no idea where they came from or who all these dead guys are. There's not a stitch of identification on any of them."

We were standing to the side, watching as EMTs and disaster-relief workers began to arrive. I noticed the girl who'd left the container car first, the one with the dark hair who'd scurried past us in the gray snorkel parka. She'd stripped off her heavy coat and pants, revealing shorts and a long-sleeved pink T-shirt with silver sequins spelling out GODDESS. She was within earshot and as we spoke, she kept glancing our way.

I smiled and crooked a finger at her. Goddess acted like she didn't understand. I went over and crouched next to her.

"You can stop pretending that you don't know any English," I said.

She looked at her lap.

"We're here to help," I said. "But we need your help in return."

There was no change in her affect, just a casual glance up, as if she were looking through me toward something far away.

"Suit yourself," I said. "But U.S. Immigration will be getting involved soon enough. If you want a chance at staying in this country, you need to start talking."

Her pupils dilated and her breath quickened. I saw both tells, shrugged at her as if I were done, stood up, and took a few steps toward Sampson.

She called after me in a thick accent, "You get me a pack of Marlboros and I try to help you."

# CHAPTER

# 49

**"YOU BELIEVE HER?" BREE ASKED** when I finally got home around eleven that night after one of the more upsetting days of my life.

"I've got no reason not to believe her," I said, eating leftover lamb kebabs with a sweet, fiery peanut sauce Nana Mama had come up with. "Several of the other young ladies who spoke English told a similar story. The young boys too."

"It's inhuman," she said.

"No argument there," I said, my thoughts traveling back to Mina Codrescu sitting on her snorkel coat and taking a long drag on that first Marlboro before she spoke.

Mina was nineteen and from the city of Balti in northern Moldova, a small, impoverished country between Hungary and Ukraine. Her mother was dead, she'd told us; her father was a drunk. She had no assets other than an ability to speak English and a dream of someday going to America, so when a Russian man she met in a bar told her there was a way she could go to the States, she'd been interested. He took her to Chişinău, the capital of Moldova, where she met a second Russian man.

"He said he would bring me to America in return for five years of work," Mina had told me, blowing out smoke from her cigarette and looking away.

"What kind of work?" Sampson had asked.

"Sex work," she'd said defiantly.

"You agreed to it?"

"I'm here, aren't I?" she said and took another drag.

I said nothing.

Mina waved her cigarette at the scenery and in the same defiant tone said, "This was worth it. For this, I would do it again. Look, I am here, in America. I can smell my dream here. If I didn't say yes, none of this happens."

"We're not judging you, Mina," I said. "Just listening. Tell me how it worked after you agreed to the deal."

Mina said she had had sex with the second Russian for three days, and then he'd handed her a ticket for Miami. A woman she knew only as Lori met her in Florida.

Lori took her passport and cell phone. She told Mina she'd get the passport back in five years and the cell phone once she was assigned to a particular locale. Lori brought Mina to a truck depot in the middle of the night. Delivery vans pulled up, and other women and boys began to pour out.

Piles of old winter clothes were dumped out on the ground and they were told to put them on. Lori had set aside the snorkel parka, pants, and boots for Mina, and she'd helped her into the refrigerated truck with assurances that her life would be much better at the other end of the drive. Luxurious, even.

"It wasn't bad for me because it gets cold where I come from," Mina had said. "But others, they barely had any clothes. We tried to keep them warm, but some of them were sick and too weak already from traveling, and they just died."

"How long were you in the truck?"

"I don't know. I didn't have a watch or phone. Two days? Maybe more?"

"Any other young Moldovan ladies here?"

"Two," she had said. "There are more from Hungary and Slovakia."

Several had been recruited as Mina had, she'd told me. Others had worked in brothels in Germany before being "transferred" to the United States, and—

"It's sad," Bree said, breaking me from my thoughts, "that there are parts of the world now where there's so little hope that young women and boys desperate for something better will sell themselves into sexual slavery."

"It sounded more like indentured servitude," I said.

Bree arched an eyebrow. "You honestly think those Russians were going to turn Mina loose after five years? No way. They were going to use her up, spit her out. Someone would have found her in a ditch."

"Maybe, but she's got a chance now," I said. "When the INS special agent in charge from Virginia Beach showed up, I had Mahoney single her out as critical to the investigation and in need of political asylum."

"That'll help her."

I nodded, trying to feel good about that rather than tired and emotional, but my exhaustion must have shown because Bree said, "You okay, Alex?"

"Not really," I said. "The whole ride back on the helicopter I was thinking about Jannie and Ali, and us. We all won the lottery at birth and got to grow up here in America, not someplace where we'd have to prostitute our way out of misery. I mean, I'm sorry, but something's wrong or out of balance when that exists. Or am I overthinking things?"

"You're just indignant," she said. "Maybe outraged."

"That bad?"

"No. It shows passion and a noble sense of fairness that I adore in you."

I smiled. "Why, thank you."

"Anytime," she said, and she smiled and yawned. "I have to sleep."

"Wait—how was *your* day, COD?"

Bree got to her feet, waved me off, and said, "I'm doing my best to forget it and start life over tomorrow morning, bright and early."

"I like that idea," I said.

"I'm full of good ideas," she said, and kissed me on the cheek.

# CHAPTER

# 50

**LATE IN THE AFTERNOON THE** Friday before Labor Day weekend, fifty members of law enforcement were crammed into the roll-call room at DC Metro for Special Agent Ned Mahoney's briefing on the massacres.

I was pleased to see the same faces from ATF, Justice, and the DEA there. It helped if the same people showed up, kept the communication lines open and clear.

If I didn't know Mahoney so well, I probably wouldn't have noticed the slight stoop to his shoulders and the tight lines around his eyes. The case was weighing on him. He was being squeezed, probably harder than Bree.

"There have been no new attacks," Mahoney said, "and we have made some progress, but we've been hampered by media leaks and the frenzy surrounding this killing spree."

That was true. The media coverage had turned red-hot and constant after the fourth massacre. Stories had been published or broadcast stating that "unnamed sources close to the investigation" said that the FBI believed ex-military, likely mercenaries, were executing the attacks and were either working on behalf of a cartel or acting as vigilantes.

Also leaked was the fact that, in addition to the human cargo, the trucks had contained a million dollars in cash and ninety kilos of cocaine, all hidden in the produce crates. DC Metro and the FBI had been hoping to keep all that inside this room.

"The leaks must stop," Mahoney said. "They're hamstringing us."

I scanned the room, seeing no one displaying obvious guilt or avoidance postures. But that didn't matter. The leaks had already made the cops distrust this group as a whole. We had decided to hold back some of the new evidence we'd found, at least for the time being.

"Moving on," Mahoney said. "There is no Littlefield Produce Company of Freehold Township, New Jersey. And six of the dead traffickers have been identified through fingerprints and IAFIS."

Six mug shots went up on a screen behind the FBI agent.

"The two on the left are Russians with ties to organized-crime syndicates out of St. Petersburg and Brighton Beach," Mahoney said. "There are agents in New York and Russia working those angles. These other four are more familiar to law enforcement. Correct, George?"

George Potter, the DEA's special agent in charge, nodded. "All four have long rap sheets in south Florida or Texas. The two there on the right, Chavez and Burton, they have loose connections to the Sinaloa cartel."

"Do any of them have a history of involvement in human trafficking?" Bree asked.

"Not that we know of," Potter said. "But they could be branching out."

"Or this could be just one branch of something bigger," I said. "These connections to both Russian mobsters and Mexican drug cartels suggests a possible alliance that is frightening when you think about it."

Potter nodded. "Like a supercartel."

Sampson said, "Or maybe they're just a crew of freight agents that transport three different kinds of criminal commodities at once: drugs, cash, and people."

"Slaves, you mean," Bree said.

Bob Taylor, a smart, African American agent over at Alcohol, Tobacco, and Firearms, asked, "Are you a slave if you sign up of your own free will?"

"They were bought and paid for," Bree said. "Even if the sellers were the girls themselves. Let's call this what it is: sexual slavery."

Taylor threw up his hands in surrender, said, "Just trying to clarify, Chief. You ask me, whoever these shooters are, they're doing the world a favor getting defects out of the gene pool."

There were a number of nods and murmurs of agreement in the room.

I couldn't argue with the sentiment in one sense. I'd had the chance to go over the dead men's rap sheets, and there was viciousness, cruelty, and depravity laced through their lives.

I don't care if you believe in Jesus, God, Allah, karma, the spirit of the universe, or a Higher Power—the crew of thugs who'd died in Ladysmith, Virginia, had been begging for a violent death like that: shot down, no mercy. I believed that was true, even if I also believed that whoever killed those thugs deserved trial and punishment.

In my book and in the blind eyes of justice, the fact that a man had it coming to him doesn't make killing him right. Especially if he's killed in an ambush. That's premeditation any way you look at it.

Mahoney went on with the briefing, giving some of the preliminary lab reports. The victims were all shot with .223 rounds, probably from AR-style rifles.

"Military?" ATF Special Agent Taylor asked. "Full-jacket?"

"No," Mahoney said. "The bulk crap you can buy at Walmart."

Sampson leaned over to me. "I gotta go. Anniversary dinner with Billie."

"Congratulations to you and Billie. How many years?"

"The big six, and thanks." He slipped out.

The big six. Somehow that was funny.

A few moments later, Bree leaned over and said, "I've got a pile of work on my desk I need to dig through."

"I'll stay here and tell you if there's anything new," I said.

There wasn't anything new, at least not from my perspective. Mahoney wrapped up the rest of the briefing in twenty minutes, and the place emptied out.

"You look like you could use a three-day weekend," I told Ned.

"Wouldn't that be something?" Mahoney said.

"Go to your place on the shore; it'll give you fresh eyes on Tuesday."

"I don't think the gods of the Bureau would appreciate me kicking back with a cold one if there's another attack on the underworld over the weekend."

"You can always keep your phone on," I said. "No one says you have to be in your office waiting for a call. There has to be some benefit to these phones beyond Facebook and texting, right?"

Mahoney half bobbed his head, getting a distracted look. "Traffic will be a bitch tonight. Maybe I can sneak away early tomorrow?"

"Now you're thinking."

"What about you? And Bree? Why don't you and the kids come? Supposed to be a beautiful weekend."

"Nothing would make me happier, but Jannie's got an invitational thing over at Johns Hopkins, and we were going to see Damon too."

"There are three days to the holiday. You could always come on Sunday morning, or even on Saturday night."

"Tempting. Let me run that by the new chief of detectives."

# CHAPTER

# 51

**ORDINARILY, THE TRACK SEASON ENDS** in mid-August, but the U.S.A. Track and Field organization had launched a program to nurture young talent, inviting high school athletes from across the country to a meet on the Johns Hopkins campus in an effort to help coaches identify those with potential.

The fact that Jannie had been invited at the age of fifteen years and eight months was a shock to us. Initially, she hadn't been among the athletes offered spots at the meet. But Ted McDonald, a well-regarded track coach who works with my daughter, showed videos of her to the right people, and she got in on discretion.

We were on the shady side of the stands an hour before she was set to run. Down on the field, the kids were warming up. Except not many of them looked like kids.

"What are they feeding them?" Bree asked.

"Human growth hormone cereal with steroid milk," Nana Mama said, and she cackled.

"I hope not, for their sake," Bree said. "Jannie said everyone had to submit urine and blood samples."

"Those can be doctored," Nana Mama said.

We knew that all too well. Earlier in the summer, a vindictive and jealous girl in North Carolina had tried to frame Jannie for drug use. Since then, we'd always demanded samples from any drug test she had to take.

A group of athletes glided by at an easy ten miles an hour. I watched them, trying to keep memories of the prior evening at bay. This was a holiday, and I'd read that it was important to take them and enjoy them or you risked burnout.

"Can I have a Coke?" Ali asked, pulling off his headphones, which were attached to the iPad we'd bought used on eBay.

"Water would be better," Nana Mama said.

"I thought this was a holiday," Ali grumbled. "Holidays are supposed to be fun. You've heard about fun, right?"

My grandmother twisted on the bleacher and fixed him with her evil-eye stare. "Are you sassing your great-grandmother?"

"No, Nana Mama," Ali said.

"I won't take sass," she said. "You've heard about that, right?"

"Yes, ma'am."

Bree and I watched in amusement at the mastery with which Nana Mama handled Ali.

"What are you listening to?" Nana Mama asked, her voice softening.

Ali brightened. "A podcast about dolphins and how they have echolocation just like bats, only in the water."

"What's the single most surprising thing you've heard so far?"

Without hesitation, he said, "Dolphins have the best hearing in the world."

"Is that true?" Bree asked.

"Humans can hear up to, like, twenty kilo-hearses. Dogs to like forty-five kilo-hearses."

"Hertz," Nana Mama said. "Forty-five kilohertz."

"Hertz," Ali said. "Big cats, like lions, hear up to sixty-five, I think. But a dolphin can hear sounds up to a hundred and twenty kilohertz. And they have, like, an electrical field around them. They say you can feel it if you swim with them. I want to do that, Dad, swim with dolphins."

"I thought you had a few questions for Neil deGrasse Tyson."

"That too," Ali said. "Can I have a Coke, Dad?"

"Yes," I said.

"What?" Nana Mama said.

I smiled. "The holiday argument gets me every time."

Someone tapped me on the shoulder. I turned around and found Damon.

"Hey!" I cried, and I stood to hug him. "Look who snuck up!"

"Hi, Dad," he said, grinning from ear to ear and hugging me back.

There was a round of hugs and kisses. We heard about orientation, and Ali got a Coke and a bag of salt-and-vinegar chips, and life was good and grounded and solid. The pressure of Bree's new job drained away too. I could see that in the way she laughed at one of Damon's tales.

She felt at ease. I did too. A rare thing in those days.

"Hey, Dad?"

# CHAPTER

# 52

**JANNIE WAS CALLING TO ME** from the fence, so I got up and started down toward her.

"Jannie, you got this," Damon said, following me. "My friends on my hall are coming to see you smoke them all."

Jannie laughed, and punched the air before hugging Damon. She has never had stage fright, at least not when it comes to running. In the past year, she'd faced women running for NCAA Division 1 schools, and she'd run well enough to be here.

"You good?" I asked.

"Always," she said, relaxed. "Coach McDonald's got good meet and race strategies worked out."

"What's the difference?"

"You'll see. Love you both."

"Love you too," I said. "Nana Mama said to run like God gave you a gift and you are grateful for every stride of it."

She smiled but with some confusion. "Tell Nana Mama I'll try, Dad. Coach Mac's up behind you, by the way."

She trotted off. We climbed back up into the stands.

Clad in his trademark gray warm-ups and a blue hoodie and wearing a pair of binoculars around his neck, Ted McDonald was moving nervously from one running-shoed foot to the other as he spoke to Bree and Nana Mama. In his fifties, with a shock of reddish-gray hair that defied gravity, Coach McDonald had a straightforward style that I appreciated.

"Dr. Cross," McDonald said, shaking my hand.

"Dr. McDonald," I said. He had a doctorate in exercise physiology.

"Ready to see a little history made today?" McDonald asked.

Ali had been listening to his podcast, but he tugged out his earbuds and asked, "What history?"

Jannie's coach said, "Anything can happen under race conditions, but I've been tracking her workout times. They're impressive. She could do something here that would really make people stand up and take notice."

"Like which people?" Nana Mama said.

McDonald gestured across the track. "Like those folks over there with the hand timers. All of them are D-One coaches. Oregon. Texas. Georgetown. Cal. Stanford. Every one of them is going to watch Jannie run."

"Does she know this?" I asked.

"No. I've got her running against the clock and herself."

"What's that mean?" Bree asked.

"I'll tell you if it happens," the coach said, looking back to the track and clapping his hands. "Here we go. Nice and easy."

Jannie lined up on the stagger in lane four. At the starter's gun, she broke into her long flowing stride and kept pace with two high school seniors from California and another from Arizona.

She was third when they crossed the finish line and didn't look winded at all.

"Eighty percent," McDonald said after looking at his stopwatch. He leaned over to me and said in a low voice, "With that run she's got every coach over there interested enough to start giving her calls in the coming months, maybe even make a few house visits."

"But she's a sophomore," I said.

"I know," McDonald said. "But later on, if she runs the way she did the other day in training, you could have every coach over there camped out in your front yard."

I didn't ask him for more. No particulars. The entire conversation had me nervous in a sour-gut sort of way, and proud, and nervous all over again.

We used the two-hour break to have lunch with Damon and two of his new friends, his roommate, William, and fellow basketball player Justin Hahn, from Boston. Both were good guys, both were very funny, and both were capable of eating a staggering amount of food. Damon too. They ate so much, we almost missed the finals.

Jannie and seven other girls were heading into the blocks when we hurried to our seats. She drew lane three of eight. The girls took their marks. The gun went off.

Jannie came up in short choppy strides, tripped, stumbled, and fell forward onto her hands and knees.

"No!" we all groaned before she sprang up and started running again.

"Oh, that sucks," Damon said.

"There goes the scholarship," his roommate said, which annoyed me but not enough to make me lower my binoculars.

Ali said, "What happened?"

"She got off balance," said Coach McDonald, who was also watching through binoculars.

"Kicked her heel and…she's maybe twenty yards in back of Bethany Kellogg, the LA girl in lane one. Odds-on favorite."

The runners in the outer lanes were almost halfway down the back straight when Jannie finally came out of the curve in dead last. But she didn't look upset. She was up to speed now, running fluidly, efficiently.

"That's not going to do it, missy," McDonald said, and it was almost like Jannie could hear him because her stride began to lengthen and her footfalls turned from springy to explosive. She didn't run so much as bound down the track, looking long-legged, loose-jointed, and strong as hell.

Through the binoculars, I was able to get a good look at her face; she was straining but not breaking with the effort.

"She just picked off the girl from Kentucky in lane four," McDonald said as the runners entered the far turn. "She's not going to be last. C'mon, young lady, show us what you've got now."

The stagger was still on, but the gaps between the athletes were narrowing fast as they drove on through the turn. Jannie was moving up with every stride. Coming onto the homestretch, she passed a Florida girl in lane two.

Damon's roommate yelled, "She's freaking flying!"

We were all on our feet now, watching Jannie dig deep into her reservoir of grit and determination. Thirty yards down the stretch, she surged past the Texas girl in lane six. She went by an Oregon racer in lane eight at the halfway mark.

"She's in fourth!" Ali shouted.

The top three girls were neck and neck, with Bethany Kellogg barely leading and ten feet between Jannie and the girl from Alabama in third.

With thirty yards to go, she closed that to six feet. With fifteen yards left, she'd pinched it to three.

Eight inches separated the two girls when they crossed the finish line.

Coach McDonald lowered his binoculars, shaking his head in wonder. "She just ran out of track, that's all that happened there."

My binoculars were still glued on Jannie, who was limping away from the finish line in pain. A television cameraman was moving toward her across the track when she bent over and started to sob.

# CHAPTER

# 53

**FOUR HOURS LATER WE HAD** the surreal experience of seeing Jannie's race on ESPN. We watched the clip on a flat-screen at Ned Mahoney's beach house on the Delaware shore.

The edited video showed the start of the race, Jannie's fall, and Jannie coming into the backstretch in dead last, then the tape jump-cut to the far turn and her go-for-broke sprint down the stretch.

A second camera caught her limping away from the finish line and doubling over, and then the screen cut to the anchor desk at ESPN's *SportsCenter*.

Carter Hayes, the Saturday coanchor, looked at his partner, Sheila Martel, and said, "That girl ran so hard after the fall, she broke her foot crossing the finish line!"

Martel stabbed her finger at her coanchor and said, "That girl ran so hard after the fall, she missed third by eight one-hundredths of a second, and first by four-tenths of a second."

Hayes jabbed his own finger Martel's way and said, "That girl ran so hard that if you subtract the conservative two seconds she lost in the fall, she would have won by one point six seconds *and* she would have been in the record books with the seventh-fastest time for the four-hundred among high school women. An amazing performance. Highlight of the day, no question."

Sheila Martel pointed at the camera and said, "Heal up, young Jannie Cross. We have a feeling we'll be hearing from you again."

The screen cut away to the next story. We all cheered and clapped.

"Seeing her run in person, I swear my heart almost stopped," Nana Mama said. "But when they called out Jannie just then, it almost stopped again."

"Dad?" Ali said. "Is Jannie famous?"

"Tonight, she is," I said.

ESPN? Highlight of the day? Jannie?

"How the hell did ESPN know about the race?" Mahoney asked.

Bree said, "Some freelance cameramen who sell to ESPN were there. They caught the whole thing."

My phone rang. It was Jannie, calling from somewhere with a lot of background noise.

"Did you see it?" she shouted.

"Of course we saw it. Where are you?"

"At a party with Damon and his friends and some people I met at the meet. Everyone cheered for me, Dad."

"Everyone cheered here too," I said, tearing up. "You deserved it."

"Yeah, but now Damon's introducing me to girls he's trying to pick up."

"Too much information," I said. "We'll be back for you tomorrow afternoon. Keep that foot elevated. No weight."

"I heard the doctor," she said. "I'm glad you were there."

"Me too," I said. "Now go have fun."

Bree and Ali went out to the beach beyond the dunes. Nana Mama and I shucked corn on the back deck of Mahoney's cottage. He'd inherited the place from his aunt, a devout Catholic who'd attended mass daily.

"I'm convinced it's why it survived Hurricane Sandy," Mahoney said as he loaded charcoal into a Weber kettle grill. "Bunch of places just to the north of here were leveled, pretty much splintered."

"So it's got good karma," I said.

"If I agreed with you on that, my aunt would probably throw a lightning bolt down at me," he said. "But yes. This place calms me."

"How couldn't it?" my grandmother said. "Cool ocean breeze. The sound of the waves. It's very tranquil."

"Glad you could come, Nana Mama," Mahoney said. "When was the last time you were at the beach?"

"I can't remember," she said, finishing the last ear of corn. "That happens a lot lately. I'll start the water on the stove."

I knew better than to argue as she got up. She was heading for the kitchen, her favorite place in any house.

"How bad is Jannie's break?" Mahoney asked, lighting the charcoal.

"Hairline fracture of one of the metatarsal bones," I said. "Crutches for two weeks, and a hard walking boot for another three. She can run in two months."

"Too bad she couldn't come out."

"Go to the beach with her stepmom, dad, great-grandmother, and little brother, or hang out with her new friends in the track world and her big brother at college for a night…"

"Enough said."

We saw Bree and Ali walking back along the

path from the dunes. He had a towel around his shoulders and a grin that made me glad to be alive.

"He's like a dolphin himself," Bree said, coming up onto the deck. "You should have seen him in the waves out there."

"Tomorrow," I said. "First thing."

Ali started toward the sliding doors, but Mahoney caught him. "Around the corner, there's an outdoor shower. Get the sand off and dry off before you go in or my lady friend will not be happy."

"I've never been in an outdoor shower," Ali said.

"It's life-changing," Mahoney said and he returned to his grill.

"I'm next," Bree called to Ali as he rounded the corner.

I went to the cooler and fished us out bottles of cold Old Dominion beer, a Delaware favorite, and opened them.

"I needed this," Bree said, taking her beer. "A break from everything."

"I think we all needed this," Mahoney said.

"We going to meet the mysterious lady friend?" Bree asked.

"Right here!" said a pretty brunette in white pedal pushers, sandals, and a gauzy blue top as she came around the corner with a plate of fresh-baked cookies.

She set down the plate, beamed at us, and said, "I'm Camille."

"Not lady-friend Camille?" I said.

Camille laughed. "Indeed. Lady-friend Camille."

"You're spicing up the party," Mahoney said.

"I try," she said, and she shook our hands. "Ned's told me so much about you both, I feel like I already know you."

Camille was a real estate agent in the area, a widow, and as bubbly as they come. She and Ned had met at a local seafood restaurant after they'd both noticed each other eating alone on two consecutive Saturday nights. On the third Saturday, Mahoney went over and showed her his badge.

"He said he was conducting an FBI investigation and needed to ask me a few questions," Camille said. "First question after my name was why I always eat alone. It was my question for him too."

They were good together and we laughed and ate and probably drank a little too much. The moon rose. Nana Mama turned in. Ali fell asleep on the couch. Mahoney and Camille took a walk north on the beach, and Bree and I walked south and admired the moon tracking on the ocean and the waves.

"It's good to be with you," I said, wrapping a blanket around both of us.

"Hard to imagine the job right now," Bree said.

"Means you're tuning out, giving your brain a needed rest."

"Parks came through surgery fine," she said. "Lincoln too."

"Good," I said, and I whispered a suggestion.

"What?" She laughed softly. "Here?"

"Back in the dunes somewhere. We've got a blanket. Be a shame to waste the opportunity."

She kissed me and said, "Sounds like the perfect end to a perfect day."

# CHAPTER

# 54

**FIVE DAYS LATER, ON THE** Thursday after Labor Day, Sampson and I climbed out of an unmarked car in the parking lot of Bayhealth Kent General Hospital in Dover, Delaware.

"Let's hope she's alert enough to help," I said.

"We knew we were taking a chance," Sampson said. "If she's not, we'll just come back."

The day before, we'd received two reports that had brought us to the Bayhealth hospital. The first report, filed the week before by a Maryland state trooper, described a Ford Taurus found flipped in Maryland just south of Millersville.

The driver, a twenty-nine-year-old waitress, was later found to have died of a .45-caliber gunshot wound to the head. The shooting had to have occurred in broad daylight, yet no witnesses had come forward.

The second report, from the sheriff's department in Kent County, Delaware, concerned a white Mustang convertible that crashed into a tree along Route 10 between Willow Grove and Woodside East. The driver, twenty-four-year-old Kerry Rutledge, a clothes buyer for Nordstrom's, was found unconscious but alive around two a.m. on Labor Day. Rutledge had broken ribs, facial injuries, a concussion, and a four-inch-long wound across the back of her head.

Ms. Rutledge regained consciousness after a few hours, but she was confused and unable to remember anything about the crash. A sheriff's detective interviewed her the following day. She told the detective she thought she'd been shot but couldn't remember how it had happened or why. The wound to the back of the head was consistent with a bullet grazing the skin, so we thought it worth the drive to try to talk to her ourselves.

At the front desk, we learned that Kerry Rutledge was out of intensive care and under observation pending the results of neurological tests. When we reached the nurses' station, we showed our badges. The head nurse said Rutledge's parents had been in to see her earlier, and the last time she'd checked, her patient was asleep.

But when we knocked softly and entered her room, the Nordstrom's buyer was propped up, sipping a cup of ice water, and gazing at a television on mute. She was a wisp of a woman with pale, freckled skin and fine copper hair that hung about the bandages that covered her bruised face.

"Ms. Rutledge?" I said, and I introduced Sampson and myself.

"You're here because I was shot," she said with a flat affect.

"That's right," Sampson said. "Did you see the person who shot you?"

Her head rotated a degree to the right and back. "I'm having trouble remembering things."

I hesitated, thinking how best to proceed, and then said, "How do you know you were shot, Ms. Rutledge?"

Her head rotated again, and stayed cocked to the right as she blinked and pursed her lips. "He was right there. He…he had a gun. I saw it."

"That's good. What kind of gun?"

"A pistol?"

"Even better. Where was he? And where were you?"

Rutledge's eyes got soft and her head started to droop ever so slightly before she frowned and came out of it and said, "I'm an idiot. What was I…"

"Ms. Rutledge?"

"I was texting," she said. "I'd been to a party and I was on my way to my parents' house in Dover. I had the top and the windows down. It was a pretty night and I was texting a friend. I remember that. Just before I was shot."

"What time was that?"

"I don't know. Late."

"So you're driving," Sampson said. "Eyes on and off the road because you're texting?"

Her mouth hung slightly open, but she gave a faint nod. "I've driven that road a thousand times. Maybe more. Oh God, what's my car look like?"

"A mess," I said. "But you were texting, and then you saw the pistol?"

"Yes. I mean, I think so."

"What happened in between? Before you saw the gun and after you stopped texting?"

She looked at me blankly, and I decided to take another approach.

"How fast do you think you were going?"

"Not fast. Fifty? I…" Rutledge said, and she paused as if noting distant and dim things.

"What are you seeing?" I said.

"There was a headlight," she said. "A single one in the rearview."

"A motorcycle headlight?"

Rutledge's eyes went wide at that. She took a

deep, sharp breath and pressed hard back into the raised mattress, not realizing how much that would hurt her ribs.

"Ohh," she moaned. "Ohh, that was just…bad."

She closed her eyes. A minute passed, then two, and gradually the spasm of pain released her and left her breathing so rhythmically I feared she'd fallen asleep.

But then her eyelids fluttered open and she looked at us more clear-eyed.

"I'm seeing more of it now," she said. "He drove up alongside of me, like he was passing, and then he backed off and pulled in behind me again. I put my phone on the console, got both hands on the wheel, and that's when he came again, right up beside me on one of those big motorcycles with a windshield. I looked to my left and he was right there, five or six feet away, with, like, a black helmet and visor, aiming the gun at me. He…he…"

Rutledge looked at us with growing disbelief. "Before he pulled the trigger, I remember now, he yelled something like 'Let this be a lesson. Never text and drive.'"

# CHAPTER

# 55

**THURSDAY AFTERNOON, IN HER OFFICE** in the Daly Building, Bree realized that by agreeing to become chief of detectives, she'd also agreed to go surfing on a tsunami of memos, overtime requests, and high-pressure meetings at which she was called upon to defend her handling of a job that she hadn't been given enough time to learn.

The good times on the Delaware shore, watching Alex and Ali playing in the waves, seemed such a distant memory that Bree wanted to throw something just to hear it break.

A knock on the doorjamb jolted her from her funk. Detective Kurt Muller ducked his head in and said, "Howdy, Chief Stone."

Looking at his waxed mustache, she couldn't help but grin. "Howdy?"

"I'm showing my inner Oklahoman today," Muller said. "Anyway, I know you're COD now and all, but I'm going to Terry Howard's storage unit. His ex-wife gave me permission to look through it, and she also gave me the combinations to two safes, which he evidently gave her in case he died."

"I didn't even know Howard had an ex-wife," Bree said.

"Patty," Muller said. "They divorced seven years ago. She's remarried to a veterinarian. Lives in Pensacola. She said she's in shock about Howard's suicide and the cancer. He never told her, or their daughter, who is nine. Anyway, I wanted to know if you felt like tagging along."

Bree almost dismissed the offer out of hand. The case was closed. Why would she want to pick through a dead man's storage unit?

But then she remembered Alex's dissent when Chief Michaels declared the homicides of Tommy McGrath and Edita Kravic solved, pinning them on the bitter ex-cop who'd blown his head off with the kind of gun he had never owned and didn't like to use.

"Sure, I'll go with you, Muller," Bree said at last, getting up from behind her desk. "It'll help me to clear my head, get me out of the spin cycle I've been on."

"I felt like that once," the detective replied. "Inner-ear infection. You would have thought I was on deck in a hurricane sea or drunk off my ass. I couldn't tell which way was up."

On the way to the storage unit in Tacoma Park, Bree actually enjoyed listening to Muller drone on about the role of the eustachian tube in regulating equilibrium.

They cut off the lock to the unit and threw open the overhead door. Near the wall to their immediate right was a baby's crib with a mattress, mobiles, and folded dusty blankets. Behind that were stacks of boxes, an old bicycle, a rolled-up volleyball net, and two large Cannon 54 safes.

"You have the combinations?" Bree asked.

"They're on here somewhere," Muller said, pulling out his phone.

Bree went to the safes, noting four green army-surplus ammunition boxes on top of one.

"You still think Howard shot himself?" Bree asked, taking one box down.

Muller shrugged, still scrolling on his phone. "Seems a little convenient in retrospect. McGrath and Howard have a bad beef. Howard kills McGrath and shoots himself because he has cancer and because he's had his revenge."

"It wraps up in a nice package, doesn't it?" Bree said.

She opened the box and found smaller cardboard boxes of .40-caliber ammunition stacked neatly inside. The second box was half full of nine-millimeter ammunition. The third box carried .30-06 rounds and a single cardboard container of Federal .45-caliber pistol ammunition.

# CHAPTER

# 56

**BREE PICKED UP THE BOX** of ammunition and opened it.

Six of the twenty bullets were missing from the plastic rack inside.

But there they were: fourteen .45-caliber bullets. Ammunition for a gun Terry Howard had claimed he never used.

"Got the combinations," Muller said. "Ready, Chief?"

"Gimme a second," Bree said, pulling out one of the bullets, noting the copper full-jacket bullet and the slight hollow spot at the tip. She inspected the primer and the rim around it and saw something that made her pause.

After a moment, she dug in her pocket and put the bullet and the box in an evidence bag.

"Ready?"

"Just let me finish here," she said, opening the fourth ammo box.

Bree found a gun-cleaning kit with jars of bore solvent, all tightly closed but still tainting the air with their peculiar smell. She reached in and pulled out a small bottle of Hoppe's #9.

She opened the top and sniffed. The liquid bore cleaner smelled like she remembered it, sweet, almost like hot caramel. It was bizarre that something that smelled that good stripped out spent gunpowder and metal fouling.

Something deep in her brain stopped her train of thought. She stared at the bottle of Hoppe's #9 and sniffed it again, grasping for a memory and not knowing exactly why.

"You ready now, or do you want some glue to sniff?"

"Funny," she said. She put the gun-cleaning kit away and stood in front of the safe's electronic keypad. "Tell me."

Muller called out a series of numbers that she entered and soon there was a chunking noise as the locks released. Bree opened the safe and shone her flashlight inside.

Muller whistled. "He's got an arsenal in there."

They would later count sixty-three guns in the two safes. There were Smith and Wesson pistols

270

in .40, .357 Magnum, and .44 Magnum calibers on one shelf in the first safe. There was a 1962 Winchester Model 70 bolt-action hunting rifle in .30-06 caliber on another shelf. The other fifty-five weapons in the safes were gleaming side-by-side double-barreled shotguns.

Bree ignored them and started to pull open the stacked drawers below the pistol shelf. Muller, however, got out his own flashlight and shone it on one of the shotguns. Then he pulled out a pair of reading glasses, got down on his knees, and looked closer at the barrel.

"Mother of God," Muller said, fishing in his pocket for latex gloves.

"What's the matter?"

"Let me make sure," he said, and he removed the gun as if it were fine crystal. He peered at the writing on the barrel and shook his head in wonder. "This was made by Purdey and Sons."

"Never heard of them," Bree said.

"They're the best," Muller said. "I had an oil-rich uncle back in Oklahoma who had one. I'll bet this one gun is worth somewhere between twenty-five and fifty thousand dollars."

Bree stopped pulling out drawers. "Is that right?"

"Purdeys are handmade in London," Muller said. "They never lose value. If all the guns in here are this fine, we could be looking at two million dollars, maybe more."

"Two million?" Bree said, shocked. "How the hell did Howard get…"

And then she knew. Of course. Howard *had* been guilty. The drugs. The money. But why shotguns?

She went back to opening drawers. The next two were empty. But the third contained a large manila envelope. Bree drew it out, seeing Howard's writing across the front: *To be opened in the likely event of my death.*

There was a second envelope in the drawer, white, legal-size.

There was a pen scrawl there too.

It read: *To COD Thomas McGrath, DC Metro.*

# CHAPTER

# 57

**BASED ON INFORMATION GLEANED FROM** Kerry Rutledge's accident report, Sampson and I found the tree her Mustang had collided with, an ancient oak off Route 10 that had a nasty gouge in it.

"Fifty miles an hour?" Sampson said doubtfully. "Looks faster."

"She said she hit the gas just before he shot," I reminded him. "So she could have been going sixty or sixty-five if she'd reacted to the bullet grazing her head by stiffening and keeping the accelerator pinned to the floor."

As we returned to the unmarked car, Sampson said, "I keep going back to his amplified voice."

Rutledge had said that when the shooter told her never to text and drive, his voice had been very loud, as if he were talking through a loud-speaker on the motorcycle.

"I know what you're thinking," I said, getting into the passenger side. "Highway patrolmen use those kinds of built-in bullhorns, but I'm pretty sure you can get them for just about any touring motorcycle these days."

"Well, whoever he is and whatever modifications he's made to his motorcycle, he's killing people for traffic violations," Sampson said as he started the car. "Three were speeding. And that girl last week, I'll bet she was texting too."

"Possible," I agreed. "All of a sudden, though, I'm starving."

"All of a sudden, me too."

We drove west toward Willow Grove, and I caught sight of something shiny in the sky far away.

"There's those blimps again," I said. "What the hell are those things for?"

"One of the great mysteries of life," Sampson said, pulling into the Brick House Tavern and Tap for lunch. I brought a road map into the tavern with me, and after ordering a chicken salad sandwich with kettle-fried potato chips, I used a pen to note where the five shootings had occurred and when.

The first was west of Fredericksburg, Virginia,

months ago. The second was in southern Pennsylvania a few weeks later. Rock Creek Park was two weeks ago. Southwest of Millersville, Maryland, four days later. Willow Grove, three days ago.

"His time between attacks is shrinking fast," I said, drawing a circle. "He could kill anytime now, and he likes it here, in this general area. He feels comfortable hunting from DC east."

The waitress brought our food. Sampson took the map and bit into a tuna melt while looking it over.

After a few minutes, he laughed, shook his head, and said, "It was staring us right in the face, and we were too close to see it."

I swallowed a gulp of Coke and said, "See what?"

He turned the map for me, picked up my pen, and traced short lines from each of the crash scenes to Denton, Maryland. The Rutledge scene was closest, no more than twenty miles away. The tavern we were eating in was closer still.

A half an hour later, as we drove down a dirt road south of Willow Grove, Sampson said, "I don't think popping in again to say hi is the smart way to go."

"Surprise is always good, though," I said.

"Unless you're surprising a lunatic-in-the-grass world-class sniper with a chip on his shoulder," Sampson said.

"If we see orange flags, we'll turn around."

"How about we call in first?"

We rounded a curve onto a straightaway about three hundred yards long, and our options narrowed. The gate to Nicholas Condon's farm was at the end of the straight, and it appeared to be opening, swinging out toward the road.

We were about one hundred and fifty feet from the gate when a Harley-Davidson appeared from the farm lane. Even though the rider wore dark leathers, a helmet, and goggles, I could tell by the beard that it was Condon.

He looked left toward us. Maybe his mercenary instincts kicked in, I don't know, but the sniper saw something he didn't like, popped the clutch, and buried the throttle. His back tire spun on the hard gravel, sliding side to side and throwing up a cloud of thick dust that curtained off the road behind him.

"Crazy sonofabitch," Sampson said, and he stomped on the gas.

# CHAPTER

# 58

**STONES AND GRAVEL HIT THE** squad-car windshield and we had to slow down for fear of crashing. Luckily the dirt road soon met asphalt at County Road 384. By the loose soil his tires had shed on the road, we knew Condon had headed north. Sampson accelerated after him.

"Stay near the speed limit," I said. "We have no jurisdiction here."

"I don't think Condon cares."

"I imagine he doesn't, but—there he is."

The sniper was weaving through the light traffic ahead and headed toward a stoplight at the intersection with Maryland Route 404. It turned red and Condon stopped, first in line. We were four cars behind him when I jumped out and started running toward him.

Condon looked over his shoulder, saw me coming two cars back, waved, and then goosed the accelerator on the Harley a split second before the light turned green again. He squealed out onto 404 heading west.

Sampson slowed as he came past and I jumped in.

"I've got to run more," I said, gasping, as the squad car swung after Condon.

"We all do," Sampson said. "Desk jockeys can't move."

Traffic heading east was heavier, but Condon was driving the Harley like a professional, roaring out and passing cars whenever he got the chance as we tried to follow him through Hillsboro and Queen Anne.

He was ten cars ahead of us when he took the ramp onto U.S. 50, a four-lane. He seemed fully aware of us, and every time we'd close the gap he'd make some crazy-ass move and put more space between us.

Condon got off at the 301, heading west again across the bay bridge. We lost him for a minute but then spotted him getting off the exit to 450 South toward the Severn River. Ahead of us entering Annapolis, he cruised down the middle of the street while we sat stalled in traffic. But by opening the door and standing up on the car frame, I was able to see him take a left on Decatur

Avenue. Three minutes passed until we could do the same.

"He's heading toward the Naval Academy," Sampson said. "It's straight ahead there."

"Academy alumnus," I said. "He's going home."

"Yeah, but where, exactly?"

I scanned the street, looking for Condon or his Harley. I wasn't spotting—

"Got him," Sampson said, pointing into a triangular parking lot at the corner of Decatur and McNair, right next to College Creek. "That's his ride, sitting there with the other motorcycles."

We pulled into the lot. A Marine Corps officer was just getting onto his bike, a midnight-blue Honda Blackbird with a partial windshield. We stopped beside him. I got out.

"Excuse me?" I said.

The officer turned, helmet in hand. He appeared to be in his late forties with the rugged build of a lifelong member of the Corps. I glanced at the nameplate: Colonel Jeb Whitaker.

"Colonel Whitaker, I'm Detective Alex Cross with DC Metro."

"Yes?" he said, frowning and looking at my identification and badge. "How can I help?"

"Did you see the man on that Harley-Davidson come in?"

Colonel Whitaker blinked and then nodded in

exasperation. "Nick Condon. What's he done now beyond parking where he's not supposed to again?"

"Nothing that we're aware of," Sampson said. "But he's been avoiding having a conversation with us."

"Regarding?"

"An investigation that we are not at liberty to talk about, sir," I said.

The colonel thought about that. "This isn't going to reflect badly on the Naval Academy, is it?"

"I have no idea," I said. "What's Condon to the academy these days?"

"He teaches shooting. On a contract basis, which means he's supposed to park in a visitors' lot, not here where you need an academy parking sticker."

He gestured to a light blue sticker with an anchor and rope on it stuck to the lower right corner of his windshield.

"So we can't park here?"

Whitaker said, "I suppose if you put something on the dash that said *Police*, you could get around it."

I glanced at Sampson, who shrugged and pulled into a space.

"Where would we go to find Mr. Condon?" I asked.

"The indoor range?" Whitaker said, and he told me how to get there.

"Thank you, Colonel," I said, shaking his hand.

"Anytime, Detective Cross," Whitaker said. "You know, now that I think about it, I've seen you on the nightly news with those shootings of the drug dealers. Is this about that?"

I smiled. "Again, Colonel, I'm not at liberty to say."

"Oh, right, of course," Whitaker said. "Well, have a nice day, Detectives."

The colonel put his helmet on and started to get on his bike, but then he stopped, patting at his pockets.

"Forgot my keys again," he said, hurrying by us. "You'd think someone who teaches military strategy could at least remember his keys."

"Age happens to the best of us," I said.

Whitaker waved his hand and trotted stiffly toward the heart of the Naval Academy. He'd disappeared from sight by the time we passed a sign saying GOD BLESS AMERICA and reached Radford Terrace, a lush, green quadrangle bustling with midshipmen and plebes during this, the first real week of classes.

"Stop," Sampson said, and he gestured across Blake Road. "Isn't that Condon right over there?"

# CHAPTER

# 59

**I CAUGHT A FLEETING GLIMPSE** of the sniper before he slipped inside the Naval Academy's chapel, an imposing limestone structure with a weathered copper dome. We hurried across the street and followed Condon in.

The interior of the chapel was spectacular, with a towering arched ceiling, balconies, and brilliant stained-glass windows depicting maritime themes. There were at least fifty people inside, some plebes, others tourists taking in the sights. We didn't spot Condon until he crossed below the dome and went through a door to the far right of the altar.

Trying to stay quiet while rushing through the hush of a famous church is no mean feat, but we managed it and followed him through the door.

We found ourselves on a stair landing. There was a closed door ahead of us, and steps that led down.

We figured the door led to the sacristy and went down the stairs. We wandered around the basement hallways, not finding Condon but seeing the tomb of Admiral John Paul Jones before returning to our last point of contact.

Back on the landing, I stood for a moment wondering where he could have gone, and then I heard Condon's distinctive voice raised in anger on the other side of the sacristy door.

"But they're following me now, Jim," Condon said. "This is persecution."

That was enough for me to rap at the door, push it open, and say, "We're not persecuting anyone."

Condon and a chaplain stood in a well-appointed room with plush purple carpet and a clean, stark orderliness. The sniper's face twisted in anger.

The chaplain said, "What is this? Who are you?"

"Really, Dr. Cross?" Condon said, taking a step toward us with his gloved hands clenched into fists. "You'd follow me in here? I thought better of you."

"We just wanted to talk," Sampson said. "And you ran. So we followed."

"I didn't run," he said. "I was late for a meeting with the chaplain."

"You saw us and played cat and mouse," I said, dubious.

"Maybe," Condon said. "But that was just entertainment."

"What's this about?" the chaplain asked, exasperated.

"You his spiritual adviser?" Sampson asked.

They glanced at each other before the chaplain said, "It's a little more complicated than that, Detective...?"

"John Sampson," he said, showing him his badge and credentials.

"Alex Cross," I said, showing mine.

"Captain Jim Healey," the chaplain said.

"What's complicated, Captain Healey?" I asked.

"This is none of their business, Jim," Condon said.

The chaplain put his hand on the sniper's arm and said, "I *am* Nicholas's spiritual adviser. I was also the father of his late fiancée, Paula."

I didn't expect that; I lost some of my confidence and stammered, "I'm—I'm sorry for your loss, Captain. For both of your losses."

"We meet to talk about Paula once a week," the chaplain said, and he smiled faintly at Condon. "It's good for us."

For a second I didn't know what to say. "I'm sorry to have interrupted," I finally told him. "We just wanted to talk to him for a few moments, Captain."

"About what?" Condon said, pugnacious again. "I already told you I didn't have anything to do with those killings."

"You actually never answered our questions about that, but this is about six motorists shot by a lone motorcyclist within an hour's drive of your house."

"One of them just up the road from your place," Sampson said. "Beyond Willow Grove."

The sniper shook his head. "I don't know what you're talking about."

"You own a forty-five-caliber handgun?" I asked.

"Somewhere," he said.

"Would you let us test it?"

"Hell no," Condon said, and then he cocked his head. "Wait, you think I shot these people from my Harley? For what?"

"Breaking traffic laws," Sampson said. "Speeding. Driving and texting."

"This is insane, Jim," the sniper said to the chaplain, throwing up his hands. "Every time a nutcase appears on the scene, they come after me. Even when a cursory glance at my medical record would show that I am not capable of shooting a forty-five-caliber handgun from a motorcycle going fast or slow."

"What are you talking about?" Sampson asked.

Condon looked over at the chaplain and then pulled off his gloves, revealing that he wore wrist braces. He tore those off too, revealing scars across his wrists.

Captain Healey said, "Nick shattered both wrists in a training exercise when he was with SEAL Team 6. He can still shoot a rifle better than any man on earth, but his wrists and hands are too weak to shoot a pistol with any accuracy. It was what got him his medical discharge."

# CHAPTER

# 60

**SAMPSON PULLED UP IN FRONT** of my house just as the sun was setting.

"Don't look so glum," Sampson said. "We'll come up with a new battle plan tomorrow."

"I feel like we had preconceptions about Condon," I said, opening the door. "He was the easy person to look to, so we did."

"We had to look at him," Sampson said. "It was our job."

"But it wasn't our job to insult a war hero and tarnish his reputation," I said, climbing out.

"Did we do that?"

"In a roundabout way, yes."

"Are we supposed to be dainty or something in a murder investigation?"

"I don't know," I said, rubbing my temples. "I

just need food and some sleep before I try to learn something from today."

"Me too, then. Best to the chief."

"And to Billie," I said and climbed up the porch steps.

When I went inside, I was blasted by the smell of curry and the sounds of home. Jannie was in the television room, her foot up and on ice.

"How's it feel?"

"Like I could run on it," she said.

"Don't you dare. You heard the doctor."

"I know." She sighed. "But my legs are starting to ache from inactivity."

"They said you can start pool therapy on Monday and the bike on Tuesday. In the meantime, stretch. Where is everyone?"

"Bree's upstairs taking a shower," she said. "Nana Mama's in the kitchen with Ali. They're working on a letter to Neil deGrasse Tyson."

"He's not going to give this up, is he?"

Jannie grinned. "He's like someone else I know once he gets something going in his brain."

"Ditto," I said. I winked at her and went through the dining room to the new kitchen and great room we'd had put on the year before.

"God, it smells good in here," I said, giving my grandmother a kiss as she stirred a simmering pot on the stove.

"Bangalore lamb," she said, tapping her wooden spoon and replacing the lid. "A new recipe."

"Can't wait," I said, and then I crossed to Ali. "How's the letter coming?"

"It's hard," he said, head down, studying his iPad. "You really have to think about what you want to say, you know?"

"Keep at it," I said, tousling his hair. "I have time for a shower?" I asked Nana Mama.

"Dinner's on the table in exactly half an hour," she said.

I hoofed it up the stairs, knocked twice on our bedroom door, and went in. Bree sat on the bed in her robe, studying a document on her lap. She didn't look up until I was almost at her side.

"Hey," she said softly and with some sadness.

"What's the matter?" I asked.

"Muller and I went to Howard's storage unit to take a look through his things on behalf of his ex-wife and daughter. We found two envelopes and…here, draw your own conclusions."

She held out the envelopes. "First one's a will and an explanation of his investing theory."

"Terry Howard had an investing theory?" I said, taking the documents.

"It's all there," she said, and she turned toward the closet. "Take five minutes to read, if that."

I read the pages while she dressed. When I was

done, I looked up. Bree had those sad eyes about her again.

"So I might be right," I said.

"Looks that way," she replied. "Which is why I'm beginning to think I am a pretty shitty chief of detectives."

# CHAPTER

# 61

**BREE PUT HER HAND TO** her mouth and tears welled in her eyes.

I got up off the bed fast and went to her. "You know that's not true."

"It is," she choked out, coming into my arms. "I was playing politics when I said Howard was good for Tommy's death, trying to clear a murder so I could get the chief and the mayor off my back."

"Is that what you were doing?"

"Well, I definitely wasn't making sure Tommy McGrath's killer was caught."

"Then the most you're guilty of is being human," I said, rubbing her back. "You were caught between a rock and a hard place, and Howard looked good for a suicide. The chief agreed."

"But you didn't," she said.

"I thought it warranted further investigation. And guess what? You further investigated. You found documents we should have looked at weeks ago, but you found them nonetheless. You made a mistake, but you corrected it. You're back on track, Chief Stone."

"Am I?" she said, unconvinced.

"I have faith in you," I said.

"Thank you. It means everything."

We kissed.

She scrunched up her nose afterward and said, "You are the love of my life, Alex, but you need a shower."

"On it now," I said and headed into the bathroom.

Letting the hot water beat on my neck, I thought back on the two documents Terry Howard had left behind. The first was a simple will that the disgraced detective wrote himself and had had notarized in duplicate. The will awarded all of Howard's property, including his shotgun collection, to his nine-year-old daughter, Cecilia.

Attached to the will was a letter explaining that he'd started investing in fine shotguns after learning that they tended to appreciate fast and were a safer bet than the stock market. Beginning with a small inheritance he'd received in his early twenties, he had been buying and trading shotguns for many years. He recommended a gun buyer in Dallas who could determine the collection's value after his death.

The second document was a brief letter to Tommy McGrath, Howard's ex-partner. In it, Howard said he bore no ill will toward McGrath and that he knew his disgrace was the result of his own actions.

*And now the cancer's got me, Tommy, or you wouldn't be reading this,* Howard wrote. *I couldn't tell you because I did not want you to pity me. I saw you with your young lady friend—you dog—and realized things were going better for you. You deserve better. May your life be long and fantastic. Remember me fondly—T.*

It didn't sound like a man who was angry and ready to commit murder. To me and to Bree, it sounded like a man trying to make peace with himself and his old partner. If he'd killed McGrath and then committed suicide, why would he have left such a note? He'd obviously written it before McGrath's death, so wouldn't he have retrieved it and destroyed it before he killed himself? Or had he just forgotten it?

The most cynical slice of me played with the idea that Howard had put the letter there as a way to throw us off the scent, but that didn't make sense in light of the suicide. Wouldn't he have left some kind of diatribe condemning McGrath?

So maybe Howard didn't commit suicide. In that scenario, whoever killed McGrath had also killed Howard and then framed the disgraced detective for McGrath's murder.

It wasn't the perfect crime. But it was close. That is, if we could prove it.

I got out of the shower and dried off. Bree came into the bathroom.

"Chief Michaels is going to need harder evidence than that letter to officially reopen the case," I said.

"I know," she said. "Can you help grease the wheels at the gun house?"

"Sure. How fast?"

"Tomorrow?"

"I'll see what I can do."

"Thanks. By the way, how'd your day go?"

I briefed her as I pulled on clothes.

When I finished, she sighed. "So we're no closer to finding Tommy's killer or the road-rage shooter."

"Or the vigilantes, for that matter. Whoever they are."

# CHAPTER
# 62

**THANK GOD FOR ALEX AND** *Ned Mahoney,* Bree thought the next afternoon as she and Muller hurried down a hallway to the Gun Room, the area of the FBI's crime lab that was dedicated to the Firearms/Toolmarks Unit. The backlog for FBI testing was weeks long, and yet here they were in Quantico, marching in the front door on less than three hours' notice.

"We're here to see Ammunition Specialist Noble," Bree told the receptionist who was inspecting their visitors' passes.

The receptionist made a call, and several minutes later a petite woman in her late forties wearing a blue skirt, a white shirt, a white lab coat, and reading glasses on a chain came out to meet them.

"Judith Noble," she said crisply. "You have friends in high places, Chief Stone."

"We're lucky," Bree said. "And thank you for agreeing to help us."

"*Not* agreeing wasn't an option," she said coolly. "What can I do for you?"

Bree handed over the evidence bag containing the .45-caliber bullets found in Howard's storage unit as well as the bullets that had killed Howard, Tommy McGrath, and Edita Kravic.

"We need a comparison done," she said. "Just to make sure we've gotten all our ducks in a row."

The ammunition specialist glanced at her watch and nodded. "Long as things don't get too complicated, I can do that."

Noble led them back to her workstation, which was immaculate.

"How do you get any work done?" Muller said. "I need a proper mess to think straight."

The ammunition tech said, "Thank God you're not in my field, Detective Muller. Defense attorneys would crucify you on the stand."

"Why's that?"

"Firearms testing is like engineering," Noble said, putting on gloves. "This is about precision, not chaos."

"Like I said, I wouldn't get a thing done,"

Muller said and he smiled at Noble in a way that Bree found kind of strange.

Noble did not respond, merely took out the three bullets that had killed Tommy McGrath, the two that had struck Edita Kravic, and the single shot that had ended Terry Howard's life.

"They're all a match for this gun," Muller said, handing over the suicide .45 in an evidence bag.

"Says who?"

"I dunno," Muller said. "Someone here."

"I can call up the report," Bree said, pulling out her phone.

Noble held up her hand. "I believe you. So all you're looking for is confirmation that the ammunition in this box matches these six rounds?"

"Exactly," Bree said.

"It should be easy," the tech said. "We have everything Federal makes in the SAF, the standard ammunition file."

She looked at the end of the box. "Personal-defense grade, two hundred and thirty grain. Pretty standard for a forty-five semiautomatic."

Noble opened the box, took out one of the fourteen remaining bullets, looked at it, and frowned. "That doesn't match."

# CHAPTER

# 63

"WHAT?" MULLER SAID. "YOU HAVEN'T even looked at the others."

"I don't need to," Noble said, miffed. "The unfired cartridges here might indeed match the killing rounds, but they do not match the labeling on the Federal box."

"No markings around the primers, right?" Bree said.

Noble cocked her head in appreciation and nodded. "That is correct, Chief Stone. All commercially made handgun ammunition has a stamp indicating manufacture and caliber on the brass around the primer."

"Which means what?" Muller asked.

"Which means that these are hand loads," the tech said. "Someone bought the components—

the brass, the powder, the primer, and the bullets—and built these to custom specifications."

"We didn't see any hand-loading equipment at Howard's apartment or in the storage unit," Muller said.

"He could have hired someone to build the bullets," Noble said.

"So do they all match?" Bree asked.

"Give me a few minutes," Noble said, and then she looked at Muller. "You neat enough to get coffee and bring it back?"

"On my best days," Muller said, and he gave her that goofy grin again.

While Noble told Muller how to get to the cafeteria, he continued to moon at her. Bree happened to look at the ammunition tech's left hand. No ring.

She fought not to laugh. Muller was smitten!

Part of her wanted to mention his kidney stones or one of his other ailments, but she took pity and said nothing when he hurried off.

"He's an odd duck," Noble said, starting to work on the bullets.

"He kind of grows on you after a while," Bree said.

"Married?" the tech asked.

"Divorced."

"Hmm," Noble said, and she kept at her work.

Twenty minutes later, Muller returned. The ammunition specialist didn't look his way. She stared at the image of a bullet on her computer screen.

He put the coffee in front of her, and she said, "The bullets in the box are a match for the used slugs. They're all Bear Creek moly-coated two-hundred-grain RNHBs. Which are about as far as could be from the specs on the box. These were made by and for an expert to exact, competition-level specs."

"You mean like three-gun competitions?" Muller asked.

"Or straight pistol on a combat range," the tech said.

"That's a problem, then," Bree said. "As far as we know, Terry Howard never competed with a pistol, never built his own bullets, and was not a gun nut. Well, not a pistol nut."

"Howard could have gotten the custom ammunition with the gun," Noble said. "Bought them from the owner."

Bree said, "Or maybe an expert shot, someone who competes with a forty-five handgun and builds his own ammo, killed all three of them and framed Howard to get away with it."

# CHAPTER

# 64

**THEY WAITED UNTIL THE HEART** of the cloudy night before turning on night-vision goggles and climbing over the chained and locked aluminum gate.

Hobbes and Fender went over smoothly, making no sound. But John Brown's bad knee was acting up again. As he straddled the gate, the chain clinked ever so softly.

Brown landed on the dirt road on the other side. A dog barked once, straight to the south, five, maybe six hundred yards. Brown saw in his night-vision goggles that Hobbes was holding up his hand for him not to move.

Another bark, and then nothing for five long minutes.

"Like a cat, now," Fender whispered through a

jawbone microphone, and he began to pad down the dirt driveway.

Fender wore fleece-bottomed booties over his sneakers. They all wore them and barely made a sound moving deeper and deeper into the property. The dog stayed quiet.

That wouldn't last long with a trained canine listening and scent-checking the wind. For the moment, however, they had it made from a scent perspective. A sturdy breeze blew right in their faces. The dog's superior nose was disabled.

But sooner or later, one of the German shepherds would hear something or perhaps see them moving into position. If the noise was blatant or the dog got a solid look at them, it would certainly bark and sound an alarm. Things would get difficult then, but not untenable.

If the movements and noises they made were soft and irregular, however, the dogs would be uncertain and would come to investigate. And that would make things easier all around.

They crossed a clearing without alerting the dogs and crept closer. Slats of light from the house were visible through the trees when Hobbes toed a rock. It rolled and tumbled into the ditch.

The dog barked once. Brown and his men froze, listening, and heard a low growl and then a heavy dog's nails clicking and scraping on porch floorboards. They'd anticipated something like this scenario and stayed with their plan. Hobbes stepped off the right side of the driveway into the ditch. He leaned against the bank there, both hands gripping a pistol with tritium night sights.

Brown and Fender did the same on the left side of the drive, back to back, with Brown facing the house with his pistol, Fender covering their trail with an ultralight, suppressed backpacking rifle.

Rather than circling to catch their scent in the wind, the dog came directly at them, trotting confidently down the driveway and into the dense pines where they waited.

When the dog was fifteen yards away, Hobbes pulled the trigger, causing a burst of pressurized air to drive a tranquilizer dart into the animal's shoulder.

It made a soft yipping sound, staggered to its left, panted, and went down.

No one budged for another five long minutes, during which Brown caught the faint sound of— cheering? And where was the second dog? Inside?

Hobbes moved first; he stalked forward to the edge of the yard, Brown right behind him. Fender passed them and stuck to the shadows, moving to the right and up onto a dirt mound where he could get a better look at the front of the house.

Brown paused next to Hobbes, hearing the voices of announcers and seeing the flicker of a television through the partially open blinds of the room to the right of the front door.

"See anything in there?" he murmured.

# CHAPTER

# 65

**A FEW MOMENTS LATER, FENDER** said, "College football highlights playing on the big-screen, but I'm not seeing anyone in there watching. Dark, though. Lot of shadows. Hard to tell."

"I'm going," Brown said, and he moved slowly across the yard, heading past a Grady-White fishing boat toward a motorcycle. He crouched by the side of the bike and worked at a leather saddlebag strap with leather gloves.

When Brown had it open, he drew out from his jacket a plastic ziplock bag that held a kit wrapped in dark cloth. He got the kit free of the plastic and placed it behind a tool kit in the saddlebag.

Then he reached into a top pocket and fished out a film canister. He opened it and spilled the contents onto the gas tank.

"I've got him," Fender whispered in Brown's earbud. "He's leaning forward in a chair. Just changed the channel."

"Kill him if you can," Brown said, buckling the saddlebag.

Fender's ultralight rifle produced a sound similar to the air pistol's. The bullet made a small tinkling noise as it passed through the screen, the blinds, and the window, and then there was the sound of lead hitting flesh and bone.

"Done," Fender said.

"Done," Brown said; he spun away from the Harley and took off in a low crouch across the yard.

Inside the house, a woman began to scream.

"Shit," Hobbes said. "He wasn't alone."

"Too late," Brown said. "Get to the car."

They sprinted into the pines, through them, and across the clearing. When they entered the wood-lot close to the road, Brown thought they were going to get away clean. The woman had stopped screaming. She was probably calling 911, but they were less than one hundred yards from the car. Nothing could—

A form hurtled out of the woods to Brown's right and sprang at him with a guttural snarl. The second dog got hold of his upper right arm and bit down viciously.

"Ahhh!" Brown cried out, feeling his flesh rip as the dog shook its head and dragged him down. Brown sprawled on his side, but he still had his pistol in his right hand.

The dog released its hold and bit again, harder this time.

Before Hobbes or Fender could do a thing to help him, Brown let go of the pistol, grabbed it with his left hand, and, at point-blank range, fired a tranquilizer dart into the attack dog's stomach.

It yelped and scratched the back of Brown's head getting off him. It didn't make it six more feet before flopping over and panting.

# Part Four

# THE REGULATORS

# CHAPTER

# 66

**AN HOUR AFTER SUNRISE,** Ned Mahoney, John Sampson, and I were looking into an open saddlebag attached to Nicholas Condon's Harley-Davidson. There was a rectangular package inside, wrapped in dark cloth.

"What's in it?" Mahoney asked.

"Haven't looked," Condon said. "Soon as I saw it, I called Dr. Cross."

"Before or after someone shot at you?" Mahoney said.

"You mean before or after someone head-shot my dummy," Condon said. "That's exactly why I've got a little winch on a timer in there. Makes the mannequin move every four or five minutes throughout the night. Handy gadget."

I didn't comment on the fact that the sniper had

to have a decoy in order to sleep soundly; I just focused on the package.

"No indication of a bomb?" Sampson asked.

"No," Condon said. "After Azore woke up, I had him sniff it."

"Could the lingering effects of the drug throw off the dog's sense of smell?" I asked.

"I'd be glad to take the package out for you if you're not up to the job."

"I'll do it," Mahoney said, and he stuck a gloved hand into the saddlebag and came out with the package. "Heavy."

He set it down and started to work at the knot that held the fabric together.

"You said they were scared off by a woman screaming," Sampson said.

"I said they were scared off by a woman's scream," Condon said. "An app on my iPhone. Goes to Bluetooth and my speakers. You'd swear she was right there, screaming her head off."

"How's the other dog?" I asked. "The one you said bit one of them?"

"Denni. She's resting inside."

"We didn't find any blood out on the road yet," Mahoney said, finally getting the knot undone.

"There's blood there somewhere," Condon said. "I could hear the guy yelling. She got into him good before he knocked her out."

"You wash her?"

"No, but I caught Azore licking her muzzle, so I don't know what you'll get from her."

"Okay," Mahoney said, folding back the fabric, revealing something silkscreened on the other side and a cardboard box.

He lifted the box up. We could see now that the fabric was a piece of a T-shirt featuring artwork for Reggae Sunsplash, a Jamaican music festival.

"I wondered where that went," Condon said.

"Stolen?"

"Or I left it at the gym. Either way, my DNA will be all over it."

Mahoney opened the cardboard box. There was a large envelope inside and a .45-caliber Remington model 1911.

"That yours?" I asked.

"No," he said. "Nice gun, though I prefer a Glock in a forty caliber."

"Me too, actually," Mahoney said, opening the envelope.

He pulled out several pages of architectural drawings and diagrams.

"Yours?" Sampson asked.

Condon looked them over and shook his head. "No. What are they?"

Mahoney shrugged and gave them to me. I

studied them and almost handed them off to Sampson before it dawned on me what they were.

"These are drawings of the attack locations," I said. "This one's the factory where they killed the meth makers. And this one shows an aerial view of the tobacco-drying sheds and the road coming down the middle."

Condon said, "Before you say anything, there is no way those are mine. This was supposed to be a diversion. Kill me and plant evidence. Keep you guys off the trail of the real vigilante crew."

The more I thought about it, the more I thought Condon was right—unless, of course, he'd shot his dummy-on-a-rope and put the evidence in his saddlebag to keep us from suspecting he was part of the vigilante group.

For the time being, however, I was going to trust him.

"So whoever they are, they think you're dead," Sampson said.

"A fair assumption," Condon said.

"Let's let them think it," I said.

Mahoney looked at me with a raised eyebrow. "What for?"

"Make them believe that they've succeeded and the investigation has shifted to looking at Condon's circle of mercenary friends."

"And we start quietly looking for a victim of a dog bite," Sampson said.

"Among other things," I said, trying to wrap my head around this entire incident. Why implicate Condon? Why not someone else? Why attempt to kill him?

The only solid answer I came up with was that they knew of Condon's past and had decided he would be the perfect fall guy.

"I thought of that while I was waiting for you to get here," Condon replied. "But maybe it was more than that. Maybe they were trying to kill me because I do know something about your vigilantes. Two of them, anyway."

# CHAPTER

# 67

**THAT MORNING, AS ALEX, SAMPSON,** and Mahoney were talking to Condon, Bree was struggling to make connections between the late chief of detectives Tom McGrath, Edita Kravic, and a competition pistol shooter.

She had the late Terry Howard's service records up on her computer screen. Four times during Howard's career, he'd failed his annual shooting qualification test. On his best day, he was evaluated as an average shot.

*Hardly the competitor,* Bree thought and shut the file.

But lots of police officers did compete. It kept their marksmanship sharp. So she couldn't discount the possibility of a cop or a former cop or a former military guy, perhaps someone McGrath and Howard knew, being the shooter.

Her desk phone rang.

"Stone," she said.

"Michaels," the police chief said. "I'm not happy."

"Chief?"

"I'm hearing rumors that you've reopened the McGrath case."

"True," she said, her heart starting to race.

"Goddamn it, Stone, I'm going to get crucified over this. Howard's our guy. You said so yourself."

"I believed it then, Chief," she said. "But not now."

She recounted her visit to the FBI lab and finished by saying, "So I think the way we look at this is, we take some lumps for jumping to the wrong conclusion, but we'll get applauded when it comes out we were dogged enough to recognize our mistake and find the real killer."

Chief Michaels sighed, said, "I can live with that. Any suspects?"

"Not yet."

"We're at square one on a dead cop?"

"Definitely not," she said. "We've got new leads we're actively working."

"Keep me posted, will you please?"

"You'll be the first to know everything, Chief," she said, and he hung up.

Bree set her phone down, thinking that that had gone smoother than she'd expected. Maybe she was getting better at the job, not as rattled by every crisis.

After Sampson and I got back from talking to Condon, I stuck my head into Bree's office. "We've had a couple of breaks you need to know about."

Bree smiled. "I could use some good news."

"Oh, we've got lots of news," Sampson said, coming in behind me. "Can't figure out if it's good or bad."

As we told her about our trip to Nicholas Condon's place, the planted evidence, and the possibility that the sniper knew two of the vigilantes, I sent two pictures to a screen on Bree's wall.

One photograph showed a wiry man in a nice suit with a face that was a fusion of Asia and Africa. He had a quarter-inch of beard and was leaning against a car, smoking a cigarette—he looked like the kind of guy who would fit in anywhere. The other picture showed a U.S. Army Green Beret officer with pale skin and a battle-gaunt face.

"The suit is Lester Hobbes, ex-CIA," Sampson said. "The soldier turned mercenary is Charles Fender."

Both men had contracted with international security firms operating in Afghanistan early on in Condon's time there. They hadn't worked directly with the sniper, but they all knew one another well enough to have a drink or two occasionally. Both Fender and Hobbes were hard-liners who thought the U.S. was bungling foreign policy in the Middle East and going to hell in a handbasket back home.

"Condon says he didn't see Hobbes or Fender for years," I said. "Then, after the death of his fiancée, the investigation in Afghanistan, and his exile on the Eastern Shore, Condon gets a call one day from Lester Hobbes."

Hobbes told Condon he thought he'd gotten a raw deal and offered his condolences. He asked the sniper if he'd be interested in having lunch sometime. Condon agreed. They met one day at a restaurant in Annapolis.

Charles Fender was there too. They all had a few too many beers as they recalled old times, and the talk turned to what was wrong with the U.S.A. Hobbes and Fender had said that people's lack of conviction and action had allowed new forms of slavery to take hold in the country.

"Slavery?" Bree said.

"'People harnessed by other people in a

criminal manner' was how they put it, evidently," Sampson said. "As in a drug user is enslaved by the drug cartels or a prostitute enslaved by her handlers. Or ordinary U.S. citizens enslaved by corrupt politicians."

I said, "Hobbes and Fender told Condon they were part of a growing group of people who thought this way. They compared themselves to John Brown and the men he led in an armed uprising against slavery."

"Violent abolitionists," Sampson said. "Willing to kill and die to free others."

"Jesus," Bree said.

"Right?" I said. "They're calling themselves the Regulators, and they asked Condon to join them. Condon declined, said he was looking to lead a quieter life, and they left it at that."

"Why didn't he tell you this the first time you talked to him?" Bree asked.

"He claims he didn't put it together until after the second attack. Even then, he couldn't see the harm in having fewer drug cartels and human traffickers in the world."

"Until Fender and Hobbes decided to frame and kill him," Bree said.

"Correct," Sampson said.

Bree sat there a few moments, absorbing it, before she leaned forward and said, "They've killed

drug dealers and human traffickers, but no corrupt politicians."

"Exactly," I said. "Which is why we need to find
Lester Hobbes and Charles Fender sooner rather
than later."

# CHAPTER

# 68

**JOHN BROWN SAT WITH SEVERAL** others at his home, his arm throbbing from the dog bite. He tried to ignore the pain as he watched the footage on the local evening news of the medical examiner's wagon rolling through the gate of Nicholas Condon's place in Denton.

A young female reporter came on in standup and gushed, "WBAL-TV Channel Eleven brings you this exclusive report. FBI and local law enforcement officials are telling us that evidence gathered at the scene of the gangland-style murder indicates a connection between the victim, former SEAL Team 6 sniper Nicholas Condon, and the massacres of drug dealers and human traffickers in the past month.

"The FBI also says the evidence has pushed the

multistate investigation in a new direction, and all of Condon's known and former associates will be coming under increased scrutiny in the days ahead," the reporter said.

"It worked," Cass said, shutting off the TV with a remote. "I have to admit, I had my doubts."

"Not me," Hobbes said. "Well played."

Fender and the rest of the eleven people gathered in Brown's living room applauded.

"We do have some breathing room now," Brown said. "Which will help us with our next target."

The group focused on Brown as he laid it all out. One by one, their faces turned somber and then skeptical.

"I don't know," Fender said when Brown finished. "Looks like a fortress."

Hobbes said, "There won't be small-timers guarding the place. We'll be facing pros with talent."

"Likely," Brown said. "But if you want to chop off a snake's head, you have to get close to the fangs."

Fender said, "How is our friend so sure this is the snake's head?"

"He says it's the snake's head for the East Coast, anyway. We chop it off, we leave their organization in total destruction. We chop it off, we'll be clear to move to the next phase of the cleanup."

"We're getting ahead of ourselves," Cass said. "Our friend's intel on the compound is solid?"

"World-class," Brown replied. "The place has been under satellite and drone surveillance for the past ten days."

"So what's the plan?" Hobbes asked. "You're the strategist."

Brown showed satellite photographs and diagrams of the next target. His followers listened intently. They had to. Their lives and cause depended on it.

When he was done, he opened the floor to questions, comments, and suggestions. They talked for hours, until long past midnight, altering and tweaking the plan until all of them agreed it could work despite the fact there would likely be casualties on their side for the first time. It seemed unavoidable, but no one backed out.

"When do we go?" Cass asked.

"The meeting's in three days," Brown said.

"That helps us," Fender said. "It will be the dark of the moon."

# CHAPTER

# 69

TRACKING POTENTIAL MASS MURDERERS CAN be a delicate job in this day and age of instant information and programs that alert someone when certain kinds of data are accessed. This is especially true when the suspects are former employees of the Central Intelligence Agency and the U.S. Special Forces.

Everything about this particular part of the investigation, Mahoney told us, had to operate under the radar. The rest of that day and on into the next, Sampson and I focused on public records. Hobbes and Fender both had Virginia driver's licenses with addresses that turned out to be mail-drop boxes in Fairfax County. Both paid income taxes from those addresses, and each listed his job as *security consultant*. Beyond that, they didn't exist.

"These guys are pros," Sampson said. "They leave no trace."

"They're probably using documented aliases and leading secret lives."

"Paranoid way to live."

"Unless you have someone hunting you."

"Point taken, but I'm feeling like we're dead in the water until Mahoney comes up with something."

My cell phone rang. A number I didn't recognize.

"Alex Cross," I said.

On the other end of the line, a woman blubbered, "Who killed Nick? Were you there?"

For a moment I was confused, and then I remembered. "Dolores?"

She stopped crying and sniffed. "I loved him. I can't...I can't believe he's gone. Were you there, Dr. Cross? Did he suffer? What do you think happened? Was he really part of this vigilante group?"

I was feeling pinched and unsure how to respond, but then I said, "What's your security clearance, Dolores?"

There was a strong tremor in her voice as she said, "I helped you, Dr. Cross. Now you help me. That's how it works in this town. I need to know."

I thought about Mahoney's investigative strategy and the need to limit the number of people who knew the truth and weighed that against the obvious grief and pain Dolores was suffering.

"He's not dead."

There was a long moment before she said in a whisper, "What?"

"You heard me. Take heart. Wait it out. There are reasons for this."

Dolores choked, and then laughed, sniffed, and laughed again, and I imagined her wiping her tears away with her sleeve.

"I'm sure," she said. "Oh God, you don't know how…I was up all night after I heard. I have never felt such regret, Dr. Cross. For what could have been."

"I think you'll get the chance to tell him that yourself before long," I said.

"Thank you," she said, sounding stuffy but ecstatic. "From the bottom of my heart, thank you. And if there's anything else I can do for you, just ask."

"There is, actually. Tell me what you know about Lester Hobbes and Charles Fender."

# CHAPTER

# 70

**THE LINE WAS QUIET FOR** several moments before Dolores said, "Interesting pair. Can I ask where this is going?"

"Not today," I said. "And please don't start poking around in any files with security clearances attached to those two. Just give me what you know."

"Fair enough," Dolores said. "I'll give you only what's in my files."

"You've got files on Hobbes and Fender?"

"I've got files on almost everyone in this business."

"Can I ask how?"

"Only if you wish to pay me for my services."

I smiled. "So, what, you're like an agent for mercenaries?"

"A broker is closer to it," Dolores said, all business now. "I'm the person you go to when you want to recruit a talented warrior, like Fender, or an assassin, like Hobbes."

"That's what Hobbes does?"

"Quite well. Very clean operator. Only takes out targets who deserve it."

I wondered at Dolores's sense of morality and justice for a moment but then pushed those concerns aside.

"Can you tell me where to find Hobbes and Fender?"

She laughed. "You want to talk to them?"

"Interrogate them is more like it."

She laughed again. "Good luck with that."

"You won't help me find them?"

"I don't know how to find them. The only time we communicate is when I have an offer for their services, and that's done by secure e-mail. Honestly, we've never even met in person."

I thought about that. "Could you make them an offer on our behalf?"

"Oh, I don't know," she said. "There are certain ethical standards in my line of work."

"Your work representing mercenaries."

"That's right."

"Next thing you'll tell me is there's an association of mercenary agents here in town."

"There's talk."

"Remember how this conversation began?" I said.

After a pause, Dolores said, "I do, and I'm grateful for the peace of mind."

"And I imagine you want to prevent further bloodshed?"

"That too."

"Then you'll help us find Hobbes and Fender?"

A longer silence followed before she said, "I'll draft a proposal for you and see if they bite."

"Make it a very lucrative offer," I said. "Then they'll definitely bite."

# CHAPTER

# 71

**OUT IN THE MOUTH OF** Mobjack Bay, close to where it meets the greater Chesapeake, John Brown's fishing boat bobbed at anchor a mile north of a fifty-acre gated and guarded compound on a point.

Cass was aboard. So were Hobbes and Fender, who were holding fishing poles, jigging for bottom fish, and studying the compound.

"If we do it right, this will be a total surprise," Brown said, handing binoculars to Fender. "We'll be in and out in twenty minutes, tops."

"That's the plan, anyway," Hobbes said, raising and lowering his rod.

That annoyed Brown. "What does that mean?"

"It means shit happens," Hobbes said. "And sometimes you have to ad-lib. I mean, who knows, a big goddamned storm comes up and we're blowing off whitecaps on our way in, we might want to ad-lib and take a different approach. That's all I'm saying."

Brown felt on edge, and he didn't know why. His arm throbbed less, but it was waking him up at night. And of course there had to be contingencies in place, but with a situation like this, he wanted specific actions to move like clockwork, the team going in and out like phantoms.

"Those are huge cigarette boats," Cass said, glued to her binoculars.

Brown shielded his eyes to look toward the big lifts that held the three boats above the water. "It's a perfect location to take advantage of the eastern shipping lanes. Less than eight miles from the Atlantic. Boats that fast can get twenty miles out in minutes, offload cargo in the middle of the night, and be back quick."

"There's another guard," said Fender, who was also glued to the binoculars. "Three so far. Looks like they're on constant patrol."

"And they'll beef up security for the meeting," Brown said. "But we are a superior fighting force."

"Damned straight on that," Fender said. "If this goes down as planned, they'll never know what hit them."

Fender had no sooner said that than his cell

phone pinged. Hobbes's phone buzzed a moment later.

Fender set his binoculars down to check his phone. Hobbes held his fishing pole one-handed to look at his message.

Brown picked up Fender's binoculars and peered through them at the compound. He'd studied the aerial view of it in the drone footage, but getting eyeballs on the target still had benefits, especially in an amphibious attack.

He lowered the glasses, saw Fender and Hobbes still at their phones.

"Heads up," Brown said. "Eyes on where we're going."

Hobbes looked up. "Sorry—short-term high-dollar employment offer."

"Same," Fender said. "Says a team of six total needed."

Brown grew angry. "You're needed here. Don't you believe in what we're doing?"

"I believe in what we're doing," Hobbes said. "But sometimes a man's gotta eat before he makes the world a better place, which means sometimes he's got to earn before he makes the world a better place."

The skin below Brown's left eye twitched. "Where I come from, desertion in a time of war is a killing offense, Hobbes."

"Who's deserting?" Fender said. "If we get the gig, we won't be gone a month. We'll be back. Think of it as us going on extended furlough without pay."

Brown didn't like it, but he said, "Get us through this phase before you go anywhere. You owe us that."

After much hesitation, Hobbes said, "Works for me."

"Me too," Fender said.

Brown glanced at Cass, who nodded.

"Let's head home, then," Brown said. "We've got thirty-two hours to—"

"Holy shit!" Hobbes cried, struggling against his bowed fishing pole. "I got a big one hooked! A monster!"

# CHAPTER

# 72

**AFTER TWO GRINDING AND UNSUCCESSFUL** days trying to track Lester Hobbes and Charles Fender, I trudged down Fifth Street, wanting home and family and a break from the pressure that had been building relentlessly.

If Condon was right, politicians were the next targets. Corrupt politicians, but politicians nonetheless, which meant we were trying to stop an assassination.

But the assassination of whom? And how many? At what level?

Federal? Mahoney had alerted U.S. Capitol Hill Police to the increased threat, but without specifics, they couldn't do much.

State? Municipal?

The truth was we could have been looking

at any pol within a hundred and fifty miles of the nation's capital. As far as limiting the pool to the dishonest, you could kick any azalea in Washington and a corrupt politician would scurry out. The number of potential targets felt overwhelming.

My cell phone beeped with a message from Judith Noble just as I walked up the steps to our home and heard symphonic music blaring.

"Turn the TV down!" Nana Mama shouted.

Stuffing my phone back in my pocket, I went in, cringing at how loud the music was and sticking my fingers in my ears. Ali sat on the couch staring at images of outer space on the screen and holding the remote away from my grandmother.

"Give it," I said, putting out my hand.

Ali grimaced but handed it to me. I hit the mute button.

The house mercifully went silent. Nana Mama was trembling, she was so angry. "He would not listen to me. He flat-out defied me."

"I didn't want to listen to Jannie crying anymore," Ali said. "Is that so hard to understand?"

"Jannie's crying?" I said.

"You better go up and talk to her," my grandmother said. "She thinks the world's come to an end."

I pointed my finger at Ali, said, "You and I are

going to have a talk later about respecting your elders. In the meantime, get in the kitchen and do whatever Nana Mama tells you to do, and do it with your lips buttoned tight and your head on straight. Understand, young man?"

Ali's lower lip began to tremble, but he nodded and got up. "Sorry, Nana Mama," he mumbled as he walked past her. "I just don't like hearing her cry."

"Doesn't give you the right to be sassing me," Nana Mama said.

I went upstairs and knocked at Jannie's door.

"Go away," Jannie said.

"It's Dad."

A few moments later the door opened. Jannie hobbled backward on her crutches, sat down hard on her bed, and burst into tears.

"Hey, hey, what's the matter?" I said, going in and putting my arm around her.

"Look at my foot," she said, sobbing. "Look at how swollen it got just from, like, a half an hour on a stationary bike with practically no pressure."

I leaned down and saw the swelling across her midfoot.

"That's not good," I said.

"What am I going to do?" Jannie said. "My physical therapist thinks there's something else wrong in there. She said what we did should not have caused this kind of reaction."

"Okay," I said after several moments of thought. "I understand you're upset. I would be too if I were you."

"Dad, what if it's real bad?" she said, starting to cry again. "What if there's something so bad I can never run again?"

"Whoa, whoa," I said. "We are not thinking that way at all. Ever. We'll just take it step by step. Does your PT have a number and a name?"

She nodded and snuggled into my chest. "I have it."

I rubbed her shoulder and said, "Don't work yourself up into a state by imagining the worst. Okay? We'll go see the best foot doctor in the country. I'm sure your coaches know who that is, and we'll have that doctor take a look and tell us what to do. Okay?"

Jannie nodded and sniffled. "I just don't want my dream to be over before it's even started."

"I don't either," I said, and I hugged her tight.

# CHAPTER

# 73

**NANA MAMA WAS WATCHING ALI** sweep the kitchen floor when I walked in.

He looked at me with watery eyes. "Is it true Jannie will never run again?"

"What? No."

"I keep telling him it's not true," Nana Mama said. "But he won't listen."

"It's what Jannie said," Ali told me.

"She was upset," I said. "Everyone, calm down. Her foot's swollen, not rotting off."

"Ugh," Ali said, but he smiled.

"Finish your sweeping, you," Nana Mama said, and then she looked to me. "Thin pork chops fried in a little bacon grease and covered with a fiery compote of onions, applesauce, and sriracha."

"That sounds great," I said. "And it smells amazing in here."

My grandmother smiled, said, "It's the caramelized onions. Ten minutes? I've got the compote made already."

"Ten minutes is fine," I said, grabbing a beer from the fridge and going out into the great room. I sat down and pulled out my cell phone to look at the message from Judith Noble.

The phone rang before I could read it.

"It's Dolores," she said. "Fender and Hobbes both replied."

I set my beer down and said, "Tell me."

"They're interested but said they're tied up overseas until Monday. Then they're open to any and all offers."

"Which means what?"

"They're busy for a few days."

"So there could be an attack in the next few days?"

"I suppose you could interpret it that way," Dolores said. "How's Nick?"

"I don't know. Mahoney's got him stashed away in Virginia somewhere."

"So how do I respond to Hobbes and Fender?"

I thought about that and said, "Tell them we look forward to hearing from them at their earliest possible convenience."

"I can do that," Dolores said, and she hung up.

I heard Bree come in the front door. It was past seven. She looked worse than I felt.

"Don't ask," she said.

"Deal," I said. "Beer?"

"Red wine," she said. "Pinot noir. And what smells so good?"

"Nana Mama's on a roll," I said and retrieved a bottle of her favorite wine.

I poured just about the time my grandmother finished the thin-sliced pork chops and set them on the table along with her mystery sauce. Jannie crutched her way in. We said grace with everyone holding hands.

Nana Mama's new dish was a hit. Every bite gave you about six different flavors, but it wasn't so spicy you screamed *Fire!* Bree and I cleared the dishes. At bedtime, Ali and I talked about respecting elders.

"Would you disrespect Neil deGrasse Tyson?"

"No," he said. "But Nana Mama's not—"

"Don't go there," I said, wagging a finger. "That argument won't work. In this house, in this universe, Nana Mama is Neil deGrasse Tyson and more."

He struggled with that, but then nodded. "Okay. I'm sorry."

"Apology accepted," I said, leaning over and kissing his head.

I went into our bedroom and found Bree already under the covers, knees up and reading her new book. I crawled into bed minutes later, and my world seemed a whole lot better than it had when I got home; I felt good and drowsy enough for sleep.

# CHAPTER

# 74

**DRESSED IN BLACK FROM HIS** Wolverine boots to his leather jacket and Bell helmet, John Brown accelerated his motorcycle down a moonless rural road. Cass rode behind him.

"I still say we could have used a car," she grumbled through a tiny earbud Brown wore.

"There's no car on earth that can stay with this bike," Brown said. "We may need that speed to get out of here alive."

The headlight beam caught parked cars ahead by the side of the road and then the lights of the high-walled compound.

"Hobbes?" Brown said.

"Here," Hobbes replied.

"Troll in to five hundred meters. Fender too."

"Roger that."

"Coming to it now," Brown said, and he down-shifted and slowed as he passed the two guards flanking the open gate.

The motorcycle rumbled when Brown pulled a U-turn and then backed into a spot between a Mercedes-Benz and a Cadillac Escalade, the bike's front tire facing the compound.

"Confidence, now," he said, shutting off the motorcycle.

"All the confidence in the world, darling," Cass said, getting down.

Brown dismounted and drew off his helmet slowly, all too aware of the guards but careful not to tug too hard on the fake beard glued to his skin. He hung the helmet on the throttle and glanced at Cass. She wore a fringed red leather jacket, a platinum-blond wig, and an Atlanta Braves cap. She held a black leather briefcase. It was hand-cuffed to her wrist.

"Three hundred meters," Brown murmured into the sensitive jawbone microphone affixed to the skin beneath his beard.

"Three hundred," Fender said.

Brown put his head up as if he owned the god-damned world and walked across the road toward the gate and the guards, Cass trailing just behind his left shoulder.

"Nice bike," the guard on the left said in Russian.

"The best," Brown replied in Russian with a perfect St. Petersburg accent.

"How fast?" the guard on the right asked.

"Three hundred and five kilometers an hour," Brown replied, smiling and looking each man in the eye. "The acceleration is breathtaking. Am I late?"

"We were close to shutting access off, but no," the guard on the left said. "Invitation, please."

Brown smiled, cocked his head, and said in English with a thick accent, "Where is the invitation, Leanne?"

"I put it in here for safekeeping, sugar," Cass said in a deep Southern twang. She came around in front of Brown, her back to the guards, and held out the briefcase. "You'll have to unlock me, boss."

Feigning exasperation, Brown dug in his pocket, came up with the key, looked at the guards, and said in Russian, "She is not a rocket scientist, this one. But in bed, my God, boys, she's a racehorse."

The guards cracked up. Cass looked at him as if she had no idea what he'd just said. Brown unlocked the handcuff and set the combination locks on the hasps.

Then he thumbed them both open, pushed up the lid, and grabbed the two sound-suppressed Glock pistols inside. He swung them out and around the sides of the briefcase and Cass and head-shot both guards at near point-blank range.

They both rocked back and crumpled.

Cass threw aside the briefcase. Brown lobbed her one of the pistols. She caught it and they went to work. They grabbed the dead men by their collars, dragged them inside the gates and out of sight, then closed the gate, barred, and locked it. After taking two-way radios from the dead men, they stepped into the shadows to pull black hoods down over their faces.

"We're in," Brown said into his mike, and they trotted down the driveway toward a cluster of buildings overlooking the bay.

Brown could hear music playing—jazz—and the clinking of cocktail glasses and the laughter of thieves and slave owners. When they were in sight of a big antebellum-style mansion that dominated the compound, Brown said, "Ready."

Brown imagined the Zodiac boats slipping toward shore, their electric trolling motors drowned out by the party din. Feeling fanatical, like God and history were on his side, Brown ran across a shadowed lawn toward the front porch and door.

"Go, Regulators," he said. "Rage against the night."

# CHAPTER

# 75

I COULD SEE BODIES FROM the air, seven of them, five males and two females, sprawled on a brightly lit terrace behind an antebellum-style mansion, right on the water near the mouth of Mobjack Bay. It was three in the morning.

"Your mystery caller wasn't lying, Ned," Sampson said from the seat beside me in the back of the FBI helicopter.

"It's another bloodbath," Mahoney said from the front seat as the chopper landed.

"We're sure they're gone?" Sampson asked.

"She said they'd left almost an hour before she called, and then she hung up," Mahoney said. "That was an hour ago, so we're two hours behind them."

"She call from in the house?" I asked as the chopper landed.

"She wasn't on with the 911 operator long enough for us to tell."

We got out, ducked under the rotor blades, and stopped to put on booties and gloves. If we were the first on the scene, we didn't want to contaminate it for the forensics investigators sure to follow.

"What's the Russian owner's name?" Sampson said.

"Antonin Guryev," Mahoney said. "Made his money in shipping and, as far as we know, clean. We've got Critical Incident Response Group agents at Quantico looking at him, but so far the name hasn't rung any bells."

Walking up onto the terrace and seeing the bodies was a bizarre experience. Judging from the way they were clustered and from their various positions, the victims seemed to have been shot down unawares.

There was a bar at one end of the terrace stocked with top-tier booze; a beefy bartender sprawled behind it. Another man had fallen near the piano. The others died in two small clusters, as if they'd been chatting when the bullets found their marks.

The lights were blazing inside. We went through open French doors into an opulently decorated home that clashed with the antebellum exterior—lots of marble, chrome, gilt, and mirrors.

"Looks like a Moscow disco, for Christ's sake," Mahoney said.

There was a long table to our left loaded with food, and four more dead people around it. To our right there was a large entertaining area and a kitchen.

Nine died in there, though at least four appeared to have died fighting. There were pistols and spent casings on the floor near them.

"I think I know this guy," Sampson said, crouching by a man in a suit with perfectly coiffed silver hair. He was in his fifties and looked vaguely familiar to me despite the wound to his throat.

"I think I do too, but I can't place him," I said.

Sampson carefully reached into the victim's breast pocket, got out his wallet.

He opened it and whistled. "Here's your first corrupt politician. That's Congressman Rory McMann."

"Shit," Mahoney said. "Justice has spent years trying to get that guy."

Rep. McMann of Virginia Beach, Virginia, had been investigated several times, but no prosecutor had ever made charges stick. He was a good ol' boy who chased skirts and liked to drink. Those vices had almost gotten him censured by the

House of Representatives, but he'd managed to wriggle free of that as well. Now here he was, the victim of vigilantes.

"It's going to take us days to process this place and identify everyone," I said, bewildered by the carnage.

"I can tell you who they are," a woman said loudly in a thick Russian accent. We started and looked around.

But there was no one alive in the room but us.

# CHAPTER

# 76

**"I WILL TELL YOU EVERYTHING,** but I...I want witness protection," she said, and we realized she was talking to us through Bluetooth speakers mounted high in the corners of the room.

"Who are you?" Mahoney asked. "Where are you?"

"My name is Elena Guryev," she said. "I am in the panic room."

"How do we find you?" Sampson asked.

"I tell you when I have witness protection."

I looked at Mahoney and said, "With this many victims, I can't see that being a hard sell."

"I can't give you the papers at the moment, Ms. Guryev," Mahoney said. "But I give you my word."

Several seconds of silence followed. "For my son too."

Mahoney sighed. "For your son too. Where is he?"

"Here, with me. He's sleeping."

"Your husband?"

The silence was longer this time. "Dead."

"Let us get you and your son out of here," Mahoney said.

"Go to wine cellar in the basement. It has door, like from a barn. Go inside. There's a camera there. Show me your badges and identifications."

The house was sprawling and we took a wrong turn or two before finding a staircase into the basement. The wine-cellar door was rough-sawn barn wood. We opened it and stepped into a brick-floored room with thousands of bottles of wine in racks along the walls.

We each held up our badge and ID to a tiny camera on the ceiling.

A moment later, we heard large metal bars disengage and slide back. A section of the wine cellar's rear wall swung open hydraulically, revealing Elena Guryev studying us from a space about the size of two prison cells.

She was tall, willowy, and in her late thirties, with sandy-blond hair and the kind of bone structure and lips that magazine editors swoon over. Black cocktail dress. Black hose and heels. Hefty diamonds at her ears, wrists, and throat.

Her hazel eyes were puffy and bloodshot, but she acted in no way distraught. Indeed, she seemed to exude a steely will as she stood with her arms crossed in front of a bunk bed. On the lower bunk, a boy of about ten slept, curled up under a blanket, his head wrapped in gauze bandages.

Across from the bed, six small screens showed six different views of the house and grounds.

"Mrs. Guryev," Mahoney began softly.

"Dimitri cannot hear us," she said. "He is stone-deaf and on pain drugs. He had a cochlear implant operation two days ago at Johns Hopkins."

I said, "Do you want a doctor to see him?"

"I am physician," she said. "He's fine and better sleeping."

"Are you okay?" I asked.

"No," she said, her fingers traveling to her lips, her eyes gazing at the floor as if contemplating horror. "I don't know what I'll tell him about his father."

A moment later, she raised her head and that toughness was back. "What do you want to know?"

Sampson gestured at the screens. "You saw what happened?"

"Some of it," she said.

"Is the feed recorded?" Mahoney asked.

"It is," she said. "But they knew where the big hard drive was stored and took it with them."

"Got away clean again," Sampson grumbled.

"They only think they got away clean," Mrs. Guryev said, reaching down to the bed. "But I make sure they will pay."

She held an iPhone in her hand like a pistol. "I videoed them, two without their hoods."

# CHAPTER

# 77

ON A SCREEN IN BREE'S office a few hours later, we watched a precision military force massacre the victims we'd found in the house, including Antonin Guryev, who begged for his life and offered the killers millions before he was shot to death in his bedroom.

The iPhone camera went haywire at that point and you heard Elena Guryev gasp and then cry out in Russian. The camera showed her shoes as she wept for several minutes and then returned to the feed from her bedroom.

"Here it comes," I said.

The gunman who killed Guryev had gotten down on his knees by the bed. He reached under it and yanked out the hard drive that recorded all security feeds on the grounds. He tucked it under one arm, tore off his hood, and wiped at his sweaty brow before he walked out of sight.

I backed the recording up and froze it at the moment the hood was off, showing a face I'd seen before, the one that was a fusion of Asia and Africa.

"Say hello to Lester Hobbes," Sampson said.

Bree sat forward, said, "No kidding."

"Wait," I said. "The second one's coming up."

The iPhone camera swung shakily to another feed in the panic room, and then it focused, showing the six hooded gunmen cleaning their way out of the entertainment area of the house, picking up their brass and even vacuuming around the bodies. When they reached the French doors that opened onto the terrace, one of them unzipped the back of the vacuum, removed the dust bag, and turned to leave while tugging off the hood.

You caught a flash of her, a woman with blond hair. It took a few tries at the computer to freeze her with her face in near profile.

"Who is she?" Bree asked

"No idea yet," Sampson said.

"Who were the victims besides the congressman?" Bree asked.

"Russian mobsters, representatives from the Sinaloa drug cartel, two bankers from New York and their wives, and someone we didn't expect."

"Who?"

"We'll get to him in a second," I said.

We explained that, according to Elena Guryev, the party had actually been a kind of emergency board meeting of a loose alliance of criminals who trafficked in everything from narcotics to humans.

"What was the meeting about?" Bree asked.

"Ironically enough, the vigilantes," Sampson said. "Every target they hit—the meth factories and the convoy—were part of the alliance's business."

"And then the vigilantes came in and wiped the leaders out," Bree said.

"Like cutting off all the hydra's heads at one time," I said.

"How did Guryev get involved?"

We told her what Elena Guryev had told us: Several years ago, her husband had overextended himself financially and gotten in huge money trouble. Members of the alliance offered him a way out of his predicament—smuggling—and his global shipping business had exploded with unseen profits.

Elena Guryev claimed she didn't know what her husband had gotten involved in until it was too late. When she discovered the depth of his criminality, she told him she wanted a divorce.

"She says he threatened to kill her and their son

if she tried to leave or tell the police," I said. "That was three months ago."

Bree thought about that. "Why was she in the panic room?"

"Her son, Dimitri, had had an operation two days before and needed to sleep somewhere he wouldn't be disturbed," I said. "She put in an appearance at the beginning of the party and then went down to be with her son. She was there when the attack began."

"Did she recognize Hobbes or the woman?"

"Said she'd never seen either of them before."

"Where are Elena and the son now?"

I shrugged. "Mahoney's got them stashed in a safe house. I suspect he'll be questioning her for days if not weeks before she goes into witness protection. Which brings us back to this guy."

I showed her a picture on my phone of a dead man in his late thirties, handsome, with a thick shock of dark hair and a bullet hole in his chest.

"Who is he?"

Sampson said, "According to Elena Guryev, his name is Karl Stavros, and he's the owner of, among other businesses, the Phoenix Club."

"Wait," Bree said. "Where Edita Kravic worked?"

"One and the same," I said. "So what are the odds that Tommy McGrath was onto something criminal going on in that club that Edita told him about?"

"I'd say very good," Bree said. "Very, very good."

"I think the answer to who killed Tommy is in that club," Sampson said.

"We'll need warrants," she said.

"The Feds are filing," I said. "Ned promised we'll be part of any search, but it's not going to be today."

I yawned. So did Sampson.

"You two look like hell," Bree said. "Go home. Get some sleep."

Sampson got up and left without any argument.

I held up my hands. "No, I'm good. Nothing a cup of coffee won't fix."

"That's a direct order, Detective Cross. Home, nap, and then I'd bet Nana Mama would appreciate you going to Ali's interview for the Washington Latin charter school this afternoon."

"Is that today?"

"It is. Five o'clock."

"Then heading home as ordered, Chief Stone. See you at dinner?"

"If I'm lucky," she said. "Love you."

"Love you too," I said, and I went out her door fantasizing about my bed and a two-hour coma.

# CHAPTER

# 78

BREE WATCHED ALEX LEAVE, FEELING a little cheated not to be an active part of Tommy McGrath's murder investigation, or not really, anyway.

If Alex and Sampson were right about the Phoenix Club, the case was essentially in the FBI's hands now. Even though Mahoney had promised that DC Metro would be part of any search, the FBI would be calling the shots.

Bree tried to put it out of her mind and deal with the barrage of paper that now dominated her working life. But after ten minutes of scanning a series of administrative memos, she couldn't take it anymore.

She had to do something that engaged her mind, that wasn't mundane, that would do some good. Wasn't that what being a cop was? Doing some good?

Bree pushed the paper pile aside and found copies of the murder books for Tommy McGrath, Edita Kravic, and Terry Howard. She started back through them, trying to suppress any preconceived ideas she had about the case, trying to see it all anew, with a beginner's mind.

As she reviewed the investigative notes and forensics reports, she realized that they'd all been looking at the case as a revenge killing of some kind, done by Howard or someone else who had a beef with McGrath, and maybe with Edita Kravic too.

Bree consciously tried to erase that filter from her mind and played with possible other motives. Bree started by asking herself who would *benefit* from Tommy McGrath dying. Or from Edita Kravic dying, for that matter.

Someone inside the Phoenix Club, she supposed. Karl Stavros? He was the owner. If Stavros thought Tommy was onto him, maybe he'd had Tommy and Edita killed to protect himself and the alliance.

She started down through a list of the evidence gathered at their apartments and, after the encryption codes were broken, from their computer hard drives. For almost an hour and a half, she studied each item in turn and tried to see it as a benefit or a loss to a killer. She ran a search for the Phoenix Club on McGrath's hard drive and got nothing. She ran a search on Edita Kravic and got the same.

Then she started through McGrath's financial affairs. The late COD had had $325,000 in his retirement account, $12,000 in his checking account, and zero debt. McGrath didn't own a home, had paid cash for his car, and paid off his credit cards every month.

His will was brief, drafted four years before. To Bree's surprise, it named Terry Howard as his sole heir. If Howard was not alive at the time of McGrath's death, the modest estate was to go to McGrath's wife, Vivian.

Bree thought about that. Tommy McGrath still cared about his old partner enough to leave him his money. Could Howard have known and killed him to collect? Or could Vivian have…

She dismissed that out of hand. McGrath's estranged wife was loaded, worth multimillions. Why would she kill Tommy for a measly three hundred grand and change?

She turned to the last page of the will and saw a reference to a document in the appendix that caused her to pause. Bree dug deeper into the financial files and found the document she was looking for. She flipped through it and then stopped at one item, thinking: *Now* that *might be something worth killing or dying for.*

Bree took the document out and went down the hall to Muller's cubicle. She found the senior detective not looking like his ordinary disheveled self; he was sharply dressed in a nice suit and freshly polished shoes.

"Kurt," she said, showing him the document. "Did we ever look into this?"

Muller took it, scanned it, and nodded. "It's unclaimed, at least as of two days ago. I check that kind of thing regularly."

Some of the wind went out of Bree's sails. She'd thought she was really onto something, something they'd missed, and she'd briefly felt like she was doing some good.

But Muller had things under control.

Some of her disappointment must have shown because he said, "We'll figure it out, Chief. We always do. But for now, I have to skip out. Got a date."

Bree smiled. "You haven't had a date in years."

"Don't I know it," Muller said, adjusting his tie.

"Who's the lucky lady?"

"The divine Ms. Noble," Muller said, and he winked.

Bree laughed and clapped her hands, feeling

better than she had all day. "I thought there was a spark between you two there in the FBI lab."

"A crackling spark," Muller said, walking past her with a grin smeared across his face. "Just crack-crack-crackling."

# CHAPTER

# 79

**NANA MAMA BEAMED AT ALI.**

"You want your dessert before dinner?" my grandmother asked him. "Blueberry pie and ice cream?"

Unnerved by this break in the routine, Ali glanced at me. I smiled and held up my hands. "You heard her."

"Yes, please, Nana," Ali said. "And less Brussels sprouts at dinner?"

"Don't push your luck," my grandmother said, fetching the pie from beneath a fine-mesh cage. "Brussels sprouts are a superfood."

"Kind of bitter," Ali said.

Nana Mama squinted hard at him.

"Just saying," Ali said.

My grandmother sighed, cut a thick slice of

blueberry pie, plopped a scoop of French vanilla ice cream beside it, then set the plate in front of Ali.

"Any boy who can charm the pants off the admissions board of a fine school deserves this," Nana Mama said, and then she handed him a spoon.

It was true. The principal and the math, science, and English teachers at Washington Latin had been waiting when we walked in. The principal introduced herself and the teachers and then asked Ali what he had been up to outside of school, on his own time. That set him off on a description of his epic quest to talk to Neil deGrasse Tyson.

"I could tell they were going to admit him about two minutes after he opened his mouth," Nana Mama said. "I think they were most impressed at how many drafts of that letter he's already written."

"Though at some point he needs to just send it," I said.

"Soon," Ali said, his mouth full of blueberry pie and ice cream.

"You do me a favor, sugar?" my grandmother said to me. "Take a twenty from my purse and go on down to Chung's and play my numbers?"

"The next drawing's not for two days," I said.

"Those jackpots are getting big," she said. "I'd rather get in on the action before the stampede."

"Get in on the action?" I said, smiling.

"Just laying my bets early, that's all. Now, are you going to help an old lady out or not, Alex Cross?"

"You knew the answer the second you asked," I said, and I got the money from her purse.

I went outside, feeling pretty good. The two-hour nap had helped. And it was only early September, but a front had come in and cooled things off. It felt nice to walk, and I did my best to focus on nothing but putting one foot in front of the other.

In my line of work, where I'm often bombarded by details and exposed to the worst of life, I have to clear my mind completely at least once a day. Otherwise, it all gets to be stressful chatter up-stairs, an endless series of questions, theories, arguments, painful memories, and regrets. It can get overwhelming.

I was feeling even better by the time I reached the grocery and went inside. Chung's was frigid, like always.

"Alex Cross, where you been, my man?" cried a woman behind the counter. "I was waiting on you or Nana Mama all day yesterday."

Chung Sun Chung, a Korean American in her

late thirties, sat framed in an arched hole in a plate of bulletproof glass. Sun, as she liked to be called, wore a puffy coat and fingerless mittens. She managed to keep an electronic cigarette in the corner of her mouth while smiling broadly at me.

I walked over to her. "We've both been busy."

"How's Damon like college?"

"Loves it."

"I saw your Jannie on the YouTube."

"Crazy, right?"

"She's gonna be famous, that one. How many chances will Nana Mama be taking at an unlimited future today?"

"That's your line?"

"Good one, huh?" She beamed and drew on her e-cigarette.

"Give her ten chances each on Powerball and Mega Millions," I said, laying down the cash.

My grandmother played only the big-money lotteries. If you're going to dream, you might as well dream big, she liked to say.

"Same number?" Sun asked.

"Sure. Wait! You know what? Let's change it up. Five each on her numbers and for the rest, add a one to the last number."

Sun glanced at me. "Nana Mama's not going to like that."

"She won't even look," I said.

"You like taking your life in your hands?"

We both laughed. We were still laughing as I left.

On my way home to dinner with my family, I decided there were still good people in the world, very good people, like Chung Sun Chung. I guess I'd needed reminding of that after the past couple of weeks I'd had.

The cumulative violence and bloodshed inflicted by the vigilantes was sobering when I thought about it. Climbing the steps to my front porch and smelling a pie Nana Mama had baked, I couldn't shake the feeling that the violence wasn't over, that Hobbes and Fender and the other vigilantes were somehow just getting started.

# CHAPTER

# 80

JOHN BROWN SAT FORWARD IN a chair, his eyes glued to the big-screen TV, where an NBC news reporter was standing in front of Antonin Guryev's compound.

"This is the fourth such massacre in less than a month," she was saying. "Up to now, the killers have left little evidence behind. But FBI special agent in charge Ned Mahoney says that has changed. Mistakes were made."

Low voices rumbled through the room behind Brown. Many of his followers were looking at one another.

"Mistakes?" Hobbes said, putting down his beer. "No way."

"Why don't you shut up and listen," Cass said, pacing and watching the screen. The scene jumped to Mahoney standing before a bank of microphones.

"We are confirming seventeen dead," Mahoney said gravely. "We are also confirming that we have a witness, a survivor who saw many of the killings on security cameras in a secret panic room in the basement of the house. This witness got solid looks at two of the killers when they took off their hoods."

"Secret panic room!" Fender said. "And who the hell took off their hoods?"

"I did," Hobbes said. "It was frickin' hot and I had the security hard drive."

"Who else broke protocol?" Brown roared.

Cass, looking stricken, said, "I did. It *was* hot and I...I thought we were good. And my hair was different. And my eyes that night."

On the screen, reporters were yelling questions at Mahoney. Who was the witness? Could the witness identify the killers?

"We're not identifying the witness for the time being," Mahoney said. "We believe the witness can identify the killers. We'll have more for you tomorrow."

The screen cut back to the standup reporter, who said, "The FBI seems confident that this is the break they needed to at last bring the vigilantes to justice."

Fender stared at Hobbes. Brown stared at Cass, who looked devastated.

"This is bullshit," Hobbes said, grabbing the remote and punching off the TV. "What are they going to get from the witness? At best, an artist's sketch."

Brown was about to explode, but then his burn phone began to buzz.

He answered, said, "You saw it?"

"Of course, I fucking saw it," the man on the other end of the line snapped. "The witness is Guryev's wife."

"That's not good," Brown said.

"No, it goddamned isn't. Our ship has a hole. You need to plug it."

Brown flushed with anger. "How the hell am I supposed to do that?"

"I have her location and a way inside."

"Attack an FBI safe house?" Brown said. "I don't know if that's such a—"

"You want to take this to the next level or not?"

The next level. Brown felt all doubt leave him then, and said, "You know it's the only long-term solution. If we don't, nothing we've done will really matter."

"Exactly. So steel yourself and get rid of Elena Guryev."

# CHAPTER

# 81

**AT EIGHT THIRTY THE MORNING** after the massacre, Ned Mahoney and I sprinted down Monroe Street in Columbia Heights. Patrol cars and an ambulance blocked the street, their lights flashing.

We showed our badges. The patrol officer pointed at the open door of a town house. The call had come into 911 only twenty minutes before. I'd been on my way to work and came straight over. Mahoney had been heading to FBI headquarters, heard about the call, and came straight over as well.

After putting on gloves and booties, we stepped inside and saw a dead man lying facedown in the entryway, another one beyond him.

"Simms and Frawley," Mahoney said angrily. "Good agents. Seasoned agents."

"Shot in the back," I said.

"They were replacing the night team," Mahoney said. "The killers must have come in right behind them."

The locations of federal safe houses are some of the most secure and heavily guarded secrets in law enforcement, so it was understood that the killers had had inside intelligence. Mahoney had a traitor in his midst, and we both knew it.

We stepped over and around the dead agents, passed a television room on our left where the carpet was smeared with blood, and went into the kitchen, where a third FBI agent lay dead. Two EMTs worked on a fourth man, George Potter, the DEA's acting special agent for the Washington, DC, office.

Potter's face was covered with blood from a nasty wound to his scalp. His shirt was off, and there was a clotting patch pressed into a chest wound. The medics had him hooked up to IVs and oxygen.

"How is he?" Mahoney asked the EMT.

Potter opened his eyes and said, gasping, "I'll live."

"How is he?" Mahoney asked again.

The EMT said, "Took a slug through his right lung, and he has a hell of a gash on his head. But he's lucky. He'll live."

"What happened?" I asked.

"We need to get him to the hospital," the medic said.

"Wait, they need to know," Potter said, looking at me. "Ned asked me to come in with the replacements and start talking to Mrs. Guryev first thing."

I glanced at Mahoney, who nodded.

"Everything looked fine coming through the door," Potter said. "I was walking down the hall with Simms and Frawley behind me. Out of nowhere there were sound-suppressed shots. Three of them. Fast. I got hit by the third shot. Spun me into that TV room. Went down, hit my head on the coffee table. When I came to, I called 911. What's happened? Has anyone gone upstairs to see?"

"No," Mahoney said, looking grim.

"We're leaving," the EMT said forcefully. "You can talk to him at GW Medical Center."

"We'll be talking to you," I said.

Potter gave a thumbs-up and closed his eyes as they wheeled him away.

I could tell from the expression on Mahoney's face that he was dreading the climb upstairs as much as I was. We found a fourth dead FBI agent on the landing, and in a bedroom, Elena Guryev, in a T-shirt and panties, lay sprawled on the floor, dead from a single gunshot wound to her forehead.

The bathroom door was open. Empty. The only other door on the second floor was shut.

I braced myself, turned the handle, and pushed the door open.

Ten-year-old Dimitri Guryev was sitting up in a twin bed, a small rose circle of dried blood showing through the gauze that wrapped his head. He had an iPad in his lap and was watching a closed-captioned Harry Potter movie.

The boy must have glimpsed my shadow because he looked up, saw me, and shrank back in fear.

"It's okay," I said, even though I knew he couldn't hear me.

I showed him my open hands, and then my badge.

Seeing the badge, he said in an odd, nasal voice that was difficult to understand, "What do you want? Where's my mother? Where's my father?"

My stomach sank.

I turned around and saw Mahoney, who was standing in the doorway, looking stricken at the boy's loss.

"Get sheets over the bodies," I said. "And close the door to his mother's bedroom. I don't want him seeing any of it."

# CHAPTER

# 82

**A FEW HOURS LATER, BREE** looked up from a memo she was writing. Alex trudged into her office, shut the door behind him, and sat down hard.

"Sometimes I hate my job," he said. "Sometimes it's just too much."

Bree rarely saw him this upset. "What happened?" she said softly.

"I had to tell a ten-year-old totally deaf boy that his mother and father had been murdered and that he was an orphan now," Alex said, his eyes watering. "I don't know if it was due to the deafness, Bree, but the grieving sounds he made were like nothing I've ever heard before, just gut-wrenching. I couldn't stop thinking about Ali as I held the poor kid."

He sat forward and put his head in his hands. "Jesus, that was hard."

Bree got up, came around the desk, and hugged him. "Maybe you were meant for the hard things, Alex. Maybe you were meant to help people through these terrible moments."

"I couldn't help that child," Alex said. "I couldn't get through to him. After I showed him the note that said his mom and dad were dead, he wouldn't read anything I wrote. He won't read anything anyone writes. He's suffering in total silence, in total isolation."

Bree hugged him tighter. "You feel too much sometimes."

"Can't help it," he said.

"I know," she said. "But we need you to buck up and push on."

Alex hugged her tight and then broke their embrace, saying, "You would have been a great cornerman in a boxing match."

"Clean them, patch them, and send them back out there with Vaseline on their brows," Bree said. "That's me."

He kissed her, said, "Thank you for being you."

Bree once again realized how much she loved him. She loved everything about him. Even when he was wounded, Alex filled her up.

Her phone rang.

"Yes?" she said.

"This is Ned," Mahoney said.

"I'm so sorry for your loss," Bree said.

The FBI agent sounded distraught and sad. "I appreciate that, Bree. They were four of my best."

"How can I help?"

"A federal judge in Alexandria just perfected our warrants. Get to Vienna ASAP if you're still interested. We're searching the Phoenix Club."

# CHAPTER

# 83

**BREE, SAMPSON, AND I MET** Mahoney and a team of ten from the FBI in the parking lot at Wolf Trap. The heat had returned, and we were sweating as we armored up, got documents in order, and rolled toward the Phoenix Club.

Based on an aerial view of the compound from Google Earth, Mahoney gave out assignments. Five agents would loop into the woods behind the property to stop any runners. The rest of us were going in the front gate.

"Pretty swank neighborhood," Bree said, seeing the mansions. "I thought where Vivian McGrath lived was big money."

"She's in the millionaires' club," Sampson said. "This is strictly billionaires."

Mahoney stopped a quarter of a mile from the

club and watched five FBI agents head up the driveway of a big Tudor estate and then disappear into the woods.

"Here we go," Mahoney said into his radio, and he put the car back in gear.

He drove us to the entrance and up the long drive. As we caught sight of the gate, it started to swing open to let a white Range Rover exit.

Mahoney blocked the way. The window of the luxury SUV rolled down and a guy with slicked-back hair wearing five-hundred-dollar sunglasses and a five-thousand-dollar suit yelled, "Move, for God's sake. I'm late for a very important meeting at the Pentagon."

"Tell it to someone who cares," Mahoney said, climbing out of the car, hand on his pistol.

"I'm a goddamned founding member of this club!" the man shouted.

"And I'm an FBI agent," Mahoney said, and then he called back to his men, "Detain him for questioning."

"What? No!" the man said, no longer belligerent but terrified as the same guard Sampson and I had seen on our previous visit appeared from the shack.

"What's going on?" he asked.

"I have a federal warrant to search the premises," Mahoney said, wielding a sheaf of papers.

"You can't just go in there," the guard said, agitated. "It's private."

"Not anymore," Mahoney said and he signaled his team to move forward.

The slick-haired suit in the Range Rover used the moment to spring from his car and start running back up the hill. Sampson thundered after him and caught him by the collar halfway up the inner drive.

"Where the hell do you think you're going?" Sampson demanded.

"Please," he said in a whine. "I'll help you. Anything you want, but my name cannot be associated with this place."

"If I were you, Mr. Founding Member, I'd shut the hell up," Sampson said, cuffing him.

Bree, Mahoney, and I kept going up the drive, past flowering gardens and trees. We rounded a corner and saw the clubhouse, a sprawling, two-story place that suggested an inn in the south of France in its design and muted colors. There were tennis courts on our right. To the left, a high whitewashed picket fence enclosed a pool and side yard. A hedge about four feet high ran out from the fence to the drive and continued on to the woods on the other side of it, effectively cutting the front yard in two, an outer manicured lawn and an inner yard of blooming gardens surrounding the clubhouse. Piano music and the sound of people laughing drifted from the pool area.

"Looks like we may be interrupting a party," I said, stepping through a gap in the hedge.

Shots rang out. Bullets slapped the pavement at our feet.

# CHAPTER

# 84

I SPUN AROUND, TACKLED BREE, and drove her down behind the hedge before another round of shots came from the house. We landed hard. Bree had the wind knocked out of her, but we were alive. So were Sampson and Mahoney, who were returning fire from behind the hedge on the other side of the drive.

I scrambled up to my knees and called to them, "Where are they?"

"Second floor!" Sampson called back.

People were screaming by the pool.

"We have multiple runners," an FBI agent said through our earbuds. "Women in bikinis and bare-chested guys with white towels around their waists."

What the hell was this place?

"Shoot them if they're armed, stop them if they're not," Mahoney said.

Ten seconds passed. Then twenty. Bree caught her breath and sat up beside me. The panic continued in the pool yard, but no more shots were fired from the clubhouse. Why? The gunmen had to know where we were hiding. They had to have seen us take cover.

Something felt strange. We'd been in the wide open in that gap between the hedges. If they'd wanted to kill us, they could have, and yet…

I thought about the layout of the property and the satellite photo we'd seen of the place. I dug in my pocket and called it up on my iPhone. Only one way in, which meant only one way out. Right?

I was about to put the phone away when I noticed something. Beyond the north security wall a good hundred feet, a stubby spur of pavement appeared out of the woods, curved, and met the driveway of the adjoining mansion. I magnified the image, looked right where the spur disappeared into the trees, and saw a thick, dark smudge about the width of the pavement.

"It was a diversion," I said, jumping to my feet.

"Alex!" Bree said.

"They've got an underground escape route," I said, and I sprinted back down the driveway, Sampson, Mahoney, and Bree behind me.

"Hey!" the suit in the cuffs said when I ran by. "I want witness protection."

"Lot of good it will do you," Sampson said as I dodged by the Range Rover and Mahoney's car.

As I ran down the long drive, I kept peering north through the trees, hoping to catch a glimpse of someone. But I hit the street and there was no one.

I turned to tell the others when I heard an engine revving and tires squealing, and then a black Chevy Suburban came hurtling out of the estate to the north. It skidded sideways and then accelerated right at me. Out of the corner of my eye, I saw Sampson, Mahoney, and Bree appear.

"Driver!" I shouted when the car was less than fifty yards from me.

All four of us opened fire on the right side of the windshield, seeing it spiderweb before we had to dive for the ditch.

The Suburban ripped by us. Then the big SUV swerved hard, went off the road, jumped the ditch, and smashed head-on into a very large granite boulder.

# CHAPTER

# 85

**BREE STONE WALKED TOWARD A** group of young women wearing terry-cloth robes and smoking cigarettes by the kidney-shaped pool. They watched her from under hooded, mistrustful eyes.

*Why should they trust me?* Bree thought. Sergei Bogrov and the three other guys in the Suburban had abandoned them, made a run for it. The driver had died. Bogrov was badly injured. The other two weren't talking, nor were the ten club members the FBI had caught trying to flee the grounds.

That left these women.

Bree had been all through the Phoenix Club by then. She'd seen a gourmet kitchen, a well-stocked wine cellar and bar, a complete workout facility, a steam room, a sauna, a massage room, and eight bedrooms designed to cater to a variety of perversions and fetishes.

There was a dungeon room, a room with mirrored walls and ceiling, a room with a bathtub you could do laps in, and a room with furniture designed for gravity-defying sex positions. There was also a storage area, where Mahoney's men found several kilos of cocaine and several kilos of crystal methamphetamine that looked remarkably similar to the high-grade stuff manufactured in the lab at the first massacre scene.

Bree stopped in front of the women. One of them, a woman with an attractive beauty mark just to the right of her ruby lips, lit a cigarette and said something in a language that wasn't English. Several of the others chuckled bitterly.

"Some of you must speak English," Bree said. "If you do, know that you are not in danger anymore."

The woman with the beauty mark made a *tsk* noise, said, "You know nothing."

"I know Stavros is dead," Bree said. "I know Bogrov is in handcuffs."

That set off a lot of chatter among the women.

Bree waited for a few moments and then spoke directly to Ms. Beauty Mark. "I am DC Metro Police chief of detectives Bree Stone. I'm telling you the truth. You are no longer in danger."

Ms. Beauty Mark's upper lip curled, "We know the better. You get some, maybe, but not all. I'm telling *you* the truth. This is so much the bigger than you think. So, smart thing for me? For us? We don't talk to no one. A lawyer comes. They always come."

"I know what you've been through," Bree said. "How you were told you'd have to work for four or five years to pay off your debt for being smuggled into America. I know some of you rode in refrigerated cars and saw people freeze to death and that you were brought here to be sex slaves. Am I right?"

Many of the women would not look at her. None of them replied.

Bree almost quit, but then she gestured at the mansion and said, "All this? That's the FBI's business. I'm here for other reasons, for someone who may have been a friend of yours. I'm here for Edita Kravic."

That caused quite a few of them, including the woman with the beauty mark, to raise their heads.

"Why for Edita?" she said. "You see her?"

"I'm sorry," Bree said, seeing the yearning in her eyes and coming closer. "Edita's dead. She was murdered."

The woman acted as if she'd been slapped, and then her hand flew to her mouth and she began to sob.

Bree went over to her. "You knew Edita?"

"I'm her sister," she said through tears. "Her baby sister, Katya."

# CHAPTER

# 86

**KATYA KRAVIC DISSOLVED INTO MISERY.** Bree stood back as her friends came over to console her. When Katya finally calmed down, her eyes puffy and bloodshot, she lit a cigarette shakily.

"Can you help me?" Bree asked.

"Can *you* help *me*?" Katya said. "All of us?"

"I'll try."

"They'll throw us out of country," Katya said. "We're not supposed to be here. At least not on the immigration computers."

"A lot depends on your cooperation," Bree said. "The more you cooperate, the more likely a judge is to look at you favorably."

Katya thought about that. Spoke to one of her friends, who nodded.

"What do you want to know?" she said.

"Tell me about Edita."

Katya said her older sister had come first, almost eight years ago. The agreement Edita had struck with the Russian broker was similar to the terms Alex had heard from the woman he and Sampson rescued from the refrigerated trucks at the tobacco-shed massacre site.

In return for five years of her life, Edita got false documents and a way into the United States. She was moved up and down the East Coast for two years before finding a permanent position with the Phoenix Club.

According to Katya, the club was not a high-volume brothel. Members paid a fifty-thousand-dollar initiation fee to join, and ten thousand a year in dues thereafter. In return, they got access to the club, its facilities, all the booze and illicit drugs they wanted, and the company of the women.

"What happened when Edita's five years were up?" Bree asked.

"They gave her back her passport and even gave her a green card, and then they said she had a choice," Katya said. "Leave, make a new life. Or become part of the management."

"She took management."

"No, Edita is…she was smart girl," Katya said. "She found an apartment in Washington and worked here. She ran the club in the evening, and Stavros and Bogrov pay her much money. She uses the money to become a lawyer."

Katya said this with such pride that Bree was touched.

"Did she ever mention a man named Tom McGrath?"

Katya's face clouded. "He is the one who killed her?"

"No, he died with her. Thomas McGrath."

"Tommy?" Katya said, her face clouding further. "Yes, Edita tells me about Tommy. Too much about Tommy."

Edita had met McGrath when he'd come to speak at her criminal law class. She was ten years older than the other students, and he was funny and handsome, and his wife had recently thrown him out of the house and said she didn't love him anymore. Edita and McGrath had had a drink after class and dinner the next night.

"They became lovers," Katya said. "Edita was the happiest I have seen her. Ever. For a month, maybe."

"Then what happened?"

Katya said McGrath ran a background check on Edita and discovered that the green card she had was fake, and there were no records in INS of an Edita Kravic applying for citizenship.

"They lie," Katya said. "Bogrov and the others. They sell to Edita a lie."

After discovering the forgery, Katya said, McGrath forced Edita to come clean and tell him everything. But the more she told him about the Phoenix Club, the more he wanted to know. Tommy asked Edita to break into the club's computers and copy things for him.

Katya stopped talking and looked up angrily. "Tommy, he says he loves Edita, but she has to prove she loves him. So he pushes and pushes, and she loves him, but she is so scared the last time I saw her. Tommy would not listen to her about Bogrov and Stavros, how they are bad men, crazy men. You ask me, Tommy got my Edita killed, and Tommy, he got himself killed too."

# Part Five

# A BLIMP RUNNETH

# CHAPTER

# 87

**THE SUN WAS SETTING AS** John Brown ended his briefing with a description of that evening's goal and the plan beyond it.

Brown looked around at the fifteen men and women in his living room, seeing mild shock in some faces, profound concern in others. He understood. His plan was bold and audacious, so audacious that—

"It's insane," Hobbes said, arms crossed.

Fender said, "We'll be either shot or hanged."

"You knew from the get-go what this was," Brown said coldly. "Wasn't it you, Hobbes, who said people would have to clean house to make way for the revolution in this country?"

"I did, but—"

"But nothing. You're in this to clean house and

see the revolution sparked or you're not in this at all. Fender, you also agreed with that strategy. Or am I wrong?"

Hobbes squirmed in his chair, said nothing. Fender glared at Brown.

Brown was about to ask the room for a vote when Cass said, "Shit."

He looked over at her, saw her staring at the muted TV tuned to CNN. Special Agent Ned Mahoney was walking toward a bank of microphones with the big FBI emblem on the wall behind them. Low on the screen, the banner read *FBI Raids Sex Club Believed Linked to Vigilante Killings.*

"Turn that up," Brown said sharply.

Cass grabbed the remote and punched off the mute. They heard Mahoney say, "I'll get to the Phoenix Club in Vienna, Virginia, but first we'd like to release two photographs of people we believe are part of the vigilante group."

The screen split in two, and images appeared of Hobbes and Cass without their hoods inside the late Antonin Guryev's house on Mobjack Bay.

"Mother of God, we're screwed," Fender said, seething.

Hobbes and Cass had both gone pale and stony.

The screen returned to Special Agent Mahoney, who said, "As of now, the woman's name is unknown. But the man is Lester Hobbes, a mercenary and an assassin. We are asking anyone who has any information on Hobbes or this woman to come forward and help us locate them."

"How do you know Hobbes and the woman are part of the vigilantes?" a reporter shouted.

Mahoney said, "Elena Guryev used her iPhone to video the feeds of several security cameras in her house during the attack."

That set off a frenzy among the reporters, all of them asking where Mrs. Guryev was.

The FBI agent turned stoic and reserved. "Gunmen broke into an FBI safe house this morning and killed four of my best men. They also severely wounded a DEA agent and shot Mrs. Guryev to death, leaving her deaf son an orphan. And, yes, we believe the gunmen were associated with the vigilantes, or the Regulators, as they evidently call themselves. Turning to the raid in Virginia—"

Fender grabbed the remote, punched mute. "Regulators?" he said, looking around the room. "How did they know that? Who used—"

"Doesn't matter," Hobbes said, looking at Cass. "We're done."

"*The both of you* did us all in," Fender said,

getting to his feet and looking like he wanted to smash things. "Taking off your hoods. Breaking the rules of engagement. What the hell's with that?"

The room around Brown erupted with accusations and demands.

Brown stood up and roared, "Enough!"

The fifteen Regulators shut up, all of them red-faced and panting.

"It's done," Brown said sharply. "They're coming after us. You knew they would eventually. So it's done. What are you going to do about it? Are you going to turn on each other? Are you going to run? Or are you going to fight back, show some spine, believe in a better tomorrow created by your sacrifices and mine?"

He let that sink in for a while and then said, "Show of hands. Who's with me?"

After several moments, hands began to go up, thirteen of them, including Cass's. Fender remained livid but eventually raised his hand. Finally, Hobbes did too.

The television screen had switched from the FBI press conference to the weather forecast.

Brown grabbed the remote, turned the sound back on, and watched the forecast. The National Weather Service was calling for gale-force winds overnight.

"There, some good news for once," Brown said. "Couldn't be better. Get your gear strapped down, and your heads screwed on straight. We go at twenty-one hundred hours."

# CHAPTER

# 88

**NANA MAMA WAS COOKING PANCAKES** for Ali the next morning when I came downstairs.

"Pancakes?" I said, rubbing Ali's head. "What did you do right this time?"

"He put that letter to Dr. deGrasse Tyson in an envelope," my grandmother said, gesturing at a stamped, addressed envelope on the counter. "In my book, seeing things through is cause for pancakes and real maple syrup."

Ali grinned as she set a plate before him. "You think he'll answer me?"

"You never know until you try," I said. "Where's Bree?"

"Up and long gone," Nana Mama said. "She's got a pile of paperwork to plow through and wanted to get at it. You hungry?"

"Tempting, but I think I'll skip the—"

"Hey, Dad, look!" Ali cried, pointing to the little TV on the counter.

I glanced over and saw the bizarre image of a bearded driver in an Amish buggy looking up at a low-flying, pale white blimp that was dragging a thick steel cable more than a mile long across fields and through trees.

The newscaster said that sometime during the night the blimp had broken free of its mooring at the U.S. Army's Aberdeen Proving Ground in Maryland, where the military tested everything from cannon rounds to chemical weapons. The blimp was part of a top secret over-the-horizon surveillance system currently being evaluated. The army believed the blimp's cable had snapped due to gale-force winds that had struck coastal Maryland overnight.

"I've seen that thing," I said. "The blimp. A couple of times last week from the Eastern Shore."

The newscaster said the heavy cable had already damaged multiple high-tension lines and several homes and buildings. The army had crews trailing the blimp and trying to figure out how to bring it down safely.

"Runaway blimp," Nana Mama said, shaking her head.

"You don't hear that every day," I said, pouring myself some coffee.

Before I could take a sip, my phone buzzed, alerting me to a text, and then another, and then a third. Annoyed, I set the coffee down and dug the phone from my pocket.

Call me.
Kerry Rutledge.
Urgent.

A fourth text came in. A phone number.

I took my coffee, went out into the great room, and called the young woman who'd survived the road-rage attack.

"Dr. Cross?" she said.

"Right here, Kerry," I said. "What's so urgent?"

"You told me to call if I remembered anything more. I did. I mean, I do."

She sounded breathless, almost panicked.

"Okay," I said. "Let's calm down a little, and then you'll tell me what's going on. Where are you?"

"At a rehab center in…I can't remember that," Kerry said, and she took a deep breath. "But I do remember now that the motorcycle was a dark Honda, big, with a windshield and, like, a lit-up dashboard, you know?"

"How do you know it was a Honda?"

"It was on the gas tank. I could see it in the light from the dashboard."

"Anything else?"

"Yes, but it's probably nothing."

"Let me be the judge of that," I said.

Kerry said, "There was something on the windshield, a decal, on the lower right-hand corner. It was square and I keep thinking that there was an anchor and a rope on it."

"An anchor and a rope on a decal?" I said. And then a memory was triggered, and my heart began to pound a little faster. "A decal like a parking sticker?"

# CHAPTER

# 89

**BREE SAT AT HER DESK** drinking her second cup of coffee and reading over reports of complaints against one of her detectives. She tried to pay close attention to the details of the report and to the detective's response, looking for differences and similarities. She hated second-guessing a cop who'd been acting in the heat of the moment, but if she was going to do the job right, she had to study the situation before rendering judgment.

For the most part, she stayed on task. But then her attention wandered and flickered over to what Katya Kravic had told her about Edita and McGrath. Had Tommy pushed her too far? Had Stavros or Bogrov shot them both and then— what, planted the gun at Terry Howard's? Made his death look like a suicide?

Those unanswered questions only raised more unanswered questions, so she took a deep breath, told herself to compartmentalize, and tried to refocus on the disciplinary report.

A knock came at her doorjamb. She sighed and looked up. Kurt Muller was standing there with that goofy grin on his face again.

"I gather the date with Ms. Noble the other night went well?" Bree asked, sitting back in her chair.

"Better than well," Muller said. "I'm smitten."

Bree laughed. "I could see that the moment you met her. Is she smitten?"

"I get that feeling," he said, the grin growing.

"Good for you. Now get back to work so I can get back to work."

Muller sobered, said, "I actually wanted to tell you we may or may not have caught a break."

Muller said he'd been checking on the status of Tommy McGrath's life insurance policy every few days since his death, and the beneficiary had not come forward to make a claim. When he'd called that morning, however, he found that an adjuster with the insurance company's claims department had learned of the chief of detectives' murder and tried to contact the beneficiary but had been directed to the beneficiary's attorney.

"So the beneficiary did not initiate contact?" Bree said, disappointed.

"Life ain't neat," Muller said, flipping through a reporter's notebook. "The attorney's name is…Lance Gordon…practices in McLean. The insurance adjuster said Gordon consulted with his client, who declined to make a claim at first. Then, three hours later, Gordon called back and filed the claim, saying his client was going to donate the money to a charity."

"This muddies everything, doesn't it?" Bree said, turning to her computer and doing an Internet search on Lance Gordon.

She found his law firm, looked at the partners' page on the website, and clicked on Gordon. A picture popped up of a handsome man in his late forties, very long and lean and dressed in a well-tailored suit.

There was something about Gordon's face that was familiar, but Bree couldn't place him at first. Then she did, in another time and location, seeing herself turn after Gordon and sniff. He'd smelled like something, hadn't he? What was it?

"Chief?"

Bree startled, looked at Muller.

"I was asking how you wanted to handle this."

"Give me a second," she said, making a possible connection in her head. She yanked open a desk drawer and rummaged around until she found what she was looking for: a small brown bottle with a yellow label. She opened the bottle and sniffed.

Bree saw Gordon again in her mind, clearer now. She sniffed again, and all sorts of distorted puzzle pieces shifted and came together.

Bree smiled at Muller and said, "Shut the door, Detective. We've got work to do."

# CHAPTER

# 90

**COLONEL JEB WHITAKER'S HONDA BLACKBIRD** was in the same U.S. Naval Academy parking lot as before when Sampson and I checked around two that afternoon. Sampson walked past the powerful motorcycle, pretended to admire the bike, and planted a GPS tracking device under its rear fender.

We knew a whole lot more about Whitaker now, and, like Tommy McGrath had felt about the Phoenix Club, the more we learned, the more we wanted to know.

Colonel Whitaker had a stellar record, first off. He'd graduated from the Naval Academy in the upper quarter of his class and later won the U.S. Navy Cross for valor, risking his life repeatedly to bring wounded Marines off the streets of war-torn

Fallujah. Then shrapnel from an IED nearly cut off his leg, ending his tour of duty.

The colonel had subsequently earned a doctorate from the War College and then joined the faculty of the Naval Academy, where he taught strategy and amphibious warfare. He was known as a charismatic teacher and was rated highly by students on several faculty-review sites we found on the web.

On paper, Whitaker did not seem like someone we should have been looking at. But then we found out his wife had died three years before in a car accident, hit head-on by a drunken, high twenty-two-year-old who had been not only speeding but texting.

Whitaker's Honda Blackbird turned out to be the fastest production motorcycle available on the planet, capable of blowing the doors off a Maserati. And Whitaker knew how to drive it. He'd raced motorcycles earlier in his life.

Sampson and I had debated bringing the colonel in for questioning but decided in the end to hang back, follow him, and learn more before we got in his face. Whitaker helped us out by appearing forty minutes after we'd set up surveillance on the Blackbird. He limped to the motorcycle, put on his helmet, and set off.

We trailed Whitaker a mile back, watching his

progress on an iPad connected via satellite to the GPS transmitter. We thought the colonel might go north to his home on Chesapeake Bay, but instead he headed west and drove to the George Washington University Medical Center in DC.

He parked in the visitors' lot, and we drove into it just in time to see Whitaker walking toward the hospital. I jumped out and trotted after him.

Because of the limp, the colonel wasn't hard to keep up with. But once we got inside the hospital, I had to hang back, and I lost Whitaker when he got an elevator. Before the doors closed, though, I heard him tell someone he was going to the ICU.

I waited a few moments. My cell beeped, alerting me to an e-mail from Judith Noble, the FBI gun tech. Subject: *Remington .45.*

I pressed the elevator call button, opened the e-mail, and read it. Then I read it again, trying to get my head around her conclusions. *Sonofabitch,* I thought. How was that possible?

The elevator dinged and the doors opened. I rode the elevator up to the ICU, thinking of all of the ramifications of the e-mail I'd just read.

Part of me wanted to back off, let Mahoney know, and stand aside, let the Feds do their job. Instead, I went to the nurses' station, showed a nurse my badge, and asked if a Marine officer with a limp had come in. She said he was down the hall, third door on the right.

"Whose room is that?"

"That would be Mr. Potter's," she said. "George Potter."

I squinted, said, "The wounded DEA agent?"

"That's the one," she said.

"George and I have worked together quite a bit lately. Think I'll pay him a visit, see how he's doing."

# CHAPTER

# 91

**SOMETIMES IT PAYS TO HANG** back. Other times it pays to rattle a few chains.

I didn't knock, just stepped quietly into Potter's room. Colonel Whitaker sat at the DEA special agent's bedside. The patient looked waxy and sallow, but alert. The two of them were deep in a heated conversation when Potter spotted me.

He tensed, said, "Alex?"

"Came by to see how you were doing, George," I said, ignoring his reaction. "Last time I saw you, you were hurting pretty bad."

"I'm still hurting pretty bad," Potter grumbled as he shifted in bed. "Do you know my old friend Jeb?"

I looked at the colonel and acted like I recognized him from somewhere but couldn't place him.

"We met once, Dr. Cross," Whitaker said, getting up from his chair. "In a parking lot at the Naval Academy."

I snapped my fingers, pointed at him, and said, "That's it. Colonel…"

"Whitaker. Jeb Whitaker."

"Small world," I said. "You knowing George and all."

"Colonel Whitaker was my commander in Iraq," Potter said. "Best damned combat officer I've ever seen."

Whitaker made a dismissive flip of his hand. "That's the painkillers talking. George was the brave one, taking a bullet like that."

"For all the good it did Elena Guryev," the DEA agent said, crestfallen.

I said nothing, just looked at Potter and then at Colonel Whitaker.

Potter licked his lips and asked, "You found anything new?"

I thought about that and then said, "When that sniper, Condon, was killed? We found a forty-five-caliber Remington in his motorcycle saddlebag. We got a report back this morning that links the Remington to a series of road-rage killings."

Whitaker was a cool character, battle hardened. He took the information in stride, even appeared uninterested.

Potter, though, suddenly looked lost in thought.

"Well," I said, making a show of checking my watch. "I've got other appointments, but I wanted to see how you were doing, George."

Potter broke from his thoughts, smiled weakly, and said, "I don't think I'll be running any marathons anytime soon. Thanks for stopping by, Alex."

"Get better, and we look forward to seeing you back at work," I said. "Colonel Whitaker? Until fate brings us together again."

"Until then," Whitaker said.

I showed them nothing but an expression of goodwill, shook their hands, and left.

Outside, I waited for Sampson to bring the car around and gazed up at the hospital, thinking how much I'd like to be a fly on the wall up there in the ICU.

# CHAPTER

# 92

JEB WHITAKER'S THOUGHTS BECAME A blur after Alex Cross left the room. The master strategist's brain sped through three different plans of response in the few seconds before Cross's footsteps faded and George Potter spoke.

"Quite the coincidence," Potter said.

Whitaker knew immediately what the DEA agent was talking about but acted as if he didn't.

"How's that?" the colonel said, crossing to the bathroom.

"We framed Condon with diagrams of the attacks and left a gun that turns out to belong to this road-rage killer?"

"Incredible," Whitaker said, going inside. "Give me a second to piss."

A few moments later, he flushed and then

washed his hands. He was drying them on a paper towel as he exited.

Potter studied him, said, "You have a special agenda, Colonel?"

Whitaker balled the paper towel loosely in his hand.

"I'm not following," he said, coming to the wounded agent's bedside and studying the lines that connected Potter to various machines.

"You've been killing drivers like that shithead who killed Lisa," Potter whispered harshly. "You stuck that gun in Condon's motorcycle bag to throw them off you."

Whitaker thought of himself as Mercury, said, "And what if I did? Isn't that what we're all about, George? Cleaning up things that need cleaning up and getting on with a better life for all?"

Potter sputtered, "Who's to say Cross is not onto you because of these road-rage killings?"

"Impossible."

"No, we have to assume Cross suspects," the DEA agent said. "Order everyone to destroy phones and computers. Tell them to—"

Whitaker thought of himself as John Brown then and said, "Who gave you command of this operation, Potter?"

"I did, sir," Potter said. "I took a goddamned bullet to make sure that the Guryev bitch shut her mouth. Your secret vendetta has threatened us all, the entire Regulator movement. From now on, I'm calling the shots, Colonel."

Whitaker stared at Potter, blinking slowly for several moments, then passed the balled-up paper towel from one hand to the other and tossed it over Potter toward the wastebasket. The DEA agent's eyes followed it as it went in.

Nothing but net.

When Potter looked back, Whitaker was gazing at him sympathetically.

*Click. Click.*

The colonel pressed the push-button device the DEA agent used to control his narcotic drip. Whitaker had used one of these hundreds of times after his war injury.

*Click. Click.*

The colonel said, "I'm giving you a monster dose of morphine here, George. It will help things go quicker."

Potter looked puzzled until he glanced at Whitaker's right hand. The colonel held a hypodermic needle attached to an empty syringe; he'd taken it from a medical-waste container in the bathroom. The colonel pulled the plunger of the syringe back and inserted the needle into the injection port of the DEA agent's IV line.

"What the hell are you doing?" Potter asked

even as the narcotic hit him in a rush and he started to swoon and slur. "What's in that…syringe, Colonel?"

"Air," Whitaker said, and he pressed the plunger down.

# CHAPTER

# 93

**BREE STONE AND KURT MULLER PULLED** into the Fort Hill Rifle and Pistol Club in rural Cumberland, Maryland. After the winds the night before, it was a calm, late-summer day in the Mid-Atlantic, a perfect afternoon for the national combat-pistol championship regional qualifier.

The place was surprisingly packed. There were twenty or more motor homes parked at the Morningside Range. With the tents, flags, food vendors, and booths selling various wares, it could have been a county fair were it not for the irregular blasts of staccato gunfire coming from the range.

Bree and Muller pushed in foam ear protectors and donned sunglasses. Acting like spectators, they worked forward through the crowd to where they could see the competitors attack the course.

A shooter with a fancy custom pistol had just finished, and the score was going up on a digital readout by a judges' table. Polite applause indicated it was only a so-so effort despite his tricked-out gun.

Next up was a Pennsylvania state trooper; he used his service pistol and shot well, knocking down two metal silhouettes at thirty yards and avoiding shooting a civilian target. When the course demanded the trooper move laterally while shooting, however, his weakness was revealed, and he turned in a score lower than the previous man's.

Bree watched the competition with interest. She'd had combat-pistol training and scored reasonably well on yearly exams, but this course was set at an entirely different level. She saw several strong runs during the next forty minutes, but nothing spectacular, nothing close to perfection.

Then out stepped a tall, lanky guy wearing a Shooter's Connection ball cap, black earmuffs, and rose-lensed sunglasses. Bree had been talking to Muller and missed the shooter's name, but heard that he was using a CK Arms Hardcore pistol in .45 caliber with a holo sight.

When the buzzer went off, the shooter drew the pistol, leaped forward to the first line, and touched off two rounds. Two metal silhouettes tipped over at thirty yards. He killed the bad guy at the window of the next building. He held off on two civilian pop-up targets and hit everything else put in front of him clean and tight. When his pistol action locked open after the last target, the sign flashed a near-perfect score.

The crowd went wild, and even the shooter seemed amazed at his skill.

He walked back, smiling, his entire body balanced and fluid. Bree barely listened to the announcer's remarks, just watched him and marveled at the shooting ability he'd just displayed.

"Best I've ever seen," Muller said.

Bree said, "I think congratulations are in order."

They angled through the spectators toward the tall shooter. He stopped at the judges' desk, took off his sunglasses, and handed his weapon over for a brief inspection. Then he shook hands with one of the judges, joked with another, retrieved his gun, and left the area.

Bree and Muller followed, seeing him go to a pretty sandy-blond woman in the crowd. She patted him on the arm and smiled. They turned and walked away, heading toward the exit.

Bree and Muller waited until the couple had gotten to where the food and merchandise vendors were set up.

When they were in range, Bree called out, "Mrs. McGrath? I thought that was you."

# CHAPTER

# 94

**TOMMY MCGRATH'S WIDOW LOOKED STARTLED.** "Detective Stone? Kurt? What are you doing here?"

"It's Chief Stone now, Vivian," Muller said.

Vivian smiled at Bree. "I heard you'd gotten Tommy's job. He would have been proud."

"Thank you for saying so," Bree said.

"Are you both competing?" Vivian said.

"Just here supporting some friends on the force," Bree said. "You?"

"I was here to watch Mr. Gordon. My attorney."

"You're a hell of a shot," Bree said to Gordon. "Where's that come from?"

He gave her an aw-shucks shrug and said, "My dad taught pistol at Ranger School, Fort Benning. I guess you could say I was a range rat."

"That explains it," Bree said before turning to

Vivian. "Tommy's insurance company notified us that you were claiming his life insurance policy."

Vivian sighed, said, "I didn't even know Tommy had that policy, Chief Stone, honestly. Not until Mr. Gordon called to say I was named as beneficiary."

"Four million dollars," Bree said.

"I had no intention of claiming the money at first," she said, her chin raised. "Then Mr. Gordon had the idea I could use it to start a charitable foundation, something in Tommy's honor."

"Is there a foundation at the moment?" Muller asked.

Gordon said, "I have associates working on it as we speak."

"Well, then," Bree said, and she smiled. "That helps. But just to tie up another loose end, how much are *you* worth these days, Mrs. McGrath?"

Gordon said, "You don't have to answer that, Vivian. That's really none of their business."

"It is if the answer is germane to a murder investigation," Bree said.

"You're asking if I need four million dollars?" Vivian said. "The answer is unequivocally no."

"Perfect—asked and answered," Muller said. "I'm sorry we had to ask."

Bree said, "Mr. Gordon, you walked by me the day of our initial interview with Mrs. McGrath. You were just leaving as we were coming in."

"Yes, I remember that."

"I caught this strangely familiar scent trailing after you."

Gordon looked confused and said, "What?"

"I couldn't name the smell until yesterday," Bree said. "It was Hoppe's Number Nine. Gun-cleaning solvent. It has a peculiar smell."

"Okay?"

"The smell made me realize that you handle guns. But then a little research revealed you're an incredible marksman. Right from the start, given the way Tommy and Edita Kravic were gunned down, we were thinking trained shooter, someone with mad skills. Someone, well, like you, Mr. Gordon."

Gordon glanced at Vivian incredulously and then back at Bree. "What possible reason would—"

"You and Viv are secret lovers," Bree said. "That's the real reason for the lack of passion in her marriage and her decision to ask Tommy to leave the house while she considered divorce."

"That is *not* true," McGrath's widow said. "None of it!"

"You hide it fairly well," Bree said. "No public

displays of affection. A lot of late-night calls and fervent secret trysts."

"We don't have to listen to this nonsense," Gordon said. "We're leaving."

Bree stepped up and stood in the way, said, "Tell me, Mr. Gordon, what bullets do you shoot in that fancy gun of yours?"

The attorney frowned. "I don't know. Whatever my sponsors send me."

"Bear Creek moly-coated two-hundred-grain RNHBs?"

"No," Gordon said, but his lower lip twitched.

Muller turned to Vivian, said, "And you're lying about your financial situation. We got a court order and looked into your investments. You've lost more than nineteen million dollars since the Chinese economy tanked, which was right before you asked Tommy to leave."

Bree said, "We figure you found out about the life insurance policy and decided that since Tommy was leaving anyway, you'd profit by making sure he checked out permanently. You'd hide that, of course, behind a foundation you could loot to build back your fortune. Sound right?"

The widow McGrath tried to maintain her poise, but her eyes got glassy. She moved her lips but made no sound before fainting dead away.

Vivian hit the ground hard, cracking her head

on the cement walkway. Bree went to her knees next to her.

Gordon put his competition pistol to the back of Bree's head and said, "We're leaving real quiet, now, you and me, Chief Stone."

# CHAPTER

# 95

**GORDON GRABBED THE LAPEL OF** Bree's jacket and jerked her to her feet, her body between him and Muller, who was going for his gun.

"Don't," Gordon said, keeping the gun on the back of Bree's head. "Toss it."

Muller looked pissed but did as he was told.

"Your backup gun."

"I don't carry one."

"C'mon," Gordon said, pushing Bree. "We're moving out."

He marched her into a maze of parked cars. She felt him relax a bit as they passed out of Muller's sight.

"You're making a big mistake," Bree said.

"No, I'm not," Gordon said.

Bree backed up fast and hard. She slammed into

the attorney's chest and grabbed for her service pistol. He pulled his gun away from her head, flipped it, caught it by its barrel, and used the grip like a hammerhead against her wrist.

The blow was excruciating. Her gun fell into the dust. Gordon flipped the gun again and had the pistol back to Bree's head before she realized her wrist was probably broken.

"You'll never get out of here alive," she said, gasping.

"That's where you're mistaken," he said, dragging her along.

"We have a SWAT team surrounding this place," Bree said.

Gordon stopped short and jerked Bree tight to him.

"Bring on the amateurs, then," he said. "I'll watch them fall one by one, starting with you, Chief Stone."

"You're just going to shoot me in cold blood?"

"Just as you would shoot me."

Bree felt the pressure from his gun barrel increase against her head, and she saw Alex and the kids and Nana Mama in her mind. It broke her.

"No," she whimpered. "Don't. Please."

"To go out in a blaze of glory, you got to start somewhere," Gordon said.

"Drop the gun, Gordon," Muller shouted.

Bree caught the old detective in her peripheral vision, crouched in a horse stance between two cars fifteen yards away and aiming a .357 Magnum Colt Python revolver at Gordon.

"Now, I'm nowhere near the shot you are, Mr. Gordon, but I can't miss from this distance," Muller said calmly. "And I won't hesitate to shoot a cop killer. So put the gun down, Mr. Gordon. Put it down real slow, and surrender."

Muller would later say that he saw Gordon's shoulders relax and his eyes turn peaceful then, as if he'd gone inside himself, preparing for whatever was to come.

Bree felt the pressure of the pistol muzzle increase, as if Gordon were squeezing the trigger. But then it eased, and Gordon dropped the gun slowly from her temple and then snapped it toward Muller.

The shots were so close, they were deafening and disorienting.

Bree staggered forward, her ears ringing. Several seconds passed before she realized that Muller was still on his feet and at her side and that Lance Gordon was dead on the ground, a bullet hole between his eyes.

# CHAPTER

# 96

**NIGHT HAD FALLEN. A RAINSTORM** was predicted. Sampson and I were sitting in a black unmarked Dodge pickup parked in a barnyard roughly a thousand yards down the road from Colonel Jeb Whitaker's place. We'd followed the signal from the bug we'd planted on his motorcycle back to his property.

We called Mahoney and learned that George Potter had died of an embolism. Colonel Whitaker had been there and called for nurses, but by the time they reached him it was too late.

It took an hour and forty minutes for Mahoney to arrive with the first of twenty heavily armed FBI agents. During that time, ten different vehicles had come up the road and then disappeared down Whitaker's driveway.

Mahoney's men were now working their way into position around the colonel's six wooded acres. Mahoney had asked two U.S. Navy CID investigators to participate, since they would have jurisdiction over the Marine colonel, and he'd even called for a U.S. Coast Guard cutter to block the way out of the Chesapeake backwater that adjoined Whitaker's land.

"Gotta stretch my legs," Sampson said as my phone rang.

"We got them," Bree said. "Tommy's killers."

"Good for you," I said, smiling. "Tell me everything."

After Bree walked me through the events at the shooting range, I said, "Don't you think you should have gone in with more force?"

"Muller was with me, and ten Maryland state troopers had the place cordoned off. I had the situation under control until Vivian keeled over."

I didn't push the point. "The important thing is you're safe and you caught Tommy's killers, and you'll see Vivian behind bars. That's a job well done no matter how you look at it, Chief Stone."

"Thank you," Bree said, the tension in her voice gone. "I love you."

"Always and forever, sugar."

"When are you going in?"

"Soon."

"Be careful."

"I'm not walking in there alone, if that's what you mean. I'm going in with a big show of force all around me."

She sighed and said, "Call me when it's over."

I set the phone down, wondering again if Bree and Muller had been foolhardy. Gordon was an exceptional pistol shot. God only knew the carnage he could have caused with his state-of-the-art gun and the six full clips they'd found on him.

Mahoney came to my window, said, "They're in position. No activity in the yard. The powwow looks to be inside the house."

"You trace the license plates we gave you?" Sampson asked, getting back in the driver's seat.

The FBI agent nodded. "A few. The black Suburban? Hobbes. The Range Rover? Fender, who is a scary SOB."

"So we heard," I said. "When do I call?"

"Now," Mahoney said.

I punched in the number of Colonel Whitaker's cell, courtesy of the Naval Academy, and put the phone on speaker. He answered on the second ring.

"Whitaker."

"This is Alex Cross, Colonel."

There was a long pause before he said, "Yes. How can I help, Dr. Cross?"

"You can give yourself up, you and your followers, the Regulators."

After another, longer pause, Whitaker chuckled
softly and said, "Now, why would we ever do such
a cowardly thing?"

"Because you're surrounded, and we want to
avoid unnecessary bloodshed," I said.

"Always the noble one, aren't you, Dr. Cross?"
Whitaker said. "Well, the Regulators are not sur-
rendering. We are prepared to fight to the last
man."

"Why?" I said.

"Ask John Brown," Whitaker said. "His goals are
our goals."

"You're wanted for murder and treason,
Colonel. The arrest warrants have already been
written and are ready to be served. It doesn't have
to end in a firefight."

"Ah, but it does, Dr. Cross," Whitaker said.
"A fight to the death is how all slave rebellions
begin."

He ended the call.

Mahoney picked up a radio and ordered his tactical team to move closer, probe for booby traps,
and try to get infrared on the house. Five minutes
later, the same report came back from all sides
of Whitaker's home: The lights were on, but the
shades and drapes were drawn. Infrared showed

fifteen people in the house, fourteen sitting around the living room and one up front talking.

"No one's moving inside and no one's posted outside," the tactical agent in charge said over the radio.

"All in one room," Mahoney said. "Take them before they fan out."

"Roger that. We are go."

Mahoney's blue sedan soon squealed out of the barnyard with us behind, tearing up the country road toward Whitaker's place. We stopped in front of the driveway, barring any exit, and got out, drawing guns even as the first flash-bang grenades went off.

Sampson said, "I promised Billie I wouldn't play cowboy."

"And you're not," I said. "We're doing the rational thing, letting the pros handle the rough stuff."

We trotted down the driveway expecting World War III to erupt at any moment, but all we heard after the grenades was doors and windows breaking and voices calling "Clear."

The wind had picked up again, and it was starting to rain as we followed Mahoney up into the house and saw the fifteen mannequins arranged around the room in various poses.

Every one of them was connected to electrical lines through sockets embedded in their heels. Their plastic skin was warm to the touch.

# CHAPTER

# 97

**A RAPID SEARCH OF THE** house revealed a fully equipped gunsmith operation in the basement, empty crates of ammunition, empty cardboard boxes for AR-rifle components, and the empty gun racks of a formidable arsenal.

Outside, in the building wind and rain, we figured out how they'd escaped. Whitaker's fishing boat was still up on its lift when we went down by the dock, but in the barn we found large, empty raft trailers and empty ten-gallon gasoline cans.

"They went to the waiting rafts the second they got here," I said.

Sampson nodded. "And they trolled out of here, probably by quiet electric motor and then by heavy outboard. They were probably out on the Chesapeake before the Coast Guard was even notified."

"Where the hell do they think they're going?" Mahoney said. "I mean, we'll have Whitaker's face everywhere within hours. He *will* be spotted. They can't escape."

"Maybe they don't mean to escape," I said. "Maybe we should take the colonel at his word: A fight to the death is how all slave rebellions begin."

"Then why didn't he stand his ground here?" Mahoney asked.

"He wants the fight to be somewhere else," I said.

"What I don't get is why," Sampson said. "What did Whitaker say on the phone, Alex? About John Brown?"

"That they had the same goals."

"Freeing slaves?" Mahoney said.

I thought about that and then did a quick Google search on my phone. After scanning the site that came up first, I said, "Brown was an abolitionist, a radical one who believed the slaves could be freed only through armed insurrection. He attacked a U.S. military arsenal in Harpers Ferry, West Virginia, trying to steal thousands of guns he planned to *give to the slaves* so they could start the rebellion."

"So, what," Sampson said. "Was Whitaker telling you he's going to attack a military installation, steal guns, and give them away?"

"They already built enough guns for a small army," Mahoney said.

"Any rebellion can use more," I said. "So if that's what their intent is, what's the target?"

"Not Harpers Ferry," Mahoney said. "There's no arsenal there anymore."

"The Naval Academy?" Sampson said. "The Coast Guard base? Or down to Norfolk? It's not that far south, and a big Zodiac boat with the right engines could handle the waves."

"Especially if there were ex–Special Forces operators driving," I said. "Those guys are like ninjas. And we can't go looking for them from helicopters with searchlights in an area as big as the Chesapeake."

"We'll have to wait for them to make a move," Mahoney said. "At least until dawn. I'll notify the Pentagon to beef up security at all military posts within five hundred miles."

"Can't they activate one of those surveillance blimps that got away the other day?" Sampson asked.

"All the blimps were grounded after that one got loose," Mahoney said, dialing his cell.

In my mind I saw that image of the bearded Amish man in his buggy looking up at the sky and the pale runaway blimp. And then it hit me.

"Ned," I said, feeling queasy.

"Hold on," he said. "The Pentagon duty officer is coming back with—"

I pulled his hand and phone away from his ear and said, "What do you know about that army blimp that got free?"

Annoyed, Mahoney said, "The cable snapped in a high wind. Big embarrassment. Went way up north into Pennsylvania, took out electricity for three hundred thousand people before the army shot it down over a big field."

"What if it was cut intentionally, Ned?" I said. "What if Whitaker or one of his followers did it so they could land on Aberdeen Proving Ground without being detected?"

# CHAPTER

# 98

**THE WIND WAS GUSTING TO** fifty knots or more. Rain flew horizontally and lashed the windshield of the U.S. Army Humvee that Sampson, Mahoney, and I were riding in. Major Frank Lacey was at the wheel.

Major Lacey was the duty officer that night at Aberdeen. He'd been waiting with the Humvee at the main gate on Hartford Boulevard when we arrived.

"What do you think Whitaker's after?" Lacey asked as we drove into the proving ground itself.

"What do you have here?" Sampson said.

"It's more like what *don't* we have here," Lacey said. "We've got everything from small arms to ship cannons, and even some real nasty stuff in labs and storage facilities spread out over one hundred and fourteen square miles of terrain."

I was riding in the backseat with Mahoney. "What's the nastiest stuff you've got here?"

"The chemicals," the major said without hesitation. "Left over from the old Edgewood Arsenal—the mustard gas, the chloropicrin, and the phosgene—all the way up to Agent Orange and the deadliest nerve agents."

I thought about Whitaker following in John Brown's footsteps, trying to arm a rebellion. He could be going for light automatic weapons, .50-caliber machine guns, maybe even rocket grenades and launchers.

But they were all awkward to move in any great quantity, and Whitaker and his followers wouldn't be able to steal or carry enough of those weapons to make it worth infiltrating a U.S. Army facility. So the colonel must be going for something portable and—

"What's the deadliest nerve agent here?" I asked.

Lacey said, "Probably a toss-up between VX and sarin."

Then the major looked at me hard over his shoulder. "You don't think he's…"

"Yeah," I said, feeling sick. "I do."

"He'll never get in. That place is a fortress," Lacey said, but he floored the Humvee and grabbed the mike to a shortwave radio.

He asked to be put through to the shift commander at Edgewater 9.

A few moments later, Lieutenant Curtis, duty officer at base headquarters, reported, "We're getting no answer from Edgewater Nine, Major."

"They're already in," Sampson said.

"That's impossible," Major Lacey snapped, but then he triggered the microphone. "Curtis, ASAP move five platoons in chemical gear south to the Edgewater Nine access off the Old Baltimore Road. Call the Coast Guard. I want Romney, Cold, and Bush Creeks sealed. I want—"

The radio began beeping loud and long, sounding like the beginning of one of those emergency-alert-system drills.

The army major stared at it. "Sonofabitch!"

"What the hell is that?" Mahoney demanded.

The major ignored him. Wrenching the Humvee onto the Michaelsville Road heading south, Lacey barked into the radio, "Report."

Curtis came back, "Storage bays one, three, and four at Edgewater Nine just opened without authorization, sir."

Lacey hesitated, and then shouted, "Go to lockdown, Curtis. I repeat, go to lockdown. No one in or out. Alert command of breach and intrusion into chemical sector. Move MPs to block the Old Baltimore Road at Abbey Point and Palmer

Roads. And all personnel in that sector are or-dered to move north immediately."

"Sound the general alarm, Major?"

"Affirmative," Lacey said.

"What's in those open bays?" I asked.

"The nerve gas VX," Lacey said. "Think of it as a pesticide for humans."

The Aberdeen Proving Ground's alert system began to groan and bray around us. It was like nothing I'd ever heard before, a two-tone blast and blare from the deepest and loudest trumpet you can imagine. Large amplifiers set up across the military base took up the alert. The sound seemed to vibrate through the Humvee and our bodies as we reached Palmer and then the Old Baltimore Road.

As we hurtled south in the Humvee, we were buf-feted by building winds and rain. Blue MP lights flickered behind us as we bore down on Edgewater 9 and the country's deadly reserves of VX.

Tasteless. Odorless. A weapon of mass destruc-tion. A pesticide for humans. The most deadly substance on earth.

What in God's name would compel Whitaker to take such a drastic step?

And why in God's name was I going to Edgewa-ter 9 to stop him?

# CHAPTER

# 99

**WITH THE ALARMS BLARING ALL** around him, Lester Hobbes calmly peered through a jeweler's loupe and dismantled a warhead built in the 1960s.

Three of the warheads had already been taken apart. Four sealed steel canisters containing a total of one gallon of VX were already tucked into Colonel Whitaker's knapsack.

*A gallon already,* Whitaker thought. Consider the destruction a tenth of a teardrop of VX could cause. Consider what a quart could do in DC.

If they were going to clean house, they had to begin with the politicians and the lobbyists, didn't they? K Street and Capitol Hill. *The lackeys of the slavers,* Whitaker thought. *The den of the slavers. They'll get a taste of their own weapons. By our sacrifice, the country will be forced to reboot and start all over—*

"Got it," Hobbes said, extracting the fifth canister of VX and lobbing it to Fender, who caught it and stuffed it into his pack.

Whitaker wasn't happy. He'd planned to control every drop of the nerve agent himself, but he didn't have time to argue.

"Move," he said. "We've got a tide to catch."

They left the army sentries bound and gagged on the storage facility's cement floor and exited the building, coming out in the driving rain. Moving in a pack with Whitaker at its center, they ran hard. The colonel's knee immediately began to throb. He gritted his teeth and hobbled on. Nothing was going to stop him now.

"Do you want me to take the pack?" Cass asked.

"No," Whitaker said. "It's mine."

The first shot rang out from the woods back by the Old Baltimore Road access. One of Whitaker's men fell. Two more shots. Another collapsed.

Hobbes, Fender, and Cass turned and opened fire, spraying bullets at their unseen enemies in the trees.

# CHAPTER

# 100

**I SHOT. MAHONEY SHOT. SO** did Sampson.

We all hit our targets before a modern John Brown and his Regulators returned fire. I had to dive behind a log to protect my head. All we had were pistols and Major Lacey's M4. They had rifles equal to Lacey's as well as a weapon of mass destruction.

Major Lacey seemed unfazed at the idea of facing a WMD. He jumped up, aimed, and shot again, attacking the retreating Regulators with short bursts that took down three more of Whitaker's people. Sampson and Mahoney broke out onto the lawn surrounding the facility.

I charged after them with Lacey just as the rain finally stopped. One of Whitaker's soldiers turned and opened up. A bullet hit Mahoney's left arm, broke bone, and knocked him down.

"Go!" he yelled when I got to his side.

I spotted an AR rifle by one of the dead Regulators, grabbed it, and kept on in a full sprint toward Sampson, who was peeking around the corner of the building. He had one of the ARs too and when I got to him he said he'd just seen the colonel and a woman running toward the sea marsh behind the storage facility.

As he swung his body around the corner, Sampson pulled the AR's trigger. I jumped out after him in time to see Whitaker vanish into the swamp. The woman, however, lurched and stumbled before she disappeared after the colonel.

"I think you hit her," I said.

I flipped on my Maglite and gripped it beneath the fore stock of the rifle. Sampson and Lacey joined me. We quickly spotted splotches of blood on the lawn. The blood flow was small but steady until we reached a maze of reeds, cattails, and towering marsh grass.

We lost the blood trail there. We cut back and forth along the edge of the marsh, seeing where the group had split up and gone in, breaking reeds. When we located the most pounded-down trail through the cattails, we took it and found blood again.

Mud sucked our shoes off in the first hundred yards, but we kept after them, Major Lacey calling in our location and direction of travel over a two-way radio.

"Coast Guard has birds in the air," Lacey said with a gasp as we fought to stay somewhere in range of Whitaker's band of fleeing Regulators.

"Here's big blood," said Sampson, shining light on a splash near a tan reed. "And more there. She's really starting to throw it now."

# CHAPTER

# 101

CASS WAS STRUGGLING. COLONEL WHITAKER could hear the liquid building in her lungs with every breath.

"Leave me, Jeb," she said. "I don't think I can make it."

Squinting to adjust the fit of his night-vision goggles, Whitaker grabbed her under the elbow. He ignored the fire in his knee and fought forward through the muck, following their back trail through the reeds as well as Hobbes and Fender, who'd gotten ahead of them.

"We just have to make the Zodiacs, Cass," Whitaker said. "Even if they bring in a Coast Guard cutter, they can't cover the whole mouth of that creek. We'll sneak out running electric. We'll disappear in the storm."

Cass stumbled and went to her knees. She coughed, and through the night-vision goggles, Whitaker saw black sprays of blood blow from her lips.

"Jesus," he said, starting to panic. "Jesus."

"Leave me, Colonel." Cass gasped.

"Can't do that, Captain," he said, trying to get her up.

"Don't worry," she said. "They'll find me. They'll make sure I live."

After a beat, Whitaker let her go. He took one long last look at Cass in the green hazy light of his goggles, pointed his rifle, and shot her through the head.

# CHAPTER

# 102

**WE HEARD THE RIFLE SHOT** loud and clear, so close it helped get us back on the track when we'd lost it. I cupped my hand over the Maglite to keep it from being seen and pushed on until I heard a sudden choked cry behind me.

I twisted around and saw Sampson about six yards back, struggling, his right leg buried to the thigh in the muck.

"I'm stuck," he said, grimacing. "Shit. Some kind of root. Go!"

"We'll come back for him," Lacey said, pushing by me.

The rain began again, and the major and I forged on through the sea of reeds, seeing blood every six or seven yards until we came upon the woman we'd seen in the images from the Guryev massacre. Blond now. There was a bullet hole in her skull.

"Whitaker can't be far," Lacey said and took off in front of me again.

I wanted to tell him to slow down, not to let his headlamp dance so far ahead of him. But the major was a man on a mission, driven to stop that nerve agent from leaving his army base.

After another hundred yards of slogging on, Lacey disappeared around a dogleg bend in the stomped-down trail through the marsh.

I reached the turn and heard the major yell, "Put down your weapons, or I'll shoot!"

I ran forward in time to hear close gunfire and see Major Lacey knocked off his feet. He landed in the trail ahead of me and lay there, unmoving.

I shut my light off and listened.

"Got that bastard," I heard one of them say.

"Nicely done, Lester," another said. "Let's get out of here."

"Fender, I need that fifth canister," Whitaker said.

"When we're at the rendezvous, Colonel," Fender said.

Keeping the light off, I groped my way forward as if reading Braille, feeling the walls of cattails to either side of me and almost tripping over the major's body. A powerful outboard engine fired to life. Then another.

"Use the electrics!" the colonel said.

"Sorry, Colonel," Hobbes said. "Fender and I are going for distance, not stealth. Come with us. Leave that raft for the others."

"I'm right behind you," Whitaker said.

The first raft roared off, and through the rain I could tell they were not far ahead of me. It sounded like Whitaker was stowing and strapping gear, and he was doing it with no discernible light source.

Night-vision goggles, I thought, and in my stocking feet I carefully stepped free of the reeds and onto a sand bar with an inch of tidal water on it.

The colonel grunted with effort. I heard the raft slide.

He grunted again, and I heard the raft slide a second time, gritty, like coarse sandpaper on soft wood.

Whitaker couldn't have been more than ten or fifteen yards from me, by the sound of it. So I eased into a crouch, raised my gun and flashlight, and whistled softly.

Then I flipped on the Maglite, trying to shine it right in his goggles.

# CHAPTER

# 103

COLONEL WHITAKER CRIED OUT IN surprise and pain. He threw up his arms to shield the goggles from magnifying my already powerful light.

I charged into point-blank range then, still shining the beam on him as he cringed, tore off the goggles, and threw them down.

"I can't see," he said, bent over and rubbing at his eyes. "Christ, I'm blind!"

"Jeb Whitaker," I said, taking another step closer. "Get on the ground, hands behind your head."

"I said I'm blind!"

"I don't care," I said. "You are under arrest for murder, treason, and—"

Whitaker uncoiled from his position so fast I never got off a shot. He spun spiral and low toward me and delivered the knife hard and underhand.

I saw the Ka-Bar knife coming but couldn't move quick enough to keep the blade from being buried deep in my right thigh. I howled in agony. My light and gun came off Whitaker long enough for him to continue his attack.

Two strides and he was on me. He grabbed my right hand, my pistol hand, and twisted it so hard, the gun dropped from my fingers.

The back-to-back shocks—being stabbed and then having my wrist nearly broken—were almost too much, and for a moment I thought I'd succumb. But before the Marine colonel could snatch my light from me, I swung the butt end of the flashlight hard at his head.

I connected.

Whitaker lurched and let go of my numb hand.

I kept after him with my good left hand, raising the flashlight to chop at him. The colonel dodged the blow and punched me so hard in the face I saw stars. Whitaker grabbed me by the straps on my bulletproof vest and punched me again in the face.

"You're not stopping me, Cross," he said, punching me a third and fourth time, breaking my nose. "Nothing's stopping me from fumigating the bugs in DC that have destroyed this great country."

My legs buckled. I sagged and began to swoon, heading toward darkness.

*Fight,* a voice deep down inside me yelled. *Fight, Alex.*

But I was barely holding on to consciousness, and I went to my knees in the water.

"You think you can stop a rebellion, Cross?" Whitaker demanded, gasping, after punching me a fifth time. "An uprising?"

The cold water against my legs roused me enough to mumble, "Using nerve gas?"

"It's how you treat any cancer. Poison the body and cut out the tumors."

"You're insane," I said.

He let go of my vest then and kneed me so hard in the face, I blacked out. I fell onto the flooded gravel bar, but even with the chill water against my skin, I lost time for a bit.

Then I was aware of Whitaker stepping over me. He stood there, straddling my chest. In a daze, I saw his silhouette above me in the beam of the flashlight I had managed to hold on to. He had my pistol.

"I'm tired of you, Cross," the colonel said. "I've got to move on, stoke the next phase of the rebellion."

He swung my gun up toward me.

I did the only thing I could think of.

I dropped the flashlight, wrenched Whitaker's knife from my thigh, turned it skyward, and swung it in an upward arc, driving the blade into the back of his left leg, high under his buttocks, and burying it to the hilt.

I felt the tip strike bone and I twisted the knife.

Whitaker screamed and fired my pistol, missing my head by an inch. He flailed, attempting to pull the blade free.

I twisted the knife again. He dropped my gun and reached back, frantically trying to stop me.

I twisted the knife a third time, then wrenched it out of him and lay there on the flooded gravel, panting.

"Ha," Whitaker said, stumbling back two feet, splashing to a stop. "See? I'm still standing, Cross. Artificial knee and I'm still standing."

"You're a dead man standing, Colonel," I said with a grunt, dropping the knife and fishing for the waterproof flashlight still shining in the water. "I just put your knife through your femoral artery."

By the time I got the flashlight beam back on him, Whitaker had gone from confident to confused. He was bent over slightly, his fingers probing the wound, no doubt feeling the blood that had to be gushing out of him. I thought the colonel would go for his belt to try to tourniquet his leg.

Instead, Whitaker went berserk. He charged, kicking me twice before diving on top of me and grabbing my neck with both hands.

As he throttled me, I tried to hit him with the flashlight again or trade it for the knife. But between my own loss of blood and the beating I'd taken, I couldn't fight him. I just couldn't.

My chest heaved for air and got none. Whitaker had this wild gleam in his eyes as my vision narrowed to blotchy darkness.

*This is the end,* I thought. *The final…*

The grip the colonel had on my throat started to weaken. I got sips of air, and my sight returned.

Whitaker was sitting on my chest, his head swaying to and fro right above mine.

"No, Cross," he said. "John Brown, he…Mercury, he never…"

He panicked then, and tried to stand.

But halfway to his feet, Whitaker lurched off me, staggered, and then crashed into three inches of cold water, dead.

# CHAPTER

# 104

**TWO DAYS LATER, MY FACE** was still swollen and bruised. The knife wound had been sutured but it hurt like hell. Bree had won a commendation for solving the murder of the late Thomas McGrath. And Jannie's orthopedist had called to say that her latest MRI showed the bone in her foot healing nicely.

"We have lots to be thankful for," I said as we sat down to dinner.

"Says a man who looks like he went four rounds with Mike Tyson," Nana Mama said, and Ali giggled.

"A man who went four rounds with Mike Tyson and survived," I said, smiling and wincing at my split lip. "Anyway, we're all here. We're all healthy. We're all safe. And for that, I for one am grateful."

We held hands and said grace and then dove into a chicken Nana Mama had roasted with Dijon mustard, pearl onions, and lemongrass. It was delicious, another triumph, and we showered praise on her.

My grandmother was pleased and in peak form as dinner went on, cracking jokes and telling stories I'd heard and loved long ago. As she did, my mind drifted to the aftermath of Colonel Whitaker's raid on Edgewater 9. Five Regulators had died in the firefight trying to escape. Two had been taken into custody by army MPs and had lawyered up.

Hobbes and Fender eluded the Coast Guard and escaped with a canister of VX, which had the country in a heightened state of alert. The men's photographs were everywhere, and Ned Mahoney, who'd come through surgery with flying colors, was saying it was only a matter of time before they were located and captured.

George Potter, the DEA SAC, was now believed to be the source of the Regulators' intelligence regarding the criminal supercartel targeted in the massacres.

The U.S. Naval Academy had taken two black eyes. Colonel Whitaker and U.S. Navy captain Cassandra "Cass" Pope were both graduates of Annapolis and on the faculty. Whitaker and Pope left vitriolic letters on their work computers declaring that slavers were destroying the country and that it was time for the slaves to arm themselves, rise up, and fight.

I shuddered to think what might have happened to Washington and to my family if they had managed to release a gallon of VX in the nation's capital. But the important thing was that the Regulators or the vigilantes or whatever you wanted to call them were no longer operating. The road-rage killer was gone too. And no one had died from—

Someone started pounding on our front door.

Then she started to yell.

# CHAPTER

# 105

"ALEX?" A WOMAN CRIED AS she rang the doorbell. "Nana Mama? You in there?"

I got up and almost went for my gun before looking through the window and seeing Chung Sun Chung. She was in her down coat, despite the heat, and she was ringing our bell and knocking like someone playing a one-note xylophone and a bongo drum.

I limped down the hall and opened the door, expecting to find a traumatized woman or a woman in peril. Instead, Sun threw her head back and let loose with a real crazy cackle of a laugh.

"Sun, what's wrong?"

"Wrong?" She chortled and then came to me and started beating her little fists lightly against my chest. "Nothing's wrong."

Sun stopped hitting me and cackled again. "Everything's right. Where is your Nana Mama?"

"I'm right here, Sun," my grandmother said, appearing in the hallway with the rest of the family. "God's sake, the way you're carrying on, you'd think I'd—"

There was a frozen moment when everyone was quiet. And then Sun howled, threw her arms over her head, and did a little jig.

"You didn't see the drawing?" the convenience-store owner cried, pushing by me. "You won! You won the Powerball!"

My grandmother looked at Sun as if she had two heads. "I did not."

"You did so!" Sun said, dancing toward her. "I've been selling you the same numbers for nine years. Seven, twelve, nine, six, one, eleven, and three in the Powerball. I saw the draw!"

Nana Mama scowled. "See there? You're wrong, Sun. I always put a two in the Powerball, so I won something, but—"

"No, Nana," I said, dumbstruck. "I changed half your tickets, added one to your last Powerball number. I asked Sun to put a three there."

"Exactly!" Sun cried and started jigging again.

"Oh my God!" Jannie yelled.

My grandmother looked about ready to keel over. Bree saw it and came up to hold her steady.

"Well, I never," Nana said, looking at all of us in total wonder and then at Sun again. "You're sure?"

"I ran six blocks in a down coat in this heat," Sun said. "I'm sure."

"How much did I win?"

Sun told her. Jannie and Ali started whooping.

Nana Mama stood there a long moment, shaking her head, mouth slack with disbelief, and then she threw her chin skyward and cackled with joy.

# ABOUT THE AUTHOR

**JAMES PATTERSON** received the Literarian Award for Outstanding Service to the American Literary Community at the 2015 National Book Awards. He holds the Guinness world record for the most #1 *New York Times* bestsellers, and his books have sold more than 325 million copies worldwide. A tireless champion of the power of books and reading, Patterson has created a new children's book imprint, JIMMY Patterson, whose mission is simple: "We want every kid who finishes a JIMMY Book to say, 'PLEASE GIVE ME ANOTHER BOOK.'" He has donated more than one million books to students and soldiers and funds over four hundred Teacher Education Scholarships at twenty-four colleges and universities. He has also donated millions to independent bookstores and school libraries. Patterson invests proceeds from the sales of JIMMY Patterson Books in pro-reading initiatives.

# BOOKS BY JAMES PATTERSON

## FEATURING ALEX CROSS

*Cross the Line* • *Cross Justice* • *Hope to Die* • *Cross My Heart* • *Alex Cross, Run* • *Merry Christmas, Alex Cross* • *Kill Alex Cross* • *Cross Fire* • *I, Alex Cross* • *Alex Cross's* Trial (with Richard DiLallo) • *Cross Country* • *Double Cross* • *Cross* (also published as *Alex Cross*) • *Mary, Mary* • *London Bridges* • *The Big Bad Wolf* • *Four Blind Mice* • *Violets Are Blue* • *Roses Are Red* • *Pop Goes the Weasel* • *Cat & Mouse* • *Jack & Jill* • *Kiss the Girls* • *Along Came a Spider*

## THE WOMEN'S MURDER CLUB

*15th Affair* (with Maxine Paetro) • *14th Deadly Sin* (with Maxine Paetro) • *Unlucky 13* (with Maxine Paetro) • *12th of Never* (with Maxine Paetro) • *11th Hour* (with Maxine Paetro) • *10th Anniversary* (with Maxine Paetro) • *The 9th Judgment* (with Maxine Paetro) • *The 8th Confession* (with Maxine Paetro) • *7th Heaven* (with Maxine Paetro) • *The 6th Target* (with Maxine Paetro) • *The 5th Horseman* (with Maxine Paetro) • *4th of July* (with Maxine Paetro) • *3rd Degree* (with Andrew Gross) • *2nd Chance* (with Andrew Gross) • *1st to Die*

## FEATURING MICHAEL BENNETT

*Bullseye* (with Michael Ledwidge) • *Alert* (with Michael Ledwidge) • *Burn* (with Michael Ledwidge) • *Gone* (with Michael Ledwidge) • *I, Michael Bennett* (with Michael Ledwidge) • *Tick Tock* (with Michael Ledwidge) • *Worst Case* (with Michael Ledwidge) • *Run for Your Life* (with Michael Ledwidge) • *Step on a Crack* (with Michael Ledwidge)

## THE PRIVATE NOVELS

*Missing: A Private Novel* (with Kathryn Fox) • *The Games* (with Mark Sullivan) • *Private Paris* (with Mark Sullivan) • *Private Vegas* (with Maxine Paetro) • *Private India: City on Fire* (with Ashwin Sanghi) • *Private Down Under* (with Michael White) • *Private L.A.* (with Mark Sullivan) • *Private Berlin* (with Mark Sullivan) • *Private London* (with Mark Pearson) • *Private Games* (with Mark Sullivan) • *Private: #1 Suspect* (with Maxine Paetro) • *Private* (with Maxine Paetro)

## NYPD RED NOVELS

*NYPD Red 4* (with Marshall Karp) • *NYPD Red 3* (with Marshall Karp) • *NYPD Red 2* (with Marshall Karp) • *NYPD Red* (with Marshall Karp)

## SUMMER NOVELS

*Second Honeymoon* (with Howard Roughan) • *Now You See Her* (with Michael Ledwidge) • *Swimsuit* (with Maxine Paetro) • *Sail* (with Howard Roughan) • *Beach Road* (with Peter de Jonge) • *Lifeguard* (with Andrew Gross) • *Honeymoon* (with Howard Roughan) • *The Beach House* (with Peter de Jonge)

## STAND-ALONE BOOKS

*Woman of God* (with Maxine Paetro) • *Filthy Rich* (with John Connolly and Timothy Malloy) • *The Murder House* (with David Ellis) • *Truth or Die* (with Howard Roughan) • *Miracle at Augusta* (with Peter de Jonge) • *Invisible* (with David Ellis) • *First Love* (with Emily Raymond) • *Mistress* (with David Ellis) • *Zoo* (with Michael Ledwidge) • *Guilty Wives* (with David Ellis) • *The Christmas Wedding* (with Richard DiLallo) • *Kill Me If You Can* (with Marshall Karp) • *Toys* (with Neil McMahon) • *Don't Blink* (with Howard Roughan) • *The Postcard Killers* (with Liza Marklund) • *The Murder of King Tut* (with Martin Dugard) • *Against Medical Advice* (with Hal Friedman) • *Sundays at Tiffany's* (with Gabrielle Charbonnet) • *You've Been Warned* (with Howard

Roughan) • *The Quickie* (with Michael Ledwidge) • *Judge & Jury* (with Andrew Gross) • *Sam's Letters to Jennifer* • *The Lake House* • *The Jester* (with Andrew Gross) • *Suzanne's Diary for Nicholas* • *Cradle and All* • *When the Wind Blows* • *Miracle on the 17th Green* (with Peter de Jonge) • *Hide & Seek* • *The Midnight Club* • *Black Friday* (originally published as *Black Market*) • *See How They Run* • *Season of the Machete* • *The Thomas Berryman Number*

## BOOK**SHOTS**

*Cross Kill* • *Zoo II* (with Max DiLallo) • *The Trial* (with Maxine Paetro) • *Little Black Dress* (with Emily Raymond) • *Chase* (with Michael Ledwidge) • *Let's Play Make-Believe* (with James O. Born) • *Hunted* (with Andrew Holmes) • *$10,000,000 Marriage Proposal* (with Harry Liftin) • *French Kiss* (with Richard DiLallo) • *Killer Chef* (with Jeffrey J. Keyes)

*Learning to Ride* by Erin Knightly • *The McCullagh Inn in Maine* by Jen McLaughlin • *Dazzling: The*

*Diamond Trilogy, Part I* by Elizabeth Haley •
*Sacking the Quarterback* by Samantha Towle •
*Radiant: The Diamond Trilogy, Part II* by Elizabeth
Haley • *Bodyguard* by Jessica Linden

## FOR READERS OF ALL AGES

### *MAXIMUM RIDE*

*Maximum Ride Forever* • *Nevermore: The Final
Maximum Ride Adventure* • *Angel: A Maximum Ride
Novel* • *Fang: A Maximum Ride Novel* • *Max: A
Maximum Ride Novel* • *The Final Warning: A
Maximum Ride Novel* • *Saving the World and Other
Extreme Sports: A Maximum Ride Novel* • *School's
Out—Forever: A Maximum Ride Novel* • *The Angel
Experiment: A Maximum Ride Novel*

### Daniel X
*Daniel X: Lights Out* (with Chris Grabenstein) •
*Daniel X: Armageddon* (with Chris Grabenstein) •
*Daniel X: Game Over* (with Ned Rust) • *Daniel X:
Demons and Druids* (with Adam Sadler) • *Daniel X:
Watch the Skies* (with Ned Rust) • *The Dangerous
Days of Daniel X* (with Michael Ledwidge)

## Witch & Wizard

*Witch & Wizard: The Lost* (with Emily Raymond) • *Witch & Wizard: The Kiss* (with Jill Dembowski) • *Witch & Wizard: The Fire* (with Jill Dembowski) • *Witch & Wizard: The Gift* (with Ned Rust) • *Witch & Wizard* (with Gabrielle Charbonnet)

## Middle School

*Middle School: Dog's Best Friend* (with Chris Tebbetts, illustrated by Jomike Tejido) • *Middle School: Just My Rotten Luck* (with Chris Tebbetts, illustrated by Laura Park) • *Middle School: Save Rafe!* (with Chris Tebbetts, illustrated by Laura Park) • *Middle School: Ultimate Showdown* (with Julia Bergen, illustrated by Alec Longstreth) • *Middle School: How I Survived Bullies, Broccoli, and Snake Hill* (with Chris Tebbetts, illustrated by Laura Park) • *Middle School: My Brother Is a Big, Fat Liar* (with Lisa Papademetriou, illustrated by Neil Swaab) • *Middle School: Get Me Out of Here!* (with Chris Tebbetts, illustrated by Laura Park) • *Middle School, The Worst Years of My Life* (with Chris Tebbetts, illustrated by Laura Park)

## OTHER BOOKS FOR READERS OF ALL AGES

*Give Please a Chance* (with Bill O'Reilly) • *Cradle and All* (teen edition) • *Jacky Ha-Ha* (with Chris Grabenstein, illustrated by Kerascoët) • *House of Robots: Robots Go Wild!* (with Chris Grabenstein, illustrated by Juliana Neufeld) • *Public School Superhero* (with Chris Tebbetts, illustrated by Cory Thomas) • *House of Robots* (with Chris Grabenstein, illustrated by Juliana Neufeld) • *Homeroom Diaries* (with Lisa Papademetriou, illustrated by Keino) • *Med Head* (with Hal Friedman) • *santaKid* (illustrated by Michael Garland)

For previews and information about the author, visit JamesPatterson.com or find him on Facebook or at your app store.